LIGHT

RADIANCE

SPLENDOR

LIGHT

RADIANCE

SPLENDOR

A NOVEL

LEAH CHYTEN

SHE WRITES PRESS

Published 2017
Printed in the United States of America
Print ISBN: 978-1-63152-178-2
E-ISBN: 978-1-63152-179-9
Library of Congress Control Number: 2016961145

For information, address:
She Writes Press
1563 Solano Ave #546
Berkeley, CA 94707

Cover design © Julie Metz, Ltd./metzdesign.com
Interior design by Tabitha Lahr

She Writes Press is a division of SparkPoint Studio, LLC.

This is a work of fiction. Names, characters, places, and incidents either are the product of the author's imagination or are used fictitiously. Any resemblance to actual persons, living or dead, is entirely coincidental.

This book is dedicated to all who work tirelessly to knit this world back together again and again.

CONTENTS

FOREWORD

Light Radiance Splendor is not a book I intended to write. My family of origin scoffed at religion and any interest in ancestry was answered with a shrug. Even our familial name was relinquished at Ellis Island. Later in life, my interest in spirituality led me to study numerous traditions, including kabbalah, the mystical aspect of Judaism. I listened with skepticism to one of my teachers, who informed me that he "saw" several ancestral guides trying to communicate with me. That night I had a dream, recalled with unusual vividness. I was hovering above a *shtetl*, a Jewish village, in Eastern Europe. The great *rebbe*, the venerable, wise spiritual leader of the community was imparting a manuscript to another man. As the manuscript changed hands a beacon of light radiated outward and morphed into the form of an exquisite feminine countenance. "I am the Goddess Shekinah, and this is my mission," She said. "Do you accept?" Was She addressing the man in the dream, or the dreamer of the dream, or perhaps the readers of the story? May this book be an inspiration and an invitation, that we all become mission keepers, and offer our unique gifts to a world slowly, slowly moving toward *tikkun olam*, toward wholeness.

EPIGRAPH

Shekinah

"*My dream was of a divine marriage between the realm of subtle perfections and physical matter. How beautiful was My original vision, and how tragic that the energies of chaos roaming the cosmos infiltrated this young world, thus planting seeds of conflict, fear, greed, and hatred. I was forced to abandon my beloved creation. I have remained near to you but the time of My return from exile is now. I need your help that together we restore the beauty and harmony of my original vision. Every righteous action brings My light into this world. My beloveds, we will prevail.*"

BOOK ONE

JAAKOV

"We must do all we can to bring Her back that She may restore balance and harmony to our world. It is Her wisdom and love that have been lost to us. She is our only hope."

—The Great Rebbe

PROLOGUE

Schtetl Bedzew, Poland, 1912
Jaakov Janowicz

Death will soon have its way with me. It whispers an invitation
to shed this crippled body, to step through the veil and enter
the realm of mystery. Death does not scare me, but I have yet
unanswered questions that stalk me like beggars thrusting empty
bowls in my face. Have I listened well enough to G-d, or have I
been swayed too much by the willfulness of my un-ripened soul?
How do I answer this question? Certainly not by attributing value
to accomplishments, or measuring the whims of joy and sorrow,
or even by counting all good deeds performed.

I long for the guidance of the Great Rebbe. Perhaps as I
approach death, the veils between now and then are thinning, for
in this moment my mind has slipped into memories of an ancient
past where I'm a young boy awed by his presence. Opening the
door to his study he gestures for me to step over the threshold
into a foreign land where piles of precariously stacked books, like
silent, benevolent creatures, encroach into the space. The acrid
odor of mildew tickles my throat, and I squelch the urge to cough.

"My young student, nothing is ever as it appears to be," the rebbe states succinctly, our eyes briefly meeting. "Are you ready to unlearn everything you think you know?"

I'm acutely aware of the clatter of hooves and the rumblings of a carriage, my father receding from my life, having dutifully delivered me here to an unfamiliar *shtetl* and into the care of a man who will provide for me what he could not. The pangs of loss are searing. At thirteen years old I'm considered a man, and yet still young enough to miss the comfort of my family. As the clatter of hooves fades I hold my breath to allay the quivering of my jaw and the tears ready to erupt. The rebbe has accepted me as his student, to live with his family, a rare honor not to be squandered. The rebbe's abrupt question, however, throws me into confusion.

"I know so little, rebbe, but I'm willing to know less than I know now."

He is so tall that his head brushes the ceiling when he stands, and the austerity of his long, black overcoat adds to his grandeur. Behind his spectacles his eyes burn like suns. I'm self-conscious from the awkward angularity of my own changing body. My arms hang loosely by my sides, too long for my torso, and my face feels scratchy from its first outburst of hair. Although tall for my age, and scholastic precocity having earned me ample praise, I feel small in this moment and unworthy of his attention.

"Come and sit here, Jaakov," he says, removing a stack of books piled on top of a chair. "Time to receive your first lesson. Your father tells me that you ask many questions." He places a stool directly in front of me and sits with back straight and feet firmly meeting the floor. His smile barely conceals unrelenting scrutiny.

"I'm curious about many things."

"That is good," he says. "Religions give answers, but kabbalah asks questions that lead us further and further into unknowing. Do you ask those kind of questions?"

"I think so, rebbe." I breathe a sigh of relief. Earlier that morning a brilliant question arose, a spark of inspiration that fills me with renewed confidence.

"Does man decide his own fate, or is it G-d that decides man's fate?"

Goldie, the rebbe's daughter, with eyes as dark and deep as his are radiant, had responded earlier with an approving nod and a shy smile, but the rebbe seems less impressed. We sit in silence, my fear of humiliation looming, made all the more awkward by the entrance of Goldie herself, the coyness of her half smile sending quivers of excitement up and down my spine.

"Mama has just taken bread from the oven and wants to know if our guest would enjoy a piece with melted butter and jam."

I would certainly enjoy a piece, particularly in this moment as the cold of looming winter chills my bones. Glancing toward the rebbe I almost respond, but he speaks instead.

"Thank you, Goldie. Jaakov is completing his lesson."

I lower my head, embarrassed by my attraction for Goldie, but the rebbe reaches out and lifts my chin with his hand until his eyes meet mine. He nods, a gesture I learn can mean many things.

"Jaakov, how would it change you to know the answer to this question?"

It is hardly the response I anticipated. "I don't understand, rebbe."

His voice is soft but it cuts right through me, as if my body is nothing but space. "No matter who is responsible, would it affect how you live your life, the decisions you make, the actions you take, the values you uphold?"

"No, yes, I don't know, rebbe," I stammer.

Tears of shame sting the inside of my eyelids. With dignified solemnity he rises, caresses his beard, straightens his jacket, walks stiffly toward the door before returning to his chair. I fight the urge to flee, to escape this crushing sense of failure. Where would I go? This is my home now. I will simply have to bear it.

"Paradox," he says, stopping to face me.

"Paradox?"

"It means that something is neither this way nor that way, neither that way nor this way." His hands gesture excitedly as he speaks. "Everything in creation is relative to something else. A question can be answered one way and then another, and both answers are true and false. Do you understand?"

"I understand, and I don't understand."

The rebbe's laughter dispels my doubt.

"That is it exactly, Jaakov." Reaching over, he pats my knee. "Now back to your question."

I've always been deemed a prodigy. Receiving raised eyebrows and nodding heads, my honored place in the *shtetl* had filled me with intoxicating specialness. Now I feel the excruciating emptiness of it all. I've become ordinary and ashamed that I've ever thought otherwise.

"I'm sorry, rebbe. I'm sorry to have asked such an unworthy question."

He looks genuinely surprised. "It is not unworthy, Jaakov."

His words confuse me. Is he mocking me?

"I'm simply demonstrating the importance of intention, of *kavanah*. G-d listens to the sincerity of intention, to whether our aspirations to receive His knowledge are pure, or skewed by a desire for personal gain."

Shame sears my heart. "Rebbe, is it wrong that I want to be a worthy student, that I want you to be proud of me?"

I wipe away tears with a quick sweep of my hand. The rebbe leans in so close that his beard tickles my chin. "Be yourself, Jaakov. This is all I ever ask of you."

Be myself. Who was I then? Who am I now?

"You will serve G-d in your own way."

Unintended words escape my lips. "I want to be like you, rebbe."

He moves his head slowly, deliberately from side to side. "I'm considered a *tzaddik,* my young student. I'm not sure that you'll want to be a *tzaddik,* at least not in this lifetime."

"Why not, rebbe?"

"A *tzaddik* knows he is nothing and everything. He lives not for himself alone but for all of humanity. The soul of a *tzaddik* has merged into the great ocean of souls, into the one Soul. A *tzaddik* suffers until every last soul is redeemed."

Suffering? I have no desire to suffer. Two years ago, the rebbe's son was killed in a *pogrom.* He was barely older than I am now. That kind of suffering terrifies me. The rebbe's hand reaches out, swallowing my own. His hands are warm and soft, pulsating with energy that calms my fright.

"We suffer when we think G-d has abandoned us, betrayed us, left us alone in this world, like orphans. On the contrary, Jaakov, in His love for us He has granted free will, that we may learn and grow from the consequences of our actions."

"Does that mean we are punished for bad deeds and rewarded for good deeds?"

"It's hardly that simple, as life will inevitably teach you."

Disturbed by his words I stubbornly cling to the belief that I'm in charge of my life. Last spring, standing at the river's edge I witnessed a man in a boat capsize as the swirling river currents caught his oar. That will never be my fate. With intelligence and determination I will always be master of the boat and the river, or so I thought then.

"We are here to purify body, heart, and mind with prayer and *mitzvoth,* with love and discipline, that we become clear vessels to receive the light of divinity. We are here to join heaven and earth, to help this beautiful world once again become a garden of delight from which every soul receives divine nourishment. Do you understand, Jaakov?"

"I think so, rebbe."

He presses his hand firmly into my shoulder. "G-d is beyond this world, for He is eternal and unchanging Truth. But the feminine aspect of G-d, the Shekinah, dwells within each of us as a spark of divinity. When we lead righteous lives the spark ignites into a flame that guides us toward our highest potential."

I tremble at the mention of Her name.

"She has already appeared to you, Jaakov, yes?"

"Yes," I whisper, baffled by the intensity of my devotion to Her.

"You have indeed been blessed. Did She ask you the question, Jaakov?"

She had appeared to me in a vision in my seventh year, a radiant column of light that transformed into an exquisite woman whose body was made of undulating filaments of light. My heart is still moved with intense devotion by this one visitation.

"Why did She ask me to serve Her, rebbe? I feel so unworthy."

"It is an honor and a responsibility to serve Her. You are worthy, Jaakov, but humility is good. She needs our help that She may return to this world."

"Return from where, rebbe? I thought She was here with us."

He shakes his head slowly. "This world was once an emanation of Her radiance and splendor, a true Garden of Eden. The fruits of this garden were love, beauty, harmony, peace, and bliss."

"What happened, rebbe?"

"It has been told that foreign entities infiltrated this world, sowing seeds of fear and hatred, greed and divisiveness. They turned brother against brother, because the more we fought among ourselves the more weakened we became, and the more they could control us. They planted their seeds among us so that now every soul carries seeds of darkness and seeds of light. She tried to intervene, but they were too powerful. She was forced to depart Her own beloved creation."

"Rebbe, is there no hope for us?"

"There is hope, Jaakov. She longs to return and take Her rightful place in this world, but She needs our participation. She cannot do it alone. That is why She is asking for help with Her mission."

"Rebbe, I'm willing to do anything She asks of me, but even if I love Her and serve Her with all my heart, how can one person make a difference?"

The rebbe reaches out and takes my hand. "That is a good question, Jaakov, a sincere question, a question with *kavanah*."

He rises slowly, unwinding his body, his movements graceful and yet ordinary. He carefully removes a book from a stack of books.

"This is how kabbalah answers your question," he says, opening the book. "*One person of pure intent can redeem the entire world*."

"I don't mean to be disrespectful, rebbe, but how can one person, no matter how pure and righteous, possibly redeem this world?"

"Excellent response, Jaakov! You are learning to think like a kabbalist. Be open to every possibility, but act only on the authority of your own wisdom."

"Thank you, rebbe." Finally I've done something right.

"We are not so separate as we might appear. Contemplate this: the entire world is contained within every one of us, and we are contained within the entire world. You may not understand, but remember, we learn by embracing paradox."

He pulls his stool even closer to mine, the scent of smoky tea accompanying his words. "Embracing paradox keeps us from being short sighted in our thinking. Seeming contradictions from one perspective are perfectly understandable from another perspective. To demonstrate paradox, I will now answer your question a different way."

He reopens the book. "*The world cannot be redeemed until every soul is redeemed. Every soul is of equal importance and significance in the redemption of the world. Until every soul is healed, none of us are fully healed*."

"As a paradox both are true? Even the wicked souls, rebbe, even the souls that murder innocent people, must they also be redeemed?"

The rebbe hesitates, blinks, and I realize too late that my careless words must have awakened the memory of his son's brutal murder.

"Yes, even those must be redeemed," he says softly. "The deluded ones are most in need of redemption, for we are one body of humanity."

I'm anticipating warm bread and sweet jam, but instead the rebbe returns to his chair. Rocking back and forth with eyes closed, he speaks in tones different from his usual voice.

"*The mission I ask you to serve is a mission of love for a world in desperate need of redemption. From whence does the notion of enemy arise? Separation in this way does not exist. We are distinct but inseparable parts of one totality. How can we condemn each other? How can the pain of one not be the pain of all?*"

Glancing up I see Goldie crouching in the doorway. Sensing my attention, she covers her face with her hands. Is she weeping? I feel an impulse to comfort her, but the Shekinah resumes speaking.

"*When we live as if this is not so, we cause harm to ourselves and to others. When we seek vengeance, the cycle of ignorance, the notion of enemy, the belief in separation is perpetuated. Love can never be harmed or destroyed. Love sees only itself in all forms. The act of forgiveness is an expression of love, and a bridge between the human and the divine. This is the true action of* tikkun olam, *the healing of the world.*"

"No!" Goldie shouts, bursting into the room. "I hate them. I will never forgive them for murdering Chaim."

Goldie's outburst shocks me, her cry of pain transforming her in my eyes from an object of my fantasy into a real person. Had the rebbe not already done so I would run to comfort her. I would do anything to ease her pain as her father is doing now, stroking her hair as she burrows her head into his chest.

"Hate what they do, my children, and take what action you must to protect yourselves from the consequences of their ignorance, but hate them, no, for that is how they take away your light."

"I'm sorry, *abba*."

He kisses her forehead, and she hastily departs. The rebbe speaks with surprising calm.

"My sweet Goldie. She and Chaim were so close, so adoring of each other."

"I'm sorry, rebbe. I wish I could do something to make it all right."

"There is something you can do." The rebbe pauses to make sure I'm listening. "You, Jaakov Janowicz, are Her first mission keeper."

"What does it mean to be Her mission keeper?"

"At the moment it means nothing, but later it will mean everything."

"When later?"

"Much later. You will know when it is time to know."

He touches my forehead with his thumb, and an exquisite and delicate blissfulness ripples through me. My mind is at peace, and I know that no matter how my life unfolds, it will be perfect in the way that She has intended.

My attention now returns to this moment, when a lifetime later I'm awaiting death. Do I still believe in the perfection of life? Memories form and dissolve, like waves upon the ocean. Seated in my familiar chair, wrapped in layers of wool blankets, I gaze slowly around the room that has held and witnessed so much of my life. This is the home that my Goldie and I shared since our wedding day, the home where our children were born and raised, the home where I will soon die alone, alone, but infused with memories. Who is to say that my son isn't studying *Talmud* at the kitchen table with Laiah, his younger sister, perched on a footstool leaning over his shoulder and trying to study along with him? Who is to say that my sweet Goldie isn't right now baking challah for *Shabbat*?

I've received many blessings. Perhaps I would be more at peace with life, accepting all as G-d's grace if it were not for Zeff. He betrayed me, or perhaps I betrayed him. Or myself. Why had I ignored the signs? Was it compassion for this orphaned boy, this magical, charismatic youth? He had been my most brilliant and promising student, but his brilliance blinded me to his cruelty. He had the heart of an undeveloped soul, not yet human. The human heart may hate, may hurt others, but not with such indifference. Goldie tried to warn me, but I refused to listen until it was too late. Stubbornly I held out hope for him, but others paid a heavy toll for my blindness.

Ironically, Zeff has just reappeared in my life. He left a note requesting that I meet with him, offering no reason other than that it is imperative that we do so. Should I meet with him? Am I once again, even in old age, blind to the consequences?

Goldie would have known what to do. Perhaps it is Goldie urging me to consult the Cup of Fortunes, an unsightly misshapen artifact with walls as thick as a finger, a handle too small for its weight and a brown crack running down its side. The Cup was bequeathed to me by the rebbe on my wedding day.

"Use it wisely, Jaakov. This is no ordinary cup, but an oracle device, a gift from my own father who bought it from a beggar, or more likely a wandering mystic who used it to read fortunes. Steep the tea and peer inside as if the Cup is a microcosm of the entire universe. The Cup of Fortunes helps you see with the eyes of your heart."

The rebbe's image recedes, and my present predicament returns. Since that day I've never consulted the Cup, but now I need whatever revelation it can offer me. Painstakingly pushing my body up out of my chair, I grasp my cane and hobble toward the kitchen where the Cup is shelved above the cook stove, too high for me to reach. Shimon will soon come for his daily visit.

Shimon, my grandson, is a sweet and handsome young man with deep sea-green eyes and a shock of red hair that embarrasses him so much that he wears a hat even in mid-summer; Shimon, who once stammered badly when he spoke, sings with the elegance of a cantor.

When he arrives, Shimon helps perform the ritual, but I form my question silently. *"Should I meet with Zeff or refuse his request? What will serve those who will remain after my death?"* Staring into the world of patterns and messages presumably hidden in the leaves, I see nothing to spawn revelation.

Shimon interrupts. "Please allow me to look." His eyes widen as he gazes. "I see the letter *tav*. Does that mean anything?"

Intrigued by his clarity of sight, I look again. The letter *tav* is completely discernible. "It means a lot, Shimon. In fact, it means everything."

Tav is the last letter of the Hebrew alphabet, and the first letter in the words *tikkun* and *teshuvah*, both alluding to the redemption and healing of the world.

"Did you receive your answer, *zeddeh?"*

"Yes, Shimon. I know what I must do."

I shuffle to bed, my body shivering under cold sheets. Goldie's face appears and transforms into the face of the Shekinah until I cannot distinguish one from the other. Her hand brushes across my brow. Her lips lightly touch my own.

"My dearest Jaakov," she whispers. Her voice is sweeter than the trickle of a forest stream. I await more words, but there are none.

CHAPTER ONE

Shtetl Bedzew, Poland, 1902

The burial place is hardly illustrious. Each plot is marked with a tiny, badly hewn stone placard, and the mounds of dirt piled over each grave are left in clumped and irregular shapes. There is no symmetry, no real order to the placing of graves, although husbands and wives are always buried side by side. The month is November and already the ground is nearly frozen. Thankfully this day is unusually warm, and digging the rebbe's grave goes quickly.

The rebbe predicted with uncanny precision when he would exhale his last breath. On the day before his death, the rebbe beckoned our family into his room. Laying his great bony hands on each of our heads, he blessed us with a prayer for well-being and continued devotion to G-d. He then whispered Laura's name. She received his last blessing, his last words, and his last request. Many were curious and more than a little resentful that she was chosen for this great honor.

Standing by her side at the site of his grave, ashamed of the biting sting of envy that leaves a bitter taste in my mouth, I shiver as the sun dissolves into the heavy gray late autumn sky. I've also been his student, and his son-in-law, and my admiration and love for him has never waned, never even faltered. I find myself wanting to find fault now of all times, now that he's passed over. I wanted to be the one chosen to sit by his side and accompany him to the doorway of death. My face flushes red with embarrassment, and I'm grateful that sunset has muted all colors. For a moment, I feel his presence, a cool breeze touching my cheek with the same gentle sternness that drew me to him in my youth.

The crowd disperses at dusk. Goldie returned earlier to the house to prepare for the first night of sitting *shiva,* the seven day gathering to mourn the deceased. Laura and I remain behind. She leans into me, and I place an arm around her shoulders, grateful to feel once again the sincerity of my fondness for her. We've known each other a long time, our relationship having been tried and strengthened by the kind of adversity that would have brought lesser souls to the point of animosity. Long ago we recognized that our destinies were bound together, like threads woven into the same tapestry.

Laura had been orphaned and left homeless as a child when a house fire killed her family. Later, when Zeff appeared, she gratefully followed this handsome, charismatic man who promised her a life of romance and adventure. Instead, with two children to care for, his abuse and violence escalating and no hope of escape, she resigned herself to a life of misery. A concerned neighbor, who happened to be my student, informed me of the situation. Rescuing Laura and the children cost me dearly.

"You are curious, am I not right, Jaakov?"

"You forgot to mention jealousy, that most lowly of human emotions."

"At last, I've made you jealous. My life is redeemed." Her laughter is a welcome relief from a day strained with consoling the bereaved.

"If something was told to you in secrecy, I will not insist."

"You're too proud for that."

"And perhaps respectful as well."

The banter ceases for a moment, and even in the last light of day, I recognize the pensive expression that comes over her at times, her head cocked slightly to one side.

"You are hurt, Jaakov."

"I trust he had his reasons. Besides, you've proven yourself an excellent kabbalist."

"Remember that you were chosen to be his successor, to take his place in the community."

Her words are accurate but make no difference to my sober mood. "We should be heading back now. The food will be gone, and I'm famished."

I try to nudge her toward the house where everybody is gathered, but her body is unyielding. I feel her thoughts, troubled, forming, struggling for words. The sting of my own hurt set aside, I become quiet, receptive, an open space. I become the night sky as her words form constellations.

"His reason was not personal, Jaakov. He should have chosen Goldie, or you, or Laiah, or any of his blood relations, but he's a *tzaddik*. His actions cannot be understood from the ordinary perspective."

She is right, and hardly to blame. How self-centered of me to be jealous of her or angry at the rebbe. My feelings disperse, like clouds on a windy day.

"He was lucid but quite weak when I met with him. His last wish was a request for our help." Standing directly in front of me, she holds my gaze. Laura is almost my height with a graceful body and alert, nervous eyes that alternately reveal innocence and alarm. "Do you remember when he named you the first mission keeper?"

"How could I forget such words, and yet he never spoke of it again."

"As cryptic as he could be at times, I don't think he received the transmission from the Shekinah until weeks before his death."

Hearing Her name releases a jolt of energy. How strange that I never connected being a mission keeper with Her visitation.

"The rebbe gave me a manuscript transmitted to him in the weeks before his death. I'm to hand it over to you at the end of the mourning period, and you are to continue decoding it until you are certain the decoding is complete. The manuscript will then be passed on through your lineage for others to decode."

"I'm not sure what I expected the mission to be, but decoding a manuscript seems almost too simple."

"I don't think it will be as simple as it appears. The manuscript is no ordinary document. It's a living consciousness that serves as a link between you and the Shekinah. She communicates with you through the manuscript. He repeated that phrase several times, so either it's important or his mind was leaving."

"If the words are true, then I'm happy to have a portal of communication with Her."

Laura sighs. "I hesitate to share the other instruction given us, but of course I must."

"Of course you must. What else did he say to you?"

"He instructed us, or rather he spoke on behalf of Her, to heal Zeff."

Outrage enflames me and then subsides. "Heal Zeff? Why would we be asked to heal Zeff? We've tried for years to heal him, and it has cost us dearly."

"Those are the instructions, Jaakov. What we do with them is our choice."

Descending with sudden rapidity, as if having momentarily forgotten its task, the sun drops into the hills, leaving behind a bloody looking red sky. The air is moist and chilling with a north wind beginning to pick up force. Laura wraps both arms around her body for warmth. We stand at the edge of the rebbe's grave, gazing down at the exposed pile of earth, as if he still resides there. Laura crouches and pats the ground.

"Rest easy, my teacher. You served us well."

Rising, her body freezes in mid-motion, her eyes riveted on the horizon. Silhouetted against the murky sky is the lone figure of a man. He senses our gaze, for he turns abruptly and disappears. Instinctively Laura reaches for my hand. I can't see him, but surely it is Zeff, and knowing Zeff and his capacity to read minds, he knows every word we spoke.

"Jaakov, I'm scared." Drawing her shivering body toward me, I wrap my arms around her tightly. "He won't hurt you anymore, Laura. I promise. He won't hurt you."

Laura and I both know that this is a promise I cannot keep. We return in silence, each of us preoccupied with Zeff, a most unwelcome ending to a difficult and emotional day. The rebbe is gone now. Despite the crowd of familiar faces, I feel more alone than I have ever felt in my life.

CHAPTER TWO

The rebbe's house is not far from the cemetery. In fact nothing in the *shtetl* is far from anything else. Although people complain incessantly about their neighbors—this one too noisy, that one small-minded, the other doesn't keep *Shabbat*—everybody chooses to live in close proximity. Houses huddle together, walls touching, windows facing into each other, clotheslines hanging from the corner of one house to the corner of the next. By the time we reach the rebbe's house I'm famished and exhausted. People mulling outside greet us warmly. Goldie rushes over the moment we step through the door.

"I've saved both of you potato soup and bread, and your favorite strudel that Effie baked. Come eat."

Grateful for her thoughtfulness, we follow her through the dense crowd until we reach the cook stove. Handing us each a steaming bowl of soup, she hovers near us, ready to ladle out second helpings. Despite her attempt at cheer, she looks weary. Her hair, wound in a bun is unwinding and falling around her face, the soft curls evoking a younger, more beautiful Goldie. But her face is shadowed by grief, her eyes swollen from weeping. As I reach out to hold her, she resists and then yields, as she often does, the softness of her body coming to rest against me.

"Let's go home," I whisper, gently kissing her forehead. "It's been a long day for both of us."

She pushes away from me. "And leave everybody here, and the kitchen still untidy and the food not put away?"

"Yes, sweetheart, let's leave all of it exactly as it is."

Laura steps in. "You should rest, Goldie. I'll make sure everything is cleaned up."

As we squeeze our way through the crowd, Moshe from across the river catches my attention. I recognize him as one of the rebbe's students, an ethereal looking young man with hair that falls in ringlets.

"Jaakov, Jaakov, you'll be taking over the rebbe's teaching, or so he told us."

"Nobody can take his place." I say far too vehemently. I cannot imagine coming close to his greatness. To Goldie, however, he was simply her adored *abba*, the father who cherished her. Preparing for sleep, huddling together under the quilt and cold bed sheets, she recounts memories of him.

"His beard, Jaakov! I used to nuzzle my face in his beard. It smelled like a pine forest and his favorite smoky tea. And I remember his deep coat pockets. When we were young, he hid little trinkets in those pockets, and if we guessed right, we got to keep them."

Goldie is resting in the crook of my arm, allowing me to stroke her hair, long and smooth with streaks of grey. Goldie takes after her mother, with dark eyes and dark complexion, high cheekbones, and a slightly pointed cleft chin. I kiss the top of her head, and she giggles softly, like a young girl.

"Do you remember how scared you were to ask *abba* for permission to marry me?"

The memory fills me with warmth. "He looked bewildered until he broke out in laughter. *"I would never stand in the way of two lovers. That would be like trying to control the moon's affinity for the earth."*

Goldie nods. "Our happiness was his happiness."

After so many years together, I hardly know my own feelings

apart from Goldie's. Is it Goldie's heart overflowing with warm memories and the gripping sadness of loss, or is it my own? Is Goldie's body relaxing into mine, or am I surrendering into hers? And yet there are surprises still. Goldie sits up suddenly as I'm drifting into sleep, and a draft of cold air slips into the warm space our bodies have created.

"Jaakov, I've felt Chaim with me all day. I hear his voice as if he is still alive." Goldie is shivering, her thin nightgown hardly a protection against the damp cold. I pull her closer to me, but she gently resists. "I want to know what he's trying to tell me."

Goldie spoke often of her older brother. "Maybe he's consoling you around *abba's* death."

"He was always protective of me, and I think he's trying to protect me now."

My body tenses. This is no time to tell Goldie about Zeff's return, no time to start the cascade of memories and regrets. Thankfully Goldie seems not to notice my alarm.

"I feel such guilt that he died fighting while I stayed hidden with my mother and the babies."

I withhold my thoughts. Chaim didn't have to fight. He chose to confront the anti-Semitic mob in a battle he couldn't possibly have won. He might have survived had he remained in hiding with the rest of the family, but he was young and outraged and unwilling to capitulate so easily.

"Did I ever share this with you, Jaakov?"

"Share what with me, sweetheart?"

Goldie curls her body into mine. "I wonder if all my miscarriages were punishment for not having stood by Chaim."

"Sweetheart, you could have done nothing to save Chaim. Instead, both of you would have been murdered, and I cannot bear to think what my life would have been without you."

My arms grip her more tightly hoping my gesture of love will extinguish her pain.

"I often wonder how Chaim would have lived his life. My

brother was always questioning, fighting, and pushing the limits of everything."

Involuntarily, I chuckle. "*Abba* once told me that Chaim knew what he was fighting against, but he didn't know what he was fighting for."

Goldie's body tightens, and I regret my words. "He died too young to know what he was fighting for, but his rebellion would have become his ideals, and his ideals would have led him to action. He would have left the confines of the *shtetl*. Perhaps . . ." Suddenly she is silent. I wait with increasing concern and curiosity for her words. Sitting up straight now, her body is taut, her mind elsewhere. Gently I reach out to pull her back to me. She responds, sinking slowly into the nest of my arms. I'm exhausted from the long day, but Goldie has more to share.

"Jaakov, do you ever feel as if your life is not large enough to hold you, not free enough to express everything inside you?"

Another ripple of fear passes through me. Only moments ago I savored the sweetness of intimacy, and the delicious unified sense of body and heart.

"Perhaps because I'm a woman, Jaakov. Sometimes I wish I'd been born a man."

"A woman bears life, a great privilege a man can never know."

Goldie sighs. "I suppose it's human nature to want what we cannot have, what seems beyond our grasp."

"Why would you want to be a man?"

Her voice softens. "I savor the privacy that a man's life offers. I so love the moments when I listen inside and hear the bliss of creation singing its delight. Even on *Shabbat,* when all men are free to study and pray, women tend to the needs of others. They take care of children and parents. There is no time for a woman to simply rest and behold."

The poignancy of her words touches me, and expands my love for her. "I want your happiness more than my own. If there is anything I can do . . ."

Goldie draws closer in to me. "Thank you, my husband. I love you."

This night I lie awake far longer than Goldie, troubled by what has been left unspoken. We know each other deeply and live inside each other in so many ways. Yet there is a part of Goldie, elusive and beautiful, like the dark side of the moon. We all have secrets hidden within, hidden even from ourselves, secrets so precious and so fragile.

"What are your secrets?" I whisper aloud to my sleeping Goldie. And what are my own secrets, I muse, before my eyes close and I slip away into other realms.

CHAPTER THREE

Startled awake by a crashing sound, I mistake the noise for a dream until, hearing footsteps, I bolt into the kitchen.

"Shmuel, is it you?" I whisper, knowing my son-in-law has no reason to be here at this hour. I proceed cautiously, my heart pounding with fear. The crackle of embers in the cook stove is the only sound. A cool breeze wafting in the thickness of the dark means a door is ajar. Lighting a candle, I find the door, equipped with an inside latch, meaning it could not have been opened from the outside. Had I been careless and left it open? The house is cold. I lift the lid off the stove and stir the embers with a poker. Slowly, vigilantly, I scan the room. Nothing seems out of order. The huge bread bowls, the baskets of potatoes, the cook pots and dishes are all in their right places. Scattered on the floor, however, are the remnants of a pitcher left on the table.

A piece of paper is set on the table, a note perhaps that Goldie wrote while I was sleeping? Holding it close to the candle, a sharp pain grips my chest. The note is in Zeff's handwriting. Why had I not guessed sooner? Who else could, and would, find a way to open a latched door? How could I have forgotten? Zeff had long ago delighted and intrigued me with his notes, resplendent with philosophical meanderings like my own, filled with poignant prophecy. Like a poisoned stream, Zeff was tempting to drink but so very toxic. Reluctantly I open the note.

What do you believe about time? Do we meet the future or create the future? Is there one past and future, or many? Do we live in certainties or probabilities? Do you see the probability that lies ahead of us, the storm cloud building on the horizon, gathering the forces of darkness in its wake? It threatens to swallow the whole world into its cavernous depths. I speak about an evil that is beyond your wildest imaginings. I tell you this, because it is the simple truth. You may try to ignore me, shut me out of your life. You may see me as vile or depraved, or you may pity me, but I will not go away. I will not be silenced. I will not be banished. You and I are bound together. There will come a time when you will need me, when your very existence will depend on the mercy I serve you, or don't. I speak the simple truth.

Memories flood through me. Zeff was the magical and wounded boy who could see into past and future. Zeff was the impassioned boy with a shock of red hair and intense sea-green eyes, Zeff, with his impressive precocity of intellect. Yet he was cruel and vindictive, causing harm to others with no remorse. Through an act of vengeful violence, Zeff fathered my cherished grandson, Shimon. Zeff is again intruding into my life, into the privacy of our home. The content of the note is also disturbing. Is he warning me or taunting me? It is hard to know with Zeff. In the flickering candlelight, I gather up the shards of pottery. Placing the note deep inside my pocket, I crouch on the floor in a corner next to the stove, and I weep.

CHAPTER FOUR

The sun is already peeking in the window by the time I open my eyes. Goldie is not beside me, and for a moment I panic that she might have found the note. Hastily I rise, shivering as the cold air contacts my skin. I find Goldie in the kitchen lighting the stove.

"Sorry to be so late this morning. I didn't sleep well last night."

"Is anything wrong?" she asks.

"Nothing is wrong. I'm missing him, that is all."

Goldie walks over to embrace me. "Jaakov, go spend time with your mistress today."

My mistress as Goldie calls her, is the viola that I inherited from the rebbe.

"You should not carry the burden. There will be an endless stream of people here today."

"I have plenty of help. Laiah and Laura and the children will be here soon."

"You know me well, sweetheart."

She smiles, and I relax. "Only a few hours with her, Jaakov. More than that will indeed be risking my wrath."

The rebbe introduced me to the viola, a precious instrument gifted to him by his own father. Learning to play was one of the great joys of my youth.

"Her music heals souls, Jaakov, just as your hands are instruments of healing. I've seen it happen. She holds the spirits of many within her body."

Stepping out into the frigid air, a sudden turn from yesterday's thaw, I hastily retreat back inside to wrap a scarf around my neck and don thick woolen gloves. The biting cold stings my face, the frozen ground crunching under the weight of my steps. Countless times I played the viola for Zeff, hoping for a miracle, hoping the magic of the music would transform his cruelty into kindness, his indifference into compassion. Zeff has returned, and all my wishes will not make him disappear.

The space I deem my office is in the loft of the old barn, now serving as our synagogue. Hoards of people were burned to death when the mob locked them inside and torched the original synagogue. We also lost a sacred Torah scroll, a part of the community for generations. This same *pogrom* took the life of Chaim. I wasn't here at the time but my own *shtetl* had endured similar violations. Fear of attack is a stark fact of our lives, ever present but intentionally ignored, for how else can we survive? How else can we live with the helplessness of not knowing if we can protect our children, our wives, our parents? How else can we preserve any sense of faith in the G-d we worship? The synagogue was never rebuilt for fear that it would meet the same fate. Such is our resourcefulness that holiness has found its home in the barn.

Last summer my students built stairs and enclosed part of the loft. The one window, cracked during installation, was left as a reminder of the precariousness of our lives. As if we need reminders. Standing at the door, the viola case pressed under one arm, I reach into my pocket for the key. For one anxious moment I fear that Zeff has intruded here as well. Thankfully I find no more notes.

The viola case I place reverently on my desk. Its leather veneer, disfigured by deep scratches, disguises the plush red lining, a breathtaking surprise every time I open the case. Taking hold of the slim and graceful neck of the viola, I lift her out of her slumber and into the familiar, intimate place between chin and shoulder. My other hand reaches for the bow, and gliding it across the strings, I tune her to near perfection. I've learned to trust, to give myself over to the music that uses my hands to make its voice known. The sound emerges and recedes, like waves cresting and dissolving back into the ocean.

"Beautiful music, Jaakov. I haven't heard you play like that for a long time."

Laura's voice startles me. She is leaning against the door jam, bundled in coat and hat, her face flushed red from the cold. "The music is enchanting."

"I had no idea that you were listening."

"You were lost in rapture, my friend. I would love to keep listening, but I've come to bring you home. It is almost noon."

"I've been playing that long?"

Laura smiles and nods vehemently. "It's freezing in here, Jaakov. How could you not have noticed?"

Now that the creative fervor has passed, my body is shivering. Warming my hands in my pockets I come upon the note from Zeff. Rapture dissolves into anger.

"I need to talk with you."

She exhales impatience. "Does it have to be now? It's already so late."

"Yes, now. It involves Zeff."

She steps back, startled, as if I've just delivered her a blow. "Let's go to my house. Sarah and Michel are already at yours."

We walk in tense silence, our eyes carefully negotiating the deep ruts in the frozen dirt road. The barn is on the edge of town, but it only takes a few moments to enter the crowded main street where each wooden house is uniquely shaped by the elements. Here a sagging roof, there a chimney partially collapsed or a porch disjointedly attached to the main structure. The sky is darkening, the air moist with impending snowfall, the first of the season. Laura walks faster than me. I follow a step behind. When she stops suddenly, I almost run into her. She turns to me, her distress revealing itself in her downturned gaze.

"Why does he keep returning, Jaakov? Will we never be free of him?"

"Perhaps we are the only family he's known."

"You're being far too kind to him. We are not his family. His children are no longer his family. The moment he abused them he lost all rights to father them."

She turns to keep walking, her pace quickening. I'm out of breath by the time we step inside her house.

"I must warn you. The children left a mess."

"They are children, Laura."

"They are old enough to know better." With sharp, quick movements, her hand sweeps across the thick wooden table, crumbs cascading to the floor.

"The water is still hot. I'll make tea."

The room is hardly a mess. In one corner is a column of wooden blocks all stacked neatly, if precariously, to reach almost waist height, likely Michel's creation. In another corner three rag dolls are propped against the wall.

"How are the children doing? I haven't seen them lately."

"They are both fine. Michel is still too hot tempered and Sarah far too timid, but they are improving. And I certainly do not want Zeff interfering in their lives ever again."

I feel a disturbing sense of helplessness. "He broke into our house last night and left a letter on the table." Her body freezes in mid-motion. "Nothing was taken or destroyed, except a pitcher that he must have knocked off the table when he heard me coming."

She looks up at me, her eyes wet with tears. "And to imagine that I once loved and trusted this man enough to marry him. I know that I was young and naïve, but his love seemed real, his promises genuine."

Her words grip my heart. I'd seen the bruises, the gashes, all the outer signs of his cruelty and betrayal.

"Try not to be hard on yourself, Laura. Remember that I also once loved him and believed in him."

Her face softens. "Was any of the good real, Jaakov? I want to believe that there is good to him, and that he fell victim to malevolent forces."

Zeff remains a disturbing mystery to me. He was so loved by all of us, and yet all he did was take advantage of our kindness. I hand Laura the note. She reads it, her face puckering with disgust.

"It's hard to tell whether this reflects his gift of prophecy or his own delusions. Why has he returned? What does he want from you, from us? The children will have to be told, warned, protected, especially Shimon. He is the youngest and most vulnerable."

"I haven't yet told Goldie. I wanted to spare her at least while she grieves her father."

"She'll have to be told soon." Laura finishes clearing the table and reaches for her coat. "I'm relieved that Josef is coming."

I've almost forgotten that my older brother is traveling here with my parents, all of them intending to stay the winter before returning to their own *shtetl.* The one-eyed widower Slosberg, whose wife recently passed away, has offered his extra room to my parents.

"Do you intend for Josef to live here with you and the children?"

She gives me a sharp look. "Please do not judge us, Jaakov. Life can sometimes be messy."

"I'm not judging you, Laura, but I don't want you to be hurt again."

"I know you want the best for me, but much has changed for your brother." Laura's face is tense, her thin lips puckered. Tears shimmer on her eyelids. "How many times have we tried to heal Zeff? How naïve I was to think that if I could offer him one moment of perfect love, his heart would open, but the more I gave the more cruel he became."

Laura dismisses her tears with a sweep of her hand. "I can't do it, Jaakov. I should be able to forgive him, but I cannot. Even Laiah, who was equally violated by him, has found more forgiveness than me."

Laiah, my beautiful daughter had befriended this boy, and this boy had returned as a vengeful young man and raped her, scarring body and psyche, impregnating her with the only child she would be able to bear. Laiah worked diligently to forgive him, because she felt it too painful to carry the child of someone she hated.

"Before we continue healing Zeff, you need to forgive yourself, Laura. You need to forgive yourself for your innocent trust, and for everything having to do with Zeff."

Laura shakes her head in agreement. "Zeff is a complexity of contradictions. Remember when a tree fell on the back of a horse, and he stayed with the horse stroking her until the tree was removed? The horse not only remained calm, but when the tree was finally moved, she stood up with no sign of injury."

How well I recall that day, the same day that Zeff lost his temper and knocked Laura unconscious.

"Yes," I say, curbing my outrage. "He is a complex soul."

"Right now we should return before Goldie presumes that I've fallen under the spell of your music."

We step outside. Sun filtering through the clouds fills the sky with diffuse yellow-grey light. We walk in silence. I think about Josef. His visits over the years have been comforting and disturbing. He is a good man, my brother, a man with his own kind of mission. Josef is a Zionist, working to reclaim the land of Palestine, the land bequeathed to our ancestors. Two thousand years of persecution we have suffered since being dispelled from our homeland by Roman conquerors. Two thousand years of ardent prayers that we may reclaim a haven in a world that has offered us no safe place to reside.

Perhaps what is disturbing about Josef is that he makes me face difficult truths about my life. Truth—the sublime elixir that liberates us from all the lies that make our lives bearable, or so we like to believe.

CHAPTER FIVE

Haunted am I, and hunted in my dreams. The world has been overtaken by darkness. The young man is being tortured. He's fallen onto a floor as hard as stone, cold as ice. Even the light is cold and casting eerie shadows on the walls of the cell. He is beaten, tortured, left for dead. Who will hear his moans? Who will rescue him? Is there mercy or is his fate written? He hovers between worlds. Good morning, good mourning.

Goldie finds Zeff's note. Refusing to meet my gaze, she hands it to me, her stark coolness a painful contrast to her usual warmth. She's been crying. Guilt pierces my heart. I try unsuccessfully to think of ways to assuage my guilt, to lay down the burden of self-blame, but the feeling weighs down my heart like an immoveable rock.

"Keep him away from me. Keep him away from all of us. Do you understand me, Jaakov?" Her words are clipped, flung like daggers.

"I understand you perfectly, Goldie. I've done what I can. What more can I do?"

"There is nothing you can do now."

"I know I should have listened to you." This conversation we've had a thousand times, the hurt unresolved still. "I will do my best to keep him from doing any more harm to any of us. I promise."

Goldie turns away, staring out the window at the parade of people walking with faces bent into prayer books, lines of children following like ducklings behind them. I venture over to join her and place my arms around her waist. Thankfully she softens. "This is the last day of sitting *shiva.*" Goldie returns my embrace, but her mind is elsewhere. What is she thinking, my Goldie? "I will visit with Laiah today." I continue talking in the hope of creating a bridge between us, trying to reach my Goldie, but I must wait until she chooses to return, always fearing that she will be lost to me forever. Please, I pray, for this reason alone, keep Zeff away. It is a prayer, I know, that won't hold. Zeff has returned, and I am powerless to contain him.

Laura is waiting for me outside the barn, walking briskly back and forth to stay warm. From a distance she reminds me of a horse nervously pacing the perimeter of the corral. Brusquely she hands me a leather binder as if it's a burden she wishes to unload. With little more than a nod she turns to leave.

"Is something wrong?" I ask.

"Nothing is wrong, Jaakov. Are not first meetings of great significance? I want to allow you time alone. First impressions are powerful."

She's right. A first meeting often reveals the totality of what will later be analyzed and understood. I climb the stairs to my office with the binder tucked under my arm, and close the door behind me. Without the fervor of musical inspiration, the damp chill of the air will make a long sitting prohibitive. Still, I need to properly prepare myself for this important meeting. Closing my eyes, chanting a prayer of gratitude, I call in the presence of the four archangels, powerful guides and protectors for the inner journey. Each one I invoke by name and by quality: Michel to my right, bold guardian of the truth; Gabriel to my left, keeper of the sacred knowledge of all time; Uriel in front of me, holding eternal wisdom, Raphael at the back, offering loving healing. Once I feel their presence, I'm ready to meet the manuscript.

The binder is soft leather, rough at the edges, with one dark stain in the center. Inside, the rebbe's handwriting meets me like a welcome and unexpected friend, each letter and word perfectly embellished in his unique style. Sensing his presence, my body relaxes in the recognition that I'm not alone.

Hear me now. How can shadow exist when all is light? How can death be real when the world has not yet been born? How can anyone be exiled when one is never apart from the Source? How can there be hatred when love is all that truly exists? To reconcile the relative world and the true condition is the state of freedom. Let all who aspire toward freedom contemplate these questions.

The initial impact is powerful, the manuscript having delivered a loving blow, an exquisite confrontation, a magnetic pull into its waiting mystery. The words are music, proclamation, poetry, thunder, prayer, invocation. I read and reread the text, slowly, deliberately listening to the sound and shape of the words, and the spaces between the words, listening for the subtleties of cadence and rhythm, listening inside the words, listening for the obvious and the hidden meaning in content and structure. These words and the consciousness embedded in these words are becoming woven into my life, into my own soul. They are catalysts, doorways, confrontations, and love songs. They will continue to transform me. I feel their energy moving within me, like yeast in bread, like the power of reciting a divine name over and over, like the impact of being seen down to the very core of one's being.

How many hours had the rebbe insisted that I engage with the practice of *gamatria*, the sacred practice of decoding a text?

Awkward at first, I became adept at changing letters, and then words into numerical values, associating words with other words having the same numerical value, or complementary value, or applying numerous other techniques, trying always to cull out the hidden meaning. Over and over I would practice until my mind in receptive unknowing would be ripened for revelation.

Momentary fear grips me. Despite my proficiency, this manuscript and this mission are of a different order. It is not proficiency that will decide success or failure, but something far more elusive. What will it mean to succeed or fail? What are the consequences either way? The will of this mission is far greater than my own, and I can only bow in humility and devotion to Her. Closing the binder, I place it under my coat, right next to my heart. The relationship—and the alchemy—has begun.

CHAPTER SIX

Despite the cold I stand on the opposite side of the street from the tailor shop where I can peer inside without being seen. It's a strange habit, perhaps, to watch my daughter without her awareness, a habit initiated when I felt her pull away from me. We were close, our temperaments and proclivities similar, and her withdrawal, subtle as it was, pained me greatly. I understand her reasons and feel gratitude that she has not condemned me, as I condemn myself for my failures.

I stand outside now, the cold deterring the usual traffic of people and wagons, making my viewing easier. The tailor shop boasts an impressive sign hung perpendicular to the building. On both sides is painted a pair of scissors. Shmuel's grandfather, the original shop owner, painted the sign himself. During the *pogrom* the window of the shop was shattered and the sign pocked with bullet holes. Inside the holes Shmuel weaves colored ribbons, and with each season he changes the colors. Since it is winter, the ribbons are white and blue.

The storefront is a large picture window. Directly in front of the window two sewing machines are perched divided by a long table. Laiah, and often Shmuel, can be seen bent over a machine.

Today Shmuel is not at his machine, but Laiah is there, bent forward, staring intently at the needle as it rises and falls with mesmerizing speed. Laiah always frowns as she works, likely from the need to pay such close attention to the task, and not from unhappiness. But it is hard to know and Laiah, for sure, will not tell me.

If Laiah were another kind of person, a less extraordinary person at least in this father's eyes, perhaps I would be more at peace with the life thrust upon her. Laiah is bright and showed an early passion for study. She is kind, almost too kind to live in a world that also requires severity. In outward appearance she resembles neither Goldie nor myself. Slender, willowy, Laiah has a high brow and marked cheekbones, and piercing silvery blue eyes.

Laiah's trusting nature left her vulnerable, and I failed to protect her as a father should protect his daughter. For this, Goldie has never completely forgiven me, nor have I forgiven myself. The choices in life are seldom clear. Perhaps if I had not rescued Laura and her children, Zeff would not have exacted revenge by raping Laiah. But Shimon was conceived in the rape and he is a gift to all of us. Shmuel, a kind and simple man, was willing to marry Laiah and adopt Shimon, even with Laiah unable to bear other children. Laiah assures me that she is content with Shmuel, and I never question her aloud. It is not a marriage of love, or, in some ways, a marriage of equals. Shmuel is a good man but is simple and lacking Laiah's textured complexity and intelligence. Is she truly content with her marriage? I know that Laiah would never tell me otherwise, and therefore I will never know. Perhaps I don't really want to know.

Stepping inside, the bell above the door tinkles with spritely welcome. The scent of sweat and wool linger in the air. The shop is empty except for the eerie presence of a mannequin and racks of clothing in need of attending. The whir of the sewing machine stops. Laiah looks up, smiles, and motions me to wait while she finishes a hem. The whir begins again, a comforting sound with its repetitive lull. When it stops, Laiah stands up and sweeps the front of her dress to remove stray threads. She greets me warmly, and then her demeanor changes.

"Abba, I know about Zeff, and I told Shimon. What are we going to do?"

"Shimon knows already?"

She shrugs. "He has to know to protect himself if Zeff tries again to kidnap him."

"How did he respond?"

Laiah's eyes gaze upward, a gesture of devotion or impatience. "Shimon is an old soul. He accepts difficulty as if it is simply part of being human. I can never tell if he is passive or wise, or both."

The tinkle of bells indicates a customer has entered. "This is Avram the butcher. I promised him his dress coat would be ready today." Laiah leaves to greet him and retrieve his garment. In a moment she returns.

"Can you imagine a child being more different from his father?" she remarks. "Except for the red hair. Shimon hates his red hair, because it's the same color as his father's hair."

"I know, I know. Thank G-d he's a bright and sensitive child, and well loved by all of us."

"And thank G-d for Shmuel. For now we've agreed that one of us will be with him all the time. It does put a strain on our work, but what else can we do?"

"Your mother and I will help as well."

"Laura and I will help each other, and soon Josef will arrive." Laiah's face relaxes. "We'll be fine, and soon Zeff will get tired of it all and disappear."

The bell tinkles again. More customers have entered. Promising to resume Shimon's lessons, I withdraw into the damp cold. Tiny ice crystals begin to fall, collecting on my beard and mustache, the high whoosh of tiny snowbells filling the air.

❧

The snowfall holds off until the next day, but by midmorning the wind picks up and the ground is blanketed in white. Agitated, Goldie paces the room, casting frequent glances out the window to stare disapprovingly at the sky.

"I hope Josef doesn't try and push through this storm. Your parents are too old to be traveling in this weather, really too old to be traveling at all."

I'm worried as well. I respect my older brother, but Josef can be a risk taker, and this is hardly a good time to take a risk.

"Josef knows what to do," I say, compelled to defend him in spite of my own concerns. "He will make sure they're safe."

Goldie's head cocks to one side. "Josef is not foolhardy. He just believes that the impossible is possible."

I laugh at the truth of her words. "At times an admirable trait."

Goldie smiles and relaxes. "Sometimes he reminds me so much of Chaim that I have to look twice to make sure he's not my brother."

This is not the first time that Goldie compares Josef to her beloved brother, nor is it the first time that it concerns me. Sensing my discomfort, Goldie wraps her arms around my waist. The scent of her, earthy and sweet, the feel of her body, now round and soft, is as familiar to me as my own body. Yet I feel increasing unease in not understanding the woman I've known most of my life. Have I held the illusion or the desire that she will stay the same forever? Relationships need to breathe—two people need to be joined but also separate, and each respected in their separateness. The lighting of the *Shabbat* candles is a reminder of this truth. One candle representing the masculine and the other the feminine, they stand close to each other, but still apart. The mutual offering of freedom is the paradoxical glue of intimacy.

"Laura tells me that he is actively seeking people to join his settlement," she says. "I wonder if he has found funding."

"I'm sure we'll hear plenty about it. In fact, it might be all we hear about. Laura also tells me that he has other news to share with us."

Goldie laughs. "You'll hear it all from him soon enough."

"Why am I the last one to know about my own brother?"

I feign annoyance, but really I know it to be a function of the distinct difference between men and women. Josef and I have our own kind of intimacy. He's a year older, but has always been a head taller, more muscular and decidedly more outspoken. He's a carpenter and works with his hands. Were it not for my proficiency in studies, and, according to my mother at least, a handsome and well-proportioned face, I might feel overshadowed by him. Instead, we mostly admire each other.

When we were both children, I also saved his life. Playing together in the barn, Josef, always daring, fell from the rafters and suffered a deep gash in his torso that bled profusely. I was about to run for help when a voice inside my mind instructed me to lay my hands on the wound and pray. The bleeding stopped, and I realized with equal degrees of fear and awe that I could call upon this strange and mysterious power to heal. Too young to realize how little ownership I had of anything in my life, I could not decide whether I was odd or special. Only later did I feel the sense of burdening responsibility that such a gift carries with it.

"They've arrived, Jaakov!"

Bursting with relief and joy, we bolt out the door to greet them and help them inside. My two elderly parents, bundled inside layers of blankets, are secured in the rear seat of the carriage. Josef and I carry them into the house, Josef hoisting my father over his shoulder while I carry my mother, delicate, frail, weighing less than a sack of potatoes. Her blue eyes sparkle as she grips my neck tightly with her arms. Goldie bustles about preparing hot tea and ladling out steaming soup. Between the weather and one close encounter with a hostile farmer who threatened to send the mob after them, it was a long and difficult journey. They are here now, thankfully, for the duration of the winter.

Exhausted and cold, the horses need tending right away. Josef and I bundle up and step back out, the wind blowing the snow in almost horizontal sheets of white. The horses snort impatiently. Josef runs his hand gently over their necks.

"Thank you for your hard work. Now is your time for a good long winter rest."

We hoist ourselves into the carriage. Josef clicks the reins and urges them toward the barn. The snow is blowing in chaotic, frenzied swirls.

"We were so worried about you, brother."

"I can imagine you were," he shouts over the wind, clicking to the horses to quicken their pace. "Traveling in a storm has advantages. It cuts down the threat of running into highway robbers and anti-Semitic gangs. These days they are a greater danger than weather."

The horses protest the increasing wind. "We're almost home now. A warm stall and hay are waiting for you."

Hearing his voice, the horses pick up the pace. Reaching the barn, I jump down from the wagon and slide open the heavy wooden doors. Josef drives the carriage inside and deftly unhitches the horses, now shivering with cold. The pungent, earthy scent of hay and the calming presence of other animals reassures them in the midst of the storm. We wipe them down, blanket them, and lead them to their stalls, pitching ample hay inside. Soon they are eating contentedly, the soft rhythmic sound of chewing interrupted by an occasional snort. After breaking the ice on the water trough, we fill two buckets, and then we have time to talk. After climbing the stairs leading to my office, we step inside. Removing his mittens and rubbing his hands together for warmth, Josef slowly scans the room.

"Why has nobody put a stove in here? How can you tolerate working in the cold?"

"I manage."

"I would think you would want to do more than just manage in life, brother. I'll install one as soon as I'm settled."

"Thank you. How long do you plan to stay this time?"

Josef's dark eyes set beneath coal black eyebrows study me intensely.

"I see that Laura has kept our secret."

"If you have a secret, she has divulged nothing to me."

He smiles, the intensity of his scrutiny relaxing. "Laura has agreed to marry me. We haven't had a lot of time with each other, but we know each other well enough to feel mutual love and respect."

"I know I shouldn't be, but I'm surprised. Have you decided to leave Sade?"

Josef sighs heavily. "I had to leave, brother. I could no longer tolerate the lack of love or affection, or even simple kindness. I remained far too long for the sake of others."

"I'm sorry, Josef. You deserve better."

Josef's face relaxes. "I'm happy to hear you say that. Knowing Laura, even as a friend, I felt her warmth and respect, and that made it even more unbearable to continue the marriage. Laura is just the opposite of Sade. She is strong, and generous, and kind, and given what she endured she deserves to be cherished. We both deserve the kind of marriage that you have with Goldie."

"I've certainly been blessed with my Goldie."

Josef shudders. "I'm freezing in here."

I laugh. "And this remark is coming from a man who just rode through a blizzard? You need warm food and hot tea. We'll have plenty of time to talk once you're more rested."

Josef stands and then hesitates. "I need to share something with you right away." Josef looks at me directly. "Laura and I intend to make *aliyah*. As you know I've been gathering resources for a settlement, and G-d willing we'll move to Palestine this spring."

His words leave me breathless. "You are not even married yet, and already you plan to move away?"

Josef fumbles nervously. "Yes, if funding comes through, we'll be leaving."

"Has Laura agreed to this?"

"She is considering."

I sit in stunned silence, absorbing the impact of his words. "Why are you doing this, Josef? Do you think it best for Laura and the children? You are many years older than her. What will happen to her if something should happen to you?"

Josef's face tightens. "Something can happen to any of us at any time, Jaakov. We've talked about it plenty, and she's not concerned. She's become strong and independent and besides, it has to be done."

"What do you mean it has to be done?"

"I would be far happier remaining here among family, but if nobody is willing to make sacrifices, then there will never be a homeland. Our lives, and the lives of our children and grand-children will continue to be run by the whims of fickle czars and power hungry anti-Semitic leaders."

My chest tightens. I feel the urge to cry. Josef notices. Placing his hand gently on my shoulder, his voice is soft and pleading.

"You don't understand the dire seriousness of the situation that Jews are facing and will continue to face in this world. We must help ourselves before it is too late."

"Of course I understand, Josef." I flash on the note that Zeff left for me with its bleak warnings about the future. "I'm just sad. Laura is my closest friend, and you are my only brother."

He softens and reaches out an arm to me. "I so wish my destiny were something other than this. The last thing I want to do is rip apart our family, and to rip Laura and the children away from the family."

I reach back to him. "I know that, Josef, and I admire your courage."

"I don't know if it's courage or fear that motivates me, brother. Whenever I have any doubt, I recall the sight of Rebbe Maslov hanging from that tree before we cut him down."

Recalling the horrific *pogrom* of three summers, ago my

body shudders. The *shtetl* that was unluckily chosen for attack was less than half a day's walk from here. It could just as easily have been me, brutally beaten and then hung from a tree. Josef was visiting at the time, and the two of us cut Rebbe Maslov down and gave him, as well as the mother and child trampled to death, a proper burial.

"We have few options, Jaakov. Any attempt to resist is futile. Every one of us would be killed. Our only hope of survival is a return to our G-d given homeland."

Josef looks away, as if he has already left, as if the brother I've known and loved has transformed into another man, a man whose personal life has come to an end, a man who has embarked on a hero's journey.

CHAPTER SEVEN

Josef wastes little time making himself useful to the community. His carpentry skills are superb and his generosity admirable. Most reassuring for me, however, is how he and Laura enjoy each other now that they are free to openly share their happiness. Sarah and Michel, Laura's children, blossom as Josef engages them in play or includes them in his work projects. They have all sacrificed plenty in this life, and their time of blessing is now.

The wedding is an expression of that blessing, a simple, heartfelt ceremony, a feast of family and sumptuous foods from last autumn's harvest. Crowded in our tiny home, we sing and dance and toast the bride and groom over and over, celebrating their union and offering blessings for the years to come.

Unnamed that evening is the sadness of their imminent departure. I can hardly imagine life without Laura, and my brother's visits have sustained my love for him throughout the years. Goldie and Laiah are feeling the loss as well. But tonight there is no mention of the future. Life is ephemeral and therefore precious. This quintessential moment of perfection will occur only this once.

The night is clear and so cold that it is hard to take a full breath without gasping. Josef arrived hours before to stoke the two stoves that inadequately heat the synagogue, a walled off space within the barn, now serving as the meeting hall. Josef is spending time this winter tightening and shoring up the old wooden structure with its precarious high-beamed roof.

Standing together at the door, we greet people as they arrive. More arrive than anticipated on this frigid evening: young Rachel, who I've known since birth, her belly protruding and two young ones pulling at her skirt; Avram the butcher who perpetually smells of blood; Asher Edelson the dreamer, who still lives with his mother; the rebbe's students, now my students from across the river; Simmy, the simpleton who has a perpetual smile. I love them all and feel privileged to serve them. When everybody is inside, Josef and I stand side by side in the front of the hall. Introducing my brother, I bask in the confidence and charisma of his presence. After the introduction I join Goldie, Laura, and the rest of my family sitting in the front row. Josef's face is tense with purpose. Despite the cold, he removes his jacket, keeping only a woolen scarf around his neck. Greeting each person with a nod, he offers reassurance that they have made the right decision to attend.

"Good evening," he begins, his voice clear and strong. "For those of you who do not know me, my name is Josef Janowicz. I am the brother of your beloved rebbe. I'm honored that you have all come on this cold winter night to hear about something of great importance to all of us, and all Jews everywhere."

He pauses, slowly looking around the room, nodding as his eyes alight on the faces of attentive listeners. A baby wails and then stops.

"What I'm about to share with you is what you yourselves already know. We, as Jews, and simply because we are Jews, are in grave danger. We live in fear. We live every day knowing that we might be attacked, our children murdered, our homes and syna-gogues destroyed. We live with indignity, tolerated at best, but mostly hated, and for no other reason than the fact that we are Jews."

He pauses again, his timing impeccable, sweeping the room with his eyes.

"For thousands of years Jews have been living in exile, never allowed to be full participants in any society or nation. We are considered pariahs, subject to the whims of the political climate, which, as we know, change as fast as the wind changes direction. And with each change our fate hangs in the balance. Our lives, our very existence is precarious. We are hated, persecuted, mur-dered out of greed, fear, envy, and ignorance. We have tried to fit in, tried to make contributions to every nation in which we live, but we are always shunned. The hatred is increasing, not decreas-ing. Acts of violence against us are increasing, not decreasing."

He gazes upward, raising his arms far above his head. "Why are we meeting in a barn? Why do we pray in a barn instead of in a holy synagogue?"

A child in the audience responds. "Bad men burned our synagogue, and everybody inside died."

Josef nods vigorously. "One of many great tragedies that has befallen us. Until now we have been powerless, forced to keep our heads low and wait for the blows to fall. If we take action now, we have a chance to change our destiny. We cannot afford to wait any longer. The time is now. Our very survival is being threatened, and we must take action."

Josef's words are captivating, his delivery forceful and com-pelling. The audience sits listening in rapt attention. Even the children are silent.

"We are not helpless unless we choose to be. At this time, and perhaps only for this limited time, we may change the course of history and reclaim Palestine, the Jewish homeland, the land bequeathed to us by our forefathers. Choosing to make *aliyah* means that our children and our children's children may reclaim their right to sovereignty and dignity."

Josef pauses and sweeps the room with his eyes. "Zionism," he says with conviction. "Zionism. Our one hope is to rebuild our homeland. This land is waiting for our return, to give it life again, to make it fertile, to draw forth its holiness."

His delivery is magnificent, imbuing me with unexpected ardor and passion.

"There are a few courageous and tireless men approaching politicians, heads of state, anyone with influence and finances. They are knocking on any door they can find to procure funding and permission to build settlements in Palestine. The more settlements we establish, the more influence we have, the closer we come to establishing our right to claim a Jewish state. I invite all who feel the call of Zionism to make *aliyah,* anybody drawn to help, to create a settlement, anyone drawn to participate in the creation of a Jewish homeland, to come forward."

People rise and walk toward him, but he gestures for them to stop. "Hear me out, for I must also warn you that the realization of our vision will take extreme courage. We must be prepared to work tirelessly, to cast aside our needs for comfort and security if we are to embark on this new journey. We may go hungry for many months. Our crops may wither. We may fall prey to illness. Our neighbors may be hostile and unwelcoming. We may cry out to return to Poland, forgetting that here we are persecuted. But if we persevere, the seeds we plant together will grow and flourish. The force of our combined effort will be unstoppable. We are interested in nothing less than changing the fate of our people. We are interested in nothing less than emerging out of defeat and claiming victory."

The people stand and cheer in a show of inspiration and solidarity, and to my surprise among those cheering loudest is Goldie.

CHAPTER EIGHT

When I rise the next morning, Goldie has already left the house. Most mornings we spend together, doing chores and sharing a simple breakfast. I'm curious but not particularly disturbed. Many people, more than usual, seem to be leaning on her. My Goldie, ever an ear, ever offering company when needed, ever bringing a meal or a prayer or a word of comfort. Goldie is not here, but I notice a binder lying open on the kitchen table. Goldie's hand-writing fills the pages. Has she left it in haste or has she left it for me to read? Assuming the latter, I read.

Who am I? Ceaselessly I ponder that question. Am I a woman, a mother, a wife, a daughter, a sister, a friend? These are my duties in life, but who am I? I try to be kind, loving, generous, and devoted to those I care about and those in need, for I am fortunate in life. I feel blessed with a husband who is kind and respectful and knows me as well as I know myself. Although I have only been able to bear two living children, I feel blessed with a remarkable daughter and son. I miss my son, Jeremiah, who chose to make his home in America, but I am proud that he followed his own path. Is that not why we are all here, to follow the destiny that G-d has prescribed for us? Some would call me selfish, but I believe it to be true.

I am blessed in life but not yet at peace. I hold a disturbing secret inside me, as if there is an unlived life inside me waiting to be born. Perhaps so many miscarriages left a longing to give birth, or perhaps I carry Chaim's soul within me. I don't know, and it scares me because when the opportunity arises, I must follow. I want to have lived a complete life. I have never spoken these words to anybody, not even to my beloved husband. If the time comes, I pray that Jaakov understands and forgives me.

My heart heavy, I close her diary and place it back on the table. I know exactly what Goldie intends to do. How will I respond? Our family is here, and being the rebbe, I'm central to the community. Will I make *aliyah* with her, with Josef and Laura? My concerns are not about my personal needs or inclinations. I would sacrifice without hesitation, but I will not leave my daughter and grandson unprotected, particularly with Zeff's reemergence.

I feel the urge to speak with my brother and head toward Laura's house. Turning a corner, I nearly bump into him. In tense silence we walk briskly to the office where earlier this week Josef installed a stove. Now he gathers kindling from the bin, fills the belly of the stove, and ignites a match. Our heads almost touching, we huddle close to the stove until the room is warm enough for us to remove our overcoats.

"I know you're angry, Jaakov."

"How long have you known, Josef?"

He chews nervously on the end of his mustache. "Goldie and I have talked about Zionism for years, but only recently has she approached me about making *aliyah*."

"How recently?"

Josef sighs loudly and looks away. "I haven't encouraged her, Jaakov. She came to me, not the other way around." I trust Josef's integrity. "The last thing I want to do is hurt you. Goldie has the passion and the vision of a Zionist, but that is not enough to risk everything to make *aliyah*. Circumstances must be right, and the body must be strong. We have limited resources. We can't afford to carry anybody unable to make a full contribution to the physical survival of the settlement. I haven't yet invited her, and there are good reasons to deny her. If you wish, I will do so."

"I could never deny Goldie her heart's yearning."

"And you, Jaakov?"

"Laiah and Shimon need me here. There is nothing for me to decide."

"I've spoken with Laiah. If it were not for Shmuel's health she'd be the first to make *aliyah*. She is a true Zionist, your daughter."

"But conditions are what they are."

"What if…"

"What if what?"

"What if Zeff agreed to keep his distance from Shimon for a year?"

His words leave me in total confusion. "Have you gone mad, brother? You don't even know how to contact him, never mind convince him of anything."

Josef's voice is a whisper. "I know how to contact him. In fact…."

"In fact what, Josef? In fact, you have spoken with him?"

Josef backs away. "Let me give you the facts, Jaakov. According to people who know more than either of us, we must act now if we are to reclaim our homeland. We must take this opportunity or the consequences for Jews will be dire."

I flash on Zeff's note.

"There are predictions, Jaakov."

"Who, besides Zeff, is making those predictions?"

"People working in high levels of government whisper about the rise of anti-Semitism, and new levels of perverted paranoid thinking."

"That has always been true, Josef. Anti-Semitism is a fact of our lives, a chronic disease that episodically flares up."

Josef's eyes widen. "This is different, Jaakov. This next anti-Semitic wave, according to people who are privy to such information, will have dire consequences for all Jews. It terrifies me, brother."

"What does this have to do with Zeff?"

"Right now there is no funding. I've had to make a difficult choice."

"Stop avoiding my question. What choice did you make?"

"Zeff offered me money, enough money to purchase land and support a group of settlers for two years."

"Zeff came to you and offered you money? For no apparent reason, he offered to pay for your settlement?"

"That is exactly how it happened, Jaakov. He left me a note, we met, and he handed me the resources I need to seed the settlement."

"You took money from a man who violently beat your wife and step-children, who raped my daughter?"

"Taking his money, as you say, is to finance a cause that could ensure our survival. Taking his money is the lesser of two evils. If I refuse, the settlement is unlikely to happen for years. Life is not perfect. Sometimes we sacrifice one thing to gain another, and here the gain is worth more than the sacrifice."

"Are you sure, Josef? He is giving you stolen money."

"This settlement needs to happen."

"Does this settlement need to happen for the right reasons? Maybe you need a purpose, Josef; maybe you want to be a champion."

Josef's face flares with rage. "Stop this, Jaakov. I have no personal desire to be anybody's hero. If you saw a terrible accident about to happen and you could prevent it, would you do so?"

I feel myself softening. "I'm sorry, brother. I trust your sincerity if not completely your judgment."

"Thank you, brother, for trusting my sincerity. As for my judgment, I'm not sure you understand how dire the situation really is, or could become. If you did, you would understand that I have no choice but to make this decision."

We sit in silence, listening to the crackle of fire.

"Why is he doing it, Josef?"

"You mean why is Zeff funding the settlement?"

"Yes, what is his motivation?"

Josef shrugs. "You would know better than me. Atoning for his sins?"

I give a cynical chuckle. "Likely he has some self-serving motivation."

"Or your healings are working, Jaakov. There is always that possibility. You and Laura are powerful healers."

Josef is a good man. He's been assigned his mission as I've been assigned mine. Reaching for our coats we share a spontaneous hug, his larger body enclosing mine.

The scent of wood smoke and steam infused with cedar embraces me as I open the door to the *mikvah,* to perform the ritual of immersing my body into blessed water, to purify the soul. Zalman Shecter, a prematurely old looking young man with a balding head and potbelly, inherited the *mikvah* from his father, who inherited it from his father. Zalman takes great pride in his bathhouse. He keeps it meticulously clean, obsessively scrubbing down the wood stained from moisture and years of use. His knowledge of *mikvah* rituals—the timing, the prayers, who can enter with whom, is indisputable. I might be the rebbe of the community, the spiritual leader, but he is definitely and rightfully in charge of this important tradition. The baths are a significant part of life for both men and women, serving to prepare for high holidays, weddings, the ending of moon cycles for women, and always to prepare for the arrival of the Shekinah on the eve of *Shabbat*, the time when She makes her ephemeral visitation and blesses us with Her presence.

"Go right in, rebbe." Zalman hands me a towel. "Sunset comes early these days."

The water is tepid as I ease my body into the tub, and I feel a deep exhale of tension, worry, and confusion. Silky, blessed water, a magical elixir for softening the mind, soothes skin and loosens knots in the heart. Who am I to think that I know what is supposed to happen? I've heard and imparted many versions of the story of the man who falls into hard times only later to find that his adverse circumstance has saved his life.

The rebbe's words come to me now. *"A kabbalist serves as a bridge from the unhealed past to the healed future."* I feel his presence holding me, reassuring me that I'm not alone. Zalman calls to me from outside the door.

"Just a few more minutes, rebbe. The sun is close to setting."

"Thank you," I say, emerging more hastily than I wish. My hair and beard still wet, I hoist on my boots and button my overcoat.

"*Shabbat Shalom*," I say goodbye to him, stepping out into the cold. The sun has already set, and dusk has painted the sky a murky purple grey. I'm late for the lighting of the candles. The streets are mostly empty of people. I feel Her hovering, waiting to join with us. Our home is not a far walk. I linger outside for a moment, peering into the frost-tinged window. All my loved ones are gathered inside, crowded around our makeshift table set with the special lace tablecloth and dishes used only for *Shabbat*. Several challahs, likely still warm from baking, adorn the table. With everybody seated, there is barely room to move, but what does it matter? On *Shabbat* the simplest of dwellings is transformed into a sanctuary, a place where holiness resides. Goldie, with head bowed, is standing at the head of the table, her eyes closed, waiting for me to share in the lighting of the two *Shabbat* candles. There are always two, one for the masculine and one for the feminine, equal, each standing upright, strong, in perfect balance with each other, thus maintaining the harmony of the world.

Pausing for a moment, my heart is overflowing with love for each precious soul sitting at the table on this *Shabbat*. I am truly blessed. Tears of gratitude spill from my eyes, freezing on my lashes. Now is the time to come in from the cold.

"There you are, *zeddeh!*" Shimon exclaims. "We've been waiting for you. *Shabbat Shalom.*"

"*Shabbat Shalom* to all of you. Are you ready for the blessing?"

Everybody, even the children, stops talking, and the room becomes silent and still in anticipation of Her descent. With exquisite delicacy, Her holy presence transforms us in that moment into divine beings inhabiting these vulnerable and uniquely precious human forms.

CHAPTER NINE

Lev is a handsome man with Josef's strong build and dark, intense eyes, a keen intellect and a wry wit. Lev, Josef's oldest son, is as passionate about Zionism as his father. He surprises us with a visit to our *shtetl* after attending the second Zionist Congressional meeting in Switzerland. He looks the same as he did several years ago when he last visited us, but he is more settled in himself. We gather around our crowded dinner table as Lev expounds on the tireless work of Theodor Herzl, the inspiring leader of the Zionist movement, who is knocking on every possible door for funding and political backing. Theodor and other young, impassioned leaders are adamant that this is the time for action. If there is a chance for the creation of a Jewish state to be recognized by the world, then it must be now. Lev's fervor for Zionism adds to his fervor for eating, as he fills and refills his plate with boiled potatoes, pickled beets, and cabbage. We jest with him that if the two are related, then Zionists make unpopular dinner guests. He good-humoredly responds with a quip that has us all roaring with laughter.

"It's good to know that there is a light side to Zionism," I remark.

"At least there is a light side to this Zionist, and yes, admittedly a rather hearty appetite."

"Lev, do you consider Zionism a social movement or a religious movement?" I query.

"There is religious fervor among some people who see Palestine as the divinely ordained Promised Land, but Zionism itself is not religious in origin. It is political and pragmatic. We don't see it as a divinely ordained mission, but as the only way to ensure the security and survival of the Jews. Land is power, and power is protection."

I feel unsettled by his response. Physical safety and security are indisputably important, but life is about more than survival. Life is bestowed upon us that we have the opportunity to transform and purify, to express G-d's will, to be vessels of Her light. We are here to heal this world, to unify and uplift, to join heaven and earth, to unite the light and wisdom of the divine with its physical counterpart. If we are not engaged in this sacred effort of *tikkun,* then what is the purpose of living?

"Lev, were our ancestors not given the land in order to live according to spiritual law?"

Lev shakes his head in bewilderment. "If someone's life is in danger, is it not the first priority to save that life? Then one can grapple with living according to spiritual law."

"Our bodies have endured the pain of exile, but our souls can also be exiled, no matter where we abide."

Lev's expression oscillates between confidence and confusion. "Zionism is a response to the question of Jewish survival. History shows us that without the protection and sovereignty that a state might offer, our survival is tenuous. We must take charge of our destiny. Nobody will come to our rescue. We will simply cease to exist, and I can't imagine that G-d by any name would wish that to be our fate."

His response makes good practical sense, and practical sense is needed in this world. What is my difficulty, I wonder. I have no words for it, only an uneasy concern that Jews not lose their spiritual bearings, for without spiritual bearings, survival is of no value. In the diaspora, with no secure physical home, all we have is a spiritual home. The holy city of Jerusalem dwells within our hearts. If we are exiled from our inner home, then what does it matter if we secure an outer home?

And yet I would be foolish to deny that our physical survival matters. We are here to bring heaven to earth, to restore holiness into this physical world. Zeff's note and Josef's words disturb me profoundly. Jews have survived many attempts at genocide. We've survived persecution, oppression, and hatred. We've maintained our divine connection and our culture in a diaspora that has lasted two thousand years. Are we more threatened than we have been in the two thousand years since expulsion from our homeland? Could Zeff be accurately predicting the future and doing what he can to shift the outcome? It may be true, but I've learned that Zeff also destroys what he professes to love.

The next morning Goldie once again leaves her diary open for me to read.

> *My choice to make aliyah is about freedom, the freedom of our people after thousands of years of persecution, and my own personal freedom. I long for the freedom to expand beyond the limits of body, of being a woman, the limits of role, or even time and space and circumstance. I long to know what it is like to be everything, to dance and wail and sing and rage and not hold anything back. I long to touch the garments of angels, but also of devils. Does that sound terrible? What I write now, I have never told anybody, including my husband. While I could not tolerate Zeff's cruelty, he also intrigued me.*

Zeff lives outside the rules set by others. Until now I never had the courage to step outside my place in life. When Josef speaks of making aliyah, my heart stirs with passion. Now is my time, my only time. Jerusalem calls to me, and I must run into the arms of my beloved. I know that life in Palestine will fall far short of my vision, for that vision lives in a different realm. And yet they are related. Kabbalists know how the realms of the holy, the realms of perfection and the immutable and often frustrating laws of this world can and must enjoin. I am my father's daughter. Making aliyah is my way of joining heaven and earth.

I place her diary back on the table. My Goldie is becoming a stranger to me. I'm scared, but my heart quickens in the thrilling recognition of her courage. I discover my heart's selfless desire to see her soar.

Fifty-two people, including Goldie and myself, are preparing to make *aliyah:* young couples with children and unmarried young adults with fervor and stamina. Plans have been set, tickets purchased, trunks mostly packed, and farewells expressed. Josef departed early for Palestine with the intention of purchasing a tract of land.

The evening before, Goldie and I lie awake, our hopes and fears tossed in the air between us. I dream of flying that night, my eyes set heavenward, wings carrying me higher and higher. In the early morning hours we savor a last cup of tea and biscuits with a dollop of butter, a luxury we will not enjoy for the whole year we have committed to Palestine.

We are startled by a loud knock at our door. Laiah stands shivering, a coat draped over her nightdress, legs bare, eyes wide with terror. "Shimon is gone. He stepped outside to the woodpile and never returned. Zeff must have kidnapped him."

"How long has it been?" I ask, my breath catching in my throat.

"A half hour perhaps. Shimon never goes anywhere without telling me. I should never have let him out of my sight, not even to the shed."

"We'll find him, Laiah. Zeff won't harm him."

"Zeff is unpredictable, and kidnapping him is already harming him."

Sprinting to the barn to borrow a horse, I pray to Zeff, knowing he will hear me.

Zeff, don't harm the boy. He is innocent. He is your son. I beg your forgiveness for anything I've done to cause you harm.

Saddling my neighbor's horse, I'm about to mount when I spot Shimon running toward me. Scooping him up in my arms, I'm shaking with relief. Shimon recounts how Zeff forced him to leave. Before reaching the edge of town Zeff slipped in a mud puddle and wrenched his ankle. Shimon seized the opportunity to make his escape.

Laiah had encouraged us to make *aliyah*, convincing us that she had the support she needed, that she and Shmuel and others in the community would be able to protect Shimon. Now I'm clear that I cannot make *aliyah* with Goldie. I'm needed here. Is the timing of this kidnapping coincidental or intentional? It is hard to know with Zeff.

Goldie is distraught. "How selfish I've been. I will also remain."

I yearn for our old lives, but Goldie has made me privy to her inner thoughts, her secret dreams, and my love for her makes me act contrary to my own inclinations. I want my beloved Goldie's life to be complete. I encourage her to live her dream and make *aliyah*.

CHAPTER TEN

Months have passed since Goldie left, and yet I sense her with me still. I can almost hear the clatter of dishes, the soft hum of her voice barely audible as she prepares dinner, the sound of the latch just before she steps inside and greets me with warm eyes. I catch the scent of lavender emanating from the sachet she carries in the cleavage of her breasts. I'm filled with her as I curl into our bed, but in the dark of night, reaching over and meeting vacuous space, I dissolve into tears. But a dream appears—a gift from Goldie perhaps. In the dream, a young Goldie is smiling and dancing in the middle of a wheat field. Her movements are fluid and graceful like stalks of wheat blowing in a soft breeze. Her belly is enormous. *These are all my lost babies. They live here with me. We have come home.* Her first letter arrives the next day.

> *Dearest and beloved husband,*
> *I miss you so much, and yet I feel you here, working alongside me. I have conversations with you all the time. I want you to know that I am happy to be here. It is difficult, sweetheart. I would not have you think otherwise. Our shelters are no more than blankets*

thrown over branches, although soon we will have real homes, but everything takes time and money and much physical labor. And physical labor takes food and we have so little. We planted crops on the land but as fast as the little shoots spring out of the ground, they are eaten away by nasty pests, and the land itself is not fertile, and our water source is sour and undrinkable. The man who sold us the land promised otherwise, but he deceived us.

The Arabs who live here have been kind and helpful. They have taught us ways to keep away pests and helped us locate another water source. But it is not all such good news with our neighbors. Our land has an olive grove on it that they have been paid to harvest for many years. It is their livelihood that we threaten. It is a big problem for all of us because we also need the olives and the income from selling the olives. Josef has generously offered that we divide the profits from the grove. So far it is working, and we all hope that as more and more settlements are built we can continue to have peaceful relations with our neighbors.

My husband, I tell you this and yet I tell you truly that my heart is joyful with purpose even if my body is aching and exhausted and my stomach always growling with hunger, even as I rise early in the morning and work until the sun disappears in the evening. We are rebuilding our homeland! I can hardly say the words without my eyes welling up with tears of gratitude. To think that this will end the diaspora, that Jews everywhere will be welcome here and safe from persecution, that we can build our synagogues with the certainty that nobody will ever again destroy them, that we do not have to worry about our children being killed by those with hearts of stone. This vision is what sustains us. Jaakov, I am doing the work that Chaim surely would have done. I am fulfilling the dream that he never got to live, and this brings peace to my heart.

All this is to say that I'm grateful to you for allowing me to make aliyah. It is of immense importance to me. I miss you and Laiah and Shimon far too much. I hope you can join me here, but I am realistic enough to accept that it might not be so. Either way I promise that I will be home within a year's time.

My darling husband, there is more to share with you, but if I don't finish this letter and make sure it is on the next ship that leaves port, you will not receive it for a while. Send my love to everybody.
Your beloved,
Goldie

As autumn arrives, Laiah surprises me by suggesting that Shimon and I travel together to Palestine. Shimon receives the news with enthusiasm. Anticipating reunion with my beloved makes this autumn a true sensual delight, with crisp golden days, the sweet scent of cut hay warming in the sun, the aroma of berries and apples simmering on every stove.

I recall with strange clarity the particulars of the afternoon when the next letter arrives. I've given Shimon his lesson and listen as he performs a song he has composed for viola. Laiah baked a blackberry pie, and I've indulged in two pieces soaked in cream. My work with the manuscript has been particularly satisfying. Twenty more days and Shimon and I will be boarding the cargo ship on our way to Palestine, on our way to Goldie.

Ezra Natalman, the postman, hands me the letter with a nod and a smile, observing it has been sent from Palestine. Anticipating Goldie's handwriting, I'm surprised to see Laura's name on the envelope.

My dearest Jaakov,

Josef and I both wish that we could be with you as you read this letter. I have sorrowful news to share. There is no easy way to tell you, Jaakov, so I will just say it. Goldie has passed on. She is dead, Jaakov. My dear friend, how I wish I didn't have to tell you. I wish it wasn't true. She died suddenly. Otherwise, we would have sent for you. She contracted malaria while working the land. There are places of stagnant water here and mosquitoes carrying the disease. She contracted a high fever, and her body didn't have the strength to fight off the disease. For a week she hovered between life and death. At times we thought the fever would surely break and that she would recover. Then, she would lapse back into a coma. Finally, her body gave out. There was no pain for her, Jaakov. That I can tell you, and I hope that it provides a small degree of comfort. I was with her throughout her illness, and at her death. I held her hand and recited the blessings. I remained with her while her soul ascended. She is at peace, Jaakov. She is at peace.

We are all devastated, as I know you will be. I came to know her well and depended on her strength, her courage, her love, and her vision. She died doing what she wanted to do. That is the only compensation we have to hold onto in this moment of such loss. She was happy, Jaakov. She missed you terribly and was counting the days until she would be reunited with you, but inside she was happy. This was the fulfillment of her dream.

I want to share with you also that before Goldie lapsed into a final coma, she whispered something about seeing a beautiful lady of light holding her hand and easing her transition. Our beloved Shekinah was here with her in those final moments. I miss you dearly,

Jaakov. We all do. I wish circumstances were different. I know we will see you soon. Feel me with you. Feel Her love with you. We will meet you when the next ship arrives in port.
In deep sorrow,
Laura

The numbness of shock lasts long enough for me to stumble into my chair, sink into its familiar cushions and wrap myself tightly in a blanket to stop the shivering. How can this be true? I feel her hands in the blanket she knitted. It cannot be true. I feel her presence with me now. But I know it is true. Laura would not have sent the letter if it were not true. I take a breath and then another, and try to focus only on this moment, and not careen down the dark tunnel of the bleak, bleak future.

CHAPTER ELEVEN

My dearest beloved Goldie,
I write you now from the deck of a cargo ship that is transporting Shimon and me to Palestine. It is a tired old ship with rusted sides and a horn so loud that the whole ship vibrates when it sounds a mournful and angry complaint. Perhaps this is the same ship that transported you when you made aliyah. Tracing your steps offers me a momentary reprieve from the despondent gloom that has befallen me. Forgive me, my darling, for writing to you, as if you are awaiting my correspondence. Death is much harder for the survivors than you who are liberated from body and identity, and now free to explore other worlds. I remember that you longed for such freedom, and now my dear Goldie, you are free. I hope that you left this life satisfied that it was complete. Shimon misses you, and does not quite understand the finality of death, but he is filled with excitement about this journey and watching him emerge and expand is yet another source of satisfaction. It is good to see him outside the confines of the shtetl with fear of kidnap always looming.

I do not mind the long, monotonous hours of travel. Most days I choose to be alone, gazing into the transparent blue of sky, time becoming as fluid as water, or chasing the sparkles as they dart across the waves. It is mostly at night that the thoughts begin to plague me.

Should I have been able to foretell what would befall you in Palestine? Was I terribly mistaken in encouraging you to follow your dreams? Perhaps it was simply meant to be so, and I could have done nothing different. I am quite certain that death is but a doorway that we have all stepped through many times. But was this the right time for you, dear Goldie? Why did I encourage you to go when you had decided to stay? Was it worth it to you, my love? Was it worth ending your life? Will I ever know, and if not, will I find peace again? And if not peace, can I befriend unknowing, for life is such a very great mystery, and death an even greater one.

Your loving husband,
Jaakov

Goldie's grave is set amidst a stand of young trees with soft green leaves rustling in a gentle breeze. Every morning I come here alone and read to her from King Solomon's *Song of Songs*. This was Goldie's favorite poem, the one we read to each other on our wedding night. *"My beloved is as a rose among thorns."* How she loved these words, often reflecting on how the beauty and the pain of life are ever intermingled. Who were you, Goldie? Did I know you at all? Who did you become during these last months of your life we spent apart from each other? I want to know the part of you that blossomed here.

Laura tells me that the best way to know her is to stay awhile and know the life that she lived here. "Sleep under the stars, Jaakov. Dig holes in this hard soil and plant seeds, and when the tender shoots spring up from the earth, see what it is like to spend endless, patient hours picking off the beetles that eat the young shoots. Teach the children to read, cut up endless vats of potatoes for the soup that sustains us, haul water from our well, and boil the water to drink, because the well water is not pure; dig countless stones from the field, help erect our simple homes, and fall asleep on one thin blanket, exhausted and yet strangely content. Goldie loved walking this land, climbing to the top of the knoll where she could touch the sky. She felt the magic of this earth, the holiness of this land, and it made her happy. There is magic here, Jaakov. I cannot explain, but when you feel it, you will know it to be true."

I take her advice, and Shimon and I stay for over three months, and at the end of three months, I feel the pull to make this my home. I will travel back with Shimon, and then return and remain here until the end of my days. It is a hard life, but I feel alive here, vibrant, purposeful, and strong. It is a life of possibility instead of coping, a life of expansion instead of confinement.

Besides, I feel it. A sacrament has been forged here, a sacrament between man and G-d. Whatever earthly events have happened here, whatever might occur in the future, this land holds divine secrets to be revealed in time. The spirit of Goldie gently brushes my cheek, or is it the wind, or the sun, or is Goldie now a part of it all?

CHAPTER TWELVE

Overflowing with cargo and passengers returning to native lands, the ship groans as she pushes away from the dock, her deafening whistle proclaiming a successful departure. Rushing to locate our bunks, Shimon dashes back up to the top deck for a last glimpse of family.

Gripping the railing with rows of passengers pressing against our backs, our voices join in the frantic communal ritual of farewell with waves and tears and promises of return. Soon the land disappears from sight and only water and sky remain, and the two of us struggle with the ambivalence of our departure. Shimon is somber, but his mood lightens as a band of children form and new adventures begin.

On this return journey I have less need for solitude. Jossi, a solidly built young man with an unkempt beard, initiates a conversation as we stand together on deck beholding the sunrise. We speak of Palestine, and the various settlements and his reason for voyage home after making *aliyah* three years ago.

"My wife and I are heartbroken about our decision. We are unwavering Zionists, but our children were suffering. There was simply not enough to feed them. When my wife became pregnant again, we made the decision to return to Poland until the children are older. We will try again when we find a more established settlement."

"Why is there no food, Jossi?"

"We know about farming in Poland, but everything is different in Palestine. The weather, the soil, the predators, the crops, the water conditions, everything is new. We didn't come prepared for what we would encounter."

In contrast, Isaac is part of a community that is slowly making progress. Isaac is barely sixteen, with alert hazel eyes that hold a perpetual smile. He is returning to spend time with his dying father, but plans to make Palestine his home.

My curiosity is curtailed when the ship runs headlong into a storm. The vessel lurches from side to side, groaning and heaving like a woman in labor, and we all retreat to our bunks. The disgusting stench of vomit and terror and the wailing of babies, make the night almost unbearable. I manage a few hours of sleep and wake to an unanticipated calm.

Shimon bolts out of bed and coaxes me to accompany him up to the open deck. Tentatively mounting the stairs, we reach the deck in time to behold a most exquisite sunrise glistening off a mirror-like sea. The moment of serenity is dispelled by the ship's horn, announcing that land has been spotted. Hopefully Laiah will have received our letter and will be waiting with Shmuel at the dock. Soon enough we will be home, both of us changed in many ways.

Crowds gather on deck, shaking off the fear and discomfort of the past night. Shimon asks permission to say farewell to his friends, and I descend once again into the belly of the ship to gather our few belongings. Fatigued from a sleepless night, I find a relatively quiet corner on the deck and likely would have dozed through the landing had it not been for the ship's horn.

Disoriented, I hoist the duffel bag over my shoulder. Where is Shimon? He cannot be far. He might be in line holding our place. I hustle up and down the snaking line of people from the top deck down two flights of stairs to the bottom deck. Shimon is not in line. I hurry back to our sleeping quarters, but he is not there, and nobody I ask has seen him. Now I'm concerned, anxiety gripping my stomach. Shimon is responsible. He may simply have lost his way. Or not. Instinct tells me otherwise.

I know what I do not want to know. Zeff has stalked us, waiting for the perfect moment. Dread creeps under my skin like writhing snakes. He has won, or almost. The ship is not yet docked, and they are still here, hidden somewhere on board. I might be able to locate them. I have the ability, at times, to see remotely, to see what is happening in other places. I had once succeeded in locating a deaf child who had wandered deep into the forest. The horn sounds again. We will soon be docking. Concentration is difficult, but I must try.

Closing my eyes, I breathe, slowly, intentionally, feeling myself relax. I catch a glimpse of them hunched up together in a compartment, a sleeping compartment perhaps, but which of the several hundred compartments is it? The number 241 flashes in my mind. The horn blares again. We are now docked. I must hurry.

Sprinting down the narrow corridor and up the iron stairs, I arrive at level two and begin reading numbers only to discover that I am on the wrong side. I sprint down the stairs and up the other staircase, arriving before the third whistle announces the opening of the gates, but compartment 241 is empty. I bolt up another set of stairs to the deck, pushing my way to the front of the line.

"My grandson is missing," I shout. "He is being kidnapped. Has anybody seen a boy and a man with red hair?"

Nobody comes forward except one man who offers to help me search. I wait at the exit, and he continues to search the ship. A man and a boy both with red hair should be easy to spot, but they don't appear. The man returns, having to leave now and join his family. He will pray for a good outcome. I panic. Are there other ways to disembark? Zeff will find them if they exist. Imploring a man in uniform for help, he points to a set of stairs cordoned off by a rope. I sprint up the stairs and down the short corridor. A metal door bears a brass plate with the captain's name. I knock, and an irritated voice asks who I am and what I want.

"A passenger," I shout. "My grandson is missing, kidnapped. I need help."

"What would you like me to do about it?"

"How can someone leave the ship without being seen?"

"Somebody could hide in a cargo box. Not the most comfortable accommodations, but if someone didn't want to get caught, it would work."

"Are the cargo boxes numbered?"

"Yes, for identification purposes."

That is it! The number refers to a cargo box. I sprint back to the door. The line of passengers is gone, just a few stragglers left, and the cargo is already loaded onto wheeled flatbeds being rolled off the ship. Shimon and Zeff could be in any one of them. Where to look? I step tentatively onto the dock, suddenly feeling waves of dizziness and nausea. My head is swirling, and my legs are wobbly. An excruciating stab of pain pierces the back of my head. My legs give way, and my body crumples. A voice screams for help as I float blissfully in a sea of light, witnessing the scene below with curious detachment.

A man I recognize as a passenger, a doctor, is bending over me checking for a pulse. How odd to be witnessing my own death. Dying? Am I dying? The thought arises with the same curious detachment. Looking down again at the crumpled body, I feel sorrow, as if the body has been a good home that I'm leaving behind. Goldie's face appears before me. Euphoric at the thought of our reunion, I see her sternly gesture for me to stop. Her hand points down toward the body. *It is not yet your time.* A young woman, my Laiah, is bent over me, her hands placed over my heart sending healing energy through her hands.

"*Abba*, don't leave me now, don't leave me." Laiah's prayer reaches my heart. I'm drawn back into my body. The impact of reentry shocks me into consciousness. When I open my eyes, the throbbing in my head has subsided.

"*Abba*, this is Laiah. Do you recognize me?"

Of course I recognize her, but as I try to speak my mouth refuses to move. The doctor kneels beside me.

"Hello, Jaakov, do you remember me? If you remember, blink twice." I do so, and he appears relieved. "You've suffered a stroke, Jaakov. Try to stay calm. You are suffering from paralysis right now, but this is likely not permanent. Blink twice if you understand what I'm telling you." I blink twice.

The doctor turns to Laiah. "His mental functioning doesn't seem to be impaired."

Laiah's face is close to mine. Her eyes are dark with fear. "*Abba*, where is Shimon? Did he return on the ship with you? If yes, blink twice." I blink twice. "Was he with you when you came off the ship?" No blink. "Did something happen to him on the ship?" Two blinks. "Was he hurt?" No blink. "Did someone kidnap him?" Two blinks. Did he take him?" Two blinks. "Were you searching for him when this happened to you?" Two blinks. Laiah bursts into tears.

My world is crumbling around me, and there is nothing I can do but blink. I can't even shed a tear. Welcome home, Jaakov. Your wife, your grandson, and now your body have all been taken from you. Welcome home to a life once filled with love and blessing. But after all, Zeff is simply being Zeff.

CHAPTER THIRTEEN

Imprisoned within a body struggling with the most basic of movements, my mind remains lucid. I think of little else but Shimon, my desire to help lending me the determination to heal. Slowly, painstakingly, I make progress. First I take a step and then a few steps hobbling with a cane. Now my hands can stir the embers in the stove back to life and fill a pot with water. Now my speech becomes comprehensible. Now it is time to try and locate him.

When I first left home to live with the rebbe's family, I discovered that my soul could leave my body and travel long distances. The first time it happened spontaneously. Lying in bed unable to sleep, I soothed my loneliness by visualizing home, imagining myself there. I felt myself lifted out of my sleeping body. Flying through the air, I was transported right to the home of my family. For many nights I practiced traveling in this way, but when I told the rebbe, he responded with alarm.

"Do not continue," he warned me. "Your body can easily be stolen if you don't know how to protect yourself. Besides, exercising special powers is a complete distraction from your real work."

Ignoring his admonition, I continued these thrilling journeys. One night I became disoriented and began drifting through space. Terrifying creatures approached me, threatening to steal my body until suddenly, to my great relief, I landed back in my body. The next morning the rebbe asked whether I'd learned my lesson. Greatly embarrassed, I realized that he'd been watching out for me, and had intervened to make sure my lesson was not a lethal one.

This time however, it is not an amusement. Three months have passed since Zeff kidnapped Shimon. My grandson needs my help, and I'm willing to take the risk. The room is still dark when I open my eyes. I lie in bed relaxing into the state between sleep and wakefulness, the intention of locating Zeff and Shimon foremost in my mind. I feel my soul separate from my body, and in the next moment I'm hovering above a small hunter's cabin nestled in a stand of spruce trees. Peering inside the cabin, I spot Shimon, still asleep. Zeff is tending the stove. When Shimon wakes, Zeff ladles gruel from a pot and hands it to him. Shimon appears calm, the relationship between them surprisingly easeful. But I feel Shimon's fear and despondency.

How can I help? Looking around, I spot several hunters hiking a short distance away. They seem jovial, enjoying their outing and their companionship. Using mental suggestion, I direct them toward the cabin. Zeff has just stepped outside, and the hunters spot him, apparently disturbed by his presence. Zeff appears angry and agitated, but the men have rifles that they point in his direction. Zeff stomps off into the forest, and the men find Shimon, frightened but unharmed. When the men understand what has happened, they accompany Shimon back to the *shtetl*.

My grandson, wise little soul that he is, speaks few words about his time with Zeff. "He is my father. He gave me life, and I'm grateful to him." Has Shimon, in his innocent love for his father, reached Zeff's heart? Could it be that Zeff's own son, conceived in an act of violence, served as the instrument of Zeff's healing? Perhaps it is so.

I recall an incident from the days of my youth. Standing on a riverbank, I lost my balance and slipped into the fast flowing water. I struggled furiously to swim to the bank, but the current was too strong. Having no recourse, I ceased fighting and was carried swiftly downstream. Soon enough the river widened, the current slowed, and I scrambled to safety.

The lesson is clear. Fighting my condition leads to misery. Ceasing the struggle, accepting my weakened body that necessitates moving with exasperating slowness and deliberation, I open to appreciating the ineffable beauty arising in the simplicity of each moment. Sitting for endless hours in my chair wrapped in Goldie's blanket, I observe the ever changing patterns of this tiny place I call home, delighting in a cricket that has wandered into a strange world, a shaft of light that dances as the leaves of the young tree just outside my window shift in the breeze. Each rising and falling of my breath is a cause for gratitude. I will not make *aliyah* again. I will not be buried next to Goldie. And so it is. And so it is that I have to accept that I may die not having completed the mission.

Time passes slowly. I receive monthly letters from Laura describing the steady progress of the settlement in Palestine. Here in the *shtetl*, one of my students takes over my duties as rebbe. The fervor for senseless killing of Jews is in a temporary lull. Laiah and I discuss my death and the fate of the manuscript. The next mission keeper has not yet appeared. Laiah will take responsibility for the manuscript and wait for someone to come forth. But I am not dead yet. Every day I work with it until I feel the manuscript as an inseparable part of myself.

Without warning or premonition, I awake one morning to a letter left on my kitchen table. A wave of alarm sweeps through me. Not now, not again. I had assumed him gone from our lives forever. Why is he writing me now? His handwriting has changed little over the years, but instead of a long philosophical treatise he writes just one line.

Agree to meet with me. It is imperative.

CHAPTER FOURTEEN

His red hair reflecting candlelight gives him the appearance of a halo. For a flicker of a moment his large sea green eyes open to reveal something that I'd seen long ago: something real and human, something delicate and vulnerable and innocent. Having once glimpsed that potential is the reason I tried so hard to find it again. The memory brings a moment of sadness, regret, and anger. Trying to save him I came close to losing everything of value to me.

Zeff is silent as he sits facing me, eyes averted, his body erect and rigid. There is so much I want to ask him. *Why did you reject my love? Why did you hurt the people who were the kindest to you? What made your heart so cold?* I don't have to ask the questions aloud. Zeff can read my mind.

"I'm not here to ponder such irrelevant questions. Human nature is quite boring, emotions irrelevant."

"Then what is relevant to you, Zeff?"

His eyes darken. "I've found very little to be of relevance. I've found life to be disappointingly empty. Thankfully, I have no investment in life being any other way. Life is so expendable. One life ends and another begins, and there seems to be no way out, or none that I've discovered."

"Emptiness can be painful or liberating. Which is it for you?"

He flinches almost imperceptibly. "I do not feel pain."

I laugh softly. "How do you manage to avoid pain? There is plenty of suffering in life."

"Long ago I discovered that the easiest way to endure life is to not feel. I have no use for sentimentality. It disgusts me. People use one another, just like you used me."

His statement hurt. I'd sacrificed so much to try and help him.

"How did I use you?"

"I filled a need for you, as you did for me, at least in the beginning. You wanted a protégé, and for a while I offered you that. I wanted to learn the secrets of the universe, and for a while you offered me that. But we outgrew each other."

I feel it. The fabrications and self-deceit, the deadness of feeling, and under it all the intense anguish of this grossly undeveloped, not-quite-human soul. To be human one has to let the heart be moved by joy and pain, desire and love and anger. In this moment of recognition, all my outrage drops away. My heart is tender with compassion for the suffering he has yet to feel. In this moment I stop trying to change him, or even heal him. I accept him completely on his terms.

"Then why are you here? Why is it imperative that we meet?"

Zeff turns his face away from me. "I don't want to be indebted to you in the next life. I want to pay my debt to you now so when we meet again, you have no power over me."

"Why are you indebted to me? For taking you in when you were a boy? For feeding you and clothing you and loving you?"

He shakes his head. "All those you did for selfish reasons. For those I owe you nothing. There is only one thing that you did for me that was completely unselfish, but that one thing makes me indebted to you."

Now I'm curious. "What did I do?"

He looks at me with disbelief. "Don't you remember?"

"I will likely remember once you remind me."

"One time you risked your life to save mine."

"I remember that event, but I didn't think about what I was doing. I just saw that you were in danger, and I took action. I couldn't stand there and watch you die."

Zeff looks exasperated. "That is why I'm indebted to you. You risked your own life for me. Luckily we both survived."

"I don't need to be rewarded for something any caring human being would have done. Besides, there is little I need at this stage of my life."

Zeff retracts. "Repaying the debt is not for you, but you will benefit. It has to be something important enough to you that my debt will be canceled."

"Then let's proceed. How do you intend to repay the debt?"

"What is not yet complete in your life?"

And then I know. The mission is not yet complete.

"Exactly," he says. "Bring the manuscript to me. I will decode it."

I stare at him, almost not comprehending his words. "How is that possible?"

"Do you want it completed or not? Time is running out."

I have nothing to lose by letting him try. I've worked on it all my life and have not yet found the key to its completion. With pained movements, I rise from my chair and retrieve the manuscript. Zeff opens the cover, and within seconds he has scanned and memorized the whole document. Retrieving pen and paper from his coat pocket, he writes, lost in concentration. Zeff's intelligence is beyond my understanding, and in that way he is as fascinating to me now as when he came to me as a young boy. I'd wrongly assumed that such high intelligence implied an empathic heart and a nobility of ethics. Suddenly he stops writing and looks up at me. His eyes are bright, his aura immense. Holding up a sheet of paper he offers me a half smile.

"Here it is," he says, handing it back to me. "The manuscript is decoded."

"Are you sure?" I ask, in awe that he has done in a few moments what I have failed to accomplish in a lifetime. "How do you know?"

"Because She guided me."

"You saw Her? She came to you?"

Zeff stands up, and for one instant he meets my gaze. A momentary exchange of love passes between us. All becomes clear to me in that moment, clear not in the sense of being able to articulate it, but clear to my heart. All was meant to happen as it did and nothing, not one action could have been different. Zeff nods, and turns toward the door. And then I see it, the divine spark of light, the initiatory light, Her gift to humanity, is now awakened in him, and this light, Her light, will ultimately heal him and guide him home.

Zeff has decoded the manuscript, but I know that I've done the necessary work to make it possible. The Great Rebbe, Laura, Josef, Laiah, Goldie, and Shimon, we've all gone through the inner and outer transformations needed for the mission to evolve. It is not for me to know the intention of the mission, nor even whether it will succeed. The next mission keeper is likely not even born yet. I know only that I've done my part and that my life is now complete.

A soft wave of blissfulness washes through me, melting away any last vestiges of fear or desire. There is only perfection in this moment, and the certainty of love. Suddenly I see Her, the Shekinah in Her light and radiant splendor. My heart is overflowing with gratitude for Her presence.

"You have served me well, Jaakov." Her voice is as sweet as wind chimes. "Rest easy, my dearest one."

Before me is a long tunnel, and at the end of the tunnel is a brilliant light. Emerging out of the light are radiant beings coming to welcome me. Goldie is there and the Great Rebbe, and all the archangels reaching out to embrace me, and then they vanish. I step into fathomless space and merge with the void and become nothing and everything.

Laiah

It is as though he has worked all night and has just fallen asleep in his favorite chair. When I approach and call his name, he does not respond, and I know that he has passed. Kissing the top of his head, I reach under and retrieve the manuscript, apparently completed in the hours before his death. He has become so thin in the months since his stroke that I'm able to move his still pliable corpse to the bed. I hold his hand, limp but still warm with life, and give voice to what is in my heart.

"*Abba*, our relationship was beautiful and complex, as were you, as am I. Your love for me, your admiration for me sustained me through all the hardship we both endured. You held yourself responsible for Zeff's violation of me, but I knew that you were not responsible. I wish I could have convinced you of that earlier, but I had to find my own way to forgiveness before I could fully release you. I release you now, *abba*. Carry no debt with you. I feel only love and respect for you and immense gratitude for all that you gave to so many. And how devotedly you served Her. Zeff was an inevitable part of this mission. Long ago I understood and accepted that. Go in peace, *abba*. I will be the guardian of the manuscript and the mission until the next mission keeper appears. I love you."

First Decoding

Hear me now
When the Sons of light and the Sons of darkness are
no longer held separate but are seen to be reflections of
the one within the other, then seeming opposites cease
to be. In the act of forgiveness, the cycle of vengeance
is broken, and there is the beginning of freedom that
leads to the True condition. To forgive is to step out
of the past and into the unformed future. Forgiveness
liberates our heart and frees us from the shackles of the
past. In this moment of forgiveness there is communion,
and in this communion is the descent of grace and the
beginning of holiness.

BOOK TWO

BENJAMIN / ZOFIA

The concept of enemy was created by man and therefore needs to be uncreated by man.

—Great Rebbe

PROLOGUE

Jerusalem, Israel, 2000
Benjamin Janowicz

Earlier today I discovered an envelope unobtrusively slipped under my front door bearing only my name. Perhaps it's from a former patient needing advice or access to old records, but would it not have been simpler to send it in the usual manner rather than driving to the Jerusalem hills? I'll read it later. Right now I'm late for my weekly breakfast date with Morris.

When I return home the envelope awaits my attention, and I settle into my reclining leather chair to discover what elusive correspondence dwells within. There is no way I could have prepared myself. The likelihood of receiving a letter from him is as remote as discovering the key to paradise, but apparently not beyond the realm of possibility, because it has happened. I feel nauseated and wish I hadn't indulged in a second piece of baklava. I'm desperately trying to convince myself that there is no reason to panic. Reason doesn't matter. My throat is clenched, and I can't manage a full breath. I'm terrified.

The content of the envelope is one handwritten page: tight, square, precise lettering, no room for misinterpretation. The letter is an imperative request that I meet with him soon because he is dying. If we meet, he writes, and I choose to hand him over to the authorities, he will not resist. My mind has lost the battle for rationality. I stare mindlessly at the wall of glass that frames the valley and distant hills, my vision meandering across the familiar vista. Without warning, the memories arise: silt stirred up from the bottom of a lake, images of a past I've spent this lifetime reconciling. Hans is at the center of those memories.

I've been alive more than eighty years. The last time I saw Hans was over forty years ago, and in that time, he has evaded being brought to justice. If the signature on the letter is genuine and my memory of his handwriting is accurate, he is here in Jerusalem. I laugh involuntarily. Hans could not possibly be in Israel, never mind Jerusalem. Last week I took a fall while walking in the park, and my head struck pavement. Perhaps I'm delusional.

Hans is dying. I'm outraged that he has lived so long. Life offers no justice. And yet the truth is that Hans twice saved my life. Life offers no consistency. What could he possibly want from me? I'm inclined to refuse his request. I'm content with life, more than content. I'm happy. I've worked hard to reconcile my past, and there is no reason to stir it all up again.

Yet there is something pulling me toward another conclusion. I feel an inexplicable gravitas, an archetypal force doing battle within me. Something is urging me to meet with him and I'm caught in an uncomfortable paralysis. I could ask someone— Morris, or my wife—for advice, but this I must alone decide, alone with the totality of my life shaping this moment, alone with my ancestors standing behind me, and future generations moving beyond me.

My father, dead for over fifty years, appears to me now in the realm of imagination. I yearn for his wisdom in this moment, even if he died before we had reconciled our mutual disillusionments. When I was young, he had introduced me to the Cup of Fortunes.

"Benjamin, G-d is speaking with us all the time. There are patterns in everything, and messages in every pattern. Even the seemingly random pattern of tea leaves at the bottom of a cup holds cosmic significance once we learn how to be far seeing."

This was after I shared with him my strange encounter with a woman who appeared to be as ancient as the world. Stooped over, leaning on a cane, Her face was a map of wrinkles. When She spoke, Her voice transformed into the sound of the wind, birdsong, gurgling brook, crickets at dusk, a baby crying. Gazing into Her ancient eyes, I felt that I had known Her forever.

My father listened attentively and then slowly nodded his head, as if in prayer.

"Did She ask you a question, Benjamin?"

"Yes, abba. She asked me if I would help Her when I was older, and I told Her I would do anything She asked me to do."

"Then you are the one," he said, staring at me for a long time, his face shifting expression but revealing little.

"What one, abba?"

"Her next mission keeper. My grandfather, your great-grandfather, Jaakov Janowicz, was the first."

Life is complex, nuanced, filled with decisions and the consequences of those decisions, including the one I must make in this moment. Perhaps it is true that I'm hallucinating, for I see my father stroking his long red beard, his face radiant.

"Remember the Cup, Benjamin. Ask it your question."

The Cup is sitting atop my desk. I haven't used it since the night of my thirteenth birthday. Despite its unsightly appearance, I choose to keep it there as a reminder of the mission imparted to me, the mission not yet completed. The mission I hope to complete before I die. I will consult the Cup. I speak my question aloud.

"What serves the highest good, to meet with Hans or refuse his request?"

Having asked my heart's question, I perform the ritual and gaze into the leaves settled into the bottom of the Cup, seeing nothing that inspires revelation. *Look again, Benjamin.* Have the leaves rearranged themselves, or has my vision shifted? The Hebrew letter *tav* appears, a most auspicious letter indicating that the answer to my question is directly related to *tikkun olam,* the healing of the world, Her mission. It is clear what I must do.

Listen, there is more, Benjamin. My memory slides back to the night I chanced upon my father sitting alone in the kitchen, the year nineteen thirty-four, the night before we were to move. Our home has been stripped of life, our possessions packed away in trunks. The night is eerily still, the fleeting scratch of a mouse the only sound. My father is staring into the Cup, his face illumined by one candle, enough for me to notice tears brimming in his eyes, like crystal droplets.

"Why are you crying, abba?"

He looks away. "Benjamin, who am I to question G-d's will?"

My stomach clenches. "What did you see?"

His voice softens. He attempts a smile.

"Look closely, Benjamin, and see the past and the future woven together, a complex and beautiful tapestry. Smell the honey and the horseradish, hear the voices of two thousand years of prayer, feel the tears of sorrow and ecstasy, two rivers meeting and becoming one great river that empties into the sea of Creation. Listen deeply, my son, and you will hear nothing at all, and this nothing is the great emptiness of G-d, deeper than Creation itself. Then you will know that nothing else matters, and that you have always been, and will forever be free."

My father is staring upward, away from this world and into the next. In the flickering candlelight his tears glisten. I do not want to see my father this way. I'm still young and filled with optimism. The vessel holding my life has not yet been shattered.

CHAPTER ONE

Schtetl Bedzew, Poland, 1934
Benjamin

My brother, Avi, proclaims that he does not believe in G-d, and refuses to hold back his disdain for those who do. His unabashed assertions, made as much for effect as a quest for truth, enliven our dinner table conversations. Avi is small for his age. Two years older than me but almost the same height, he is nimble and muscular and can outrun almost every boy in the *shtetl*.

"If there really is a G-d", he exclaims, "then why are we, His Chosen People, always persecuted? If there is a G-d, then He is a cruel G-d, or a stupid G-d."

"Stop talking like that!" My mother reaches across the table and places an extra serving of beets on his plate.

Channah, my younger sister, protests. "Why is he rewarded for saying such mean things?"

My father offers her a slice of challah, warmed and greased. "Now you are rewarded for being such a good girl."

The frequent play of provocations and peace offerings enacted during family meals leaves me amused and unaffected.

It is Avi's way of diverting my mother from the litany of complaints about her life—"my children are not obedient, my uncle's wife looks down on me, and she of all people has nothing to brag about. The oven cooks unevenly so how can anything be baked right"— recited over and over again like a prayer at every meal.

My mother is beautiful to me, with thick dark hair piled like a crown on her head, but her beauty is marred by furrows of worried tension that make her look perpetually angry. My grandmother, Laiah, offers a stark contrast. Laiah is tall, slender, and graceful, with delicate features, sharp blue eyes, and white hair she wears in a bun. She never complains even when there is good reason. She does, however, protest when my mother insists on limiting my time with her.

"Rivkah, please try and understand. Benjamin is a mission keeper. He must learn what he needs to fulfill his responsibility."

Rivkah throws up her hands. "We are living in a different century. He must learn to live in the world, provide for his family. Don't you think so, Shimon?"

My father sighs. "What do you want to do, Benjamin?"

"I want to learn kabbalah."

My mother's face contorts with disgust. Later they will argue. Laiah's eyes are moist with tears, but we both know that she is the only one who can prepare me to serve Her mission. Laiah takes every opportunity to impart her wisdom to me.

"Kabbalah is about union with G-d," she says. "It is a beautiful and difficult path. We must be humble enough to move beyond the many obstacles and challenges we encounter. We must learn to live a righteous life based not on the whims of emotion but on the higher principles of the Good. We become instruments of *tikkun olam*, the healing of the world. This is kabbalah, Benjamin."

My mother's litany abates for a time, and our family experiences relative peace. Avi is skeptical. "If mother is not complaining, then something is wrong."

While playing together in the barn, Channah finally reveals the secret. "Mother says we are moving to Warsaw."

Avi and I bolt into the kitchen. Our mother is slicing green beans for canning.

"Be careful of the boiling pots of water."

"Are we moving?" Avi demands.

"Who told you that?"

"Channah overheard you talking with *abba*. Is it true? Are we moving?"

She slices with greater fervor.

"Are we moving?"

Avi insists as only Avi can. I'm distraught. My home is here in this *shtetl*, not in Warsaw. My family has lived in this same home for generations. Besides, Laiah is here, and Laiah will surely not be moving with us.

"Laiah, why is my father allowing this to happen?"

Laiah sweeps away tears she wishes me not to see. "Your father is too kind, or G-d forbid I say it, too weak to speak up to your mother. I adore your father, Benjamin. He is my only child, and he has always been a loving, gentle soul, but he lacks strength to stand up for what he believes."

I know this about my father. I want to respect him, but too often he disappoints me.

"Do they treat Jews better in Warsaw than they do here?"

Laiah blinks, swallows hard. "You must be careful there, and promise me you will not forget your responsibility as mission keeper. The manuscript must remain here with me. We'll place it in hiding, and when you're old enough, you will come and retrieve it, yes?"

"I promise you that I will retrieve it."

"G-d's will," Laiah whispers, as we stoop inside the musty root cellar, not much more than a large hole with wooden scaffolding supporting the sides. Digging through encrusted earth is tedious work, but my dedication to Her, and to Laiah, is unwavering. With renewed fervor, I dig a hole as deep as the length of my arm.

CHAPTER TWO

Warsaw, Poland, 1935
Benjamin

Laiah's absence from my life is a painful emptiness in my heart. The *shtetl* holds the memories of my childhood, and the chain of my lineage with its mythic significance, the Great Rebbe and my great-grandfather, Jaakov, still revered in the community. But it takes little time for me to realize how confining life in the *shtetl* has been. Warsaw offers a colorful and unending array of tantalizing adventures; smoky cafes with enticing music and lively conversation, museums and galleries, and the freedom of anonymity. My father frets as I venture farther and farther from the safety of the Jewish ghetto, slipping incognito into the world of Gentiles.

"Why are you doing this, Benjamin?" He implores, standing like a sentinel guarding the door of our apartment. "Are you suddenly not a Jew any more?"

"I'm a Jew, *abba*. I just want to explore their world."

Avi laughs, disdainful of me as always. "Don't be a fool, Benjamin. They might appear friendly to you, even generous, but the next moment they'll stab you in the back, and I mean that literally."

"I'm careful," I say. But I'm hardly careful, and I meet with good fortune, with people at least tolerant of Jews. I avail myself of opportunities, such as the night I slip through the ornate door of the magnificent music hall in the center of Warsaw. Marble sculptures of men with perfectly muscled bodies, sensuous women with ecstatic smiles, wall hangings depicting battles and religious scenes, the scent of perfume and cigars, and the elegantly dressed audience. Like me, they have come to enjoy the music of the famous violist, Bartel Barzowski.

I'm here because my father plays the viola, and he taught me to play when I was young. I've had no formal training, but I know how to discern a skilled musician from a master by whether the music touches my heart. Bartel is unmistakably a master. Beholding the grace with which he unites bow and string stirs a longing in me to study with him. The strength of my desire imbues me with the courage and confidence to approach him after the performance.

The air is bitingly cold. Futilely attempting to keep warm, I sprint up and down the steep steps in the rear of the elegant stone building, my hope of meeting him waning. I'm about to walk away when the doors open, and Bartel emerges. His appearance off-stage is decidedly unglamorous. Short and stocky, he waddles with a disjointed gait. His viola, held with such naturalness during his performance, hangs by his side like an awkward extension of his arm. He looks up, startled, as I dash forward to meet him.

"Mr. Barzowski, may I have a word with you?"

Instinctively he clutches the viola to his chest, and I realize, with embarrassment, that I've frightened him.

"At this time of night I don't talk to strangers." He turns sharply and keeps walking.

I follow him, carefully remaining a step behind. "I know I'm a stranger to you, but you are no stranger to me. Your music touches me. You gave a beautiful performance."

He slows.

"Mr. Barzowski, I play the viola, and I want to study with you."

Perhaps he hears my sincerity, or he wishes to rid himself of my intrusion, but either way he turns to face me.

"Do you have a name, young man?"

"My name is Benjamin Janowicz."

"Benjamin, are you a Jew?"

"My family is Jewish. Why do you ask? Do you not accept Jewish students?"

"If a student is talented, I don't care what God he supplicates to. I don't care who or what he sleeps with. I only care about the quality of his music."

"In that case, you'll not be disappointed in me. I promise to become your brightest protégé."

A smile flashes across his face. "You are quite confident, young man."

"I'm confident, sir, that you will not regret allowing me an opportunity." I'm incredulous at my own audacity.

"I like confidence, Benjamin. We'll find out whether or not your talent warrants it." Reaching inside his pocket, he retrieves paper and a pen. "Tomorrow afternoon come ready to perform."

Brusquely handing me his address, he turns and walks away. I'm left holding my breath, my body pulsating with terror and elation.

His apartment is located in a section of Warsaw I've not yet explored. Buildings with intricate carvings, and carefully tended gardens, here is wealth and gentility, and most certainly no Jews. Bartel graciously invites me inside.

"I've been fortunate in life, Benjamin. I hope to extend my good fortune in hearing you perform."

Opening a set of double doors, he motions for me to enter a

room as large as my family's entire living quarters, painted a deep plum with gold trim. Antique instruments are arranged along the perimeter of the room while in the center is showcased a shiny black baby grand piano with delicate gold inlays on the cover and legs. I feel an empty pit in my stomach, but there is no turning back. Taking a breath to calm my anxiety, I lift the viola from inside the case.

Bartel's eyebrows pique with interest. "Where did you obtain this instrument? It's made with a unique kind of wood, and the inlays are original designs. May I play?"

"I'm honored."

He performs a short waltz, an uplifting piece in his capable hands. "It has an unusual sound, rich and resonant, and yet nuanced. What is its origin?"

"I don't know its maker. It has been in my family for generations."

"Time to hear you perform."

Once I start to play, my confidence returns and the music flows effortlessly. Bartel listens with eyes closed, so motionless that I wonder if he's sleeping through my performance, but in the next moment he springs to life.

"Excellent work, Benjamin."

"Thank you, Mr. Barzowski."

"Call me Bartel," he says. "Your confidence is well earned. We'll begin lessons next week."

I'm elated, even knowing there is yet another obstacle to overcome.

"Sir, I forgot to ask your fee."

He laughs, and I wonder if he is mocking me.

"Come a half hour early, and help me with transcriptions. That will be your payment."

"Thank you, Mr. Barzowski—I mean, Bartel. How may I express my gratitude?"

He places a reassuring hand on my shoulder. "Become the best musician you can be."

My proficiency as a musician soars with Bartel as my mentor. Not only is he an inspiring teacher, but he also opens his world to me, sweeping me with graciousness into the center of the intellectual and cultural elite of Warsaw. Introduced into this world of wealth and culture as his promising protégé, people's heads turn in my direction. Nobody asks or cares whether or not I'm a Jew, and for a brief moment I've reached the pinnacle of life. Invited into the homes of the elite, paid well for my performances, written up as a promising new musician, even my father stops voicing disapproval. For one glorious moment, I'm a star among stars, obstinately refusing to see that my star is rising at a time when the world around me is fast descending into darkness.

Poland has been invaded by Russia and Germany, fighting for dominance on our soil. In the midst of poverty, chaos and dissolving social structures, anti-Semitism—always an insidious undercurrent—is increasing with frightening rapidity. I refuse to accept the implications for my own life. Bartel wisely recognizes the danger in my youthful denial. Fearing for my safety, he reluctantly forbids me to attend salons or performances.

"This will pass, Benjamin. Sanity will return to the world."

My star plummets into a maelstrom of anti-Semitic hatred and violence. Lootings, attacks on innocent people, and cold-blooded murders occur with terrifying frequency. Businesses and factories are torched and vandalized. My exotic life is now a memory, a painful contrast to the grey and somber existence that is forced upon all of us. I must work long hours in my uncle's factory alongside my father and brother. Business is dying and wages are drastically cut. We barely have enough money to sustain our family even with three of us working. My life with Bartel has overnight become a dream.

The factory has increasing incidents of looting, one involving an employee nearly beaten to death. The next week my father stays late, and while returning home, is attacked by a roaming gang of hoodlums. Stumbling through the door, blood dripping from a huge gash above his eye makes his face a macabre mask. His nose is broken and swollen to twice its usual size. My brother runs to find the doctor, who does his best to stitch up the deep gashes. Wounded but alive, my father is lucky this time. When the doctor leaves, my brother admonishes me.

"You said you were going to stay late and come home with *abba*."

"*Abba* told me to leave and finish my studies."

"Grow up, Benjamin."

"Stop fighting, boys," my mother pleads. "Don't let them ruin our family."

"What are we going to do now, Shimon? You can't go back to work."

"Of course I'll go back, Rivkah. I'll wake up tomorrow morning and go to work. What choice do I have?"

CHAPTER THREE

1936

Benjamin

A few Jews are still slipping through the cracks in the system and entering the halls of universities. Noting my interest in medical school, Bartel uses his influence to gain me acceptance, his kindness and concern touching me deeply.

"Consider this my small contribution to a world precariously perched on a fulcrum of good and evil."

Thus it is that I'm waiting anxiously outside the austere university building, sweating profusely despite a cool breeze. We are fifty-three altogether—fifty young men and three women — and likely not another Jew among us. A beautiful autumn morning, a cloudless, crystal clear blue sky, the day lends itself to optimism. Yet I'm hardly optimistic. The universities are waging their own moral struggle with the "Jewish problem." New laws require Jewish students to be segregated from the rest of the student body. Not all institutions agree to enforce these laws, but they most certainly exist. Bartel informs me that the university president is not in principle opposed to admitting Jews, but he wants no trouble, and Jews mean trouble. My acceptance is tenuous at best. Too much trouble, even if not of my creation, will mean expulsion.

My face holds no resemblance to the beak-nosed stereotype of the Jew depicted in the graffiti. I'm tall, lean, with large green eyes and a full head of curly auburn hair. I've intentionally removed my yarmulke and dress like other students, and yet somehow they know. Gangs of hoodlums are everywhere, skulking about, hunting for Jews to harass. I feel their gaze as I stand in line with fellow students. They wait restlessly for the right moment to make their move.

If the doors had opened on time, I might have entered unscathed. Instead they find their moment, and despite my vigilance, I'm not prepared for the attack. Grabbing me from behind, they strike before I have time to brace myself for the blows that send blood spilling from my nose and knock the wind out of me. Doubled over in pain, one pins me to the ground, and the other is about to send a fist flying into my face when a fellow student jumps him from behind. Other students join in my defense. The two thugs escape, shouting death threats to any Jews who dare desecrate the university with their vile presence. Reeling from shock and pain, I'm helped to my feet, fighting the urge to vomit, slowing my breath to still my pounding heart.

"Are you all right?" a woman's voice asks, but I can't articulate a response. "Let me check for a concussion."

Kneeling beside me, she directs me to open my eyes and look into hers. Gratefully, I receive the welcome, soothing balm of her kindness.

"I didn't see them coming. I should have been more watchful." My attempted smile sends shooting pain down the left side of my face. Her steady, relentless gaze holds my own.

"Tell me your name."

"Benjamin. And yours?"

"Zofia," she shares succinctly. "Where do you live, Benjamin?"

"I live in the Jewish Ghetto. The address would mean nothing to you." Zofia is decidedly beautiful, her face delicate with a straight, narrow nose and soft lips that seem to naturally smile, but I'm Jewish and she is not. Waves of unintended attraction washing through me, I force myself to look away.

"It's my fault for thinking this could work." My body shudders, throwing off the shock of the attack. "I don't want to make you late for class."

She ignores my words. "Nor should you be late. Let me help you inside."

Awkwardly rising to my feet, I gasp involuntarily from the stabbing pain in my left torso.

"You might have fractured a rib."

"It's just badly bruised."

She shakes her head. "I think it's fractured, Benjamin. The attack was vicious. My father is a doctor, and I'm sure he would see you."

I smile, attempting to conceal the pain. "Thank you, Zofia. I'll recover. You've been more than kind to me." She returns the smile. "I've gotten blood all over your clothing." Why does such a statement feel so intimate?

Zofia glances down at her blouse, and then up at me. "We're studying to become doctors. A little blood should not deter us."

I want to prolong our conversation, to bask in her company, to know more about her, everything about her. Before I can censor myself, I blurt out the unthinkable.

"Zofia, will you meet me after class? I want to know more about you." My face reddens with shame. "I'm sorry. I should not ask that of you."

Looking me directly in the eye she responds. "I accept your invitation, Benjamin."

CHAPTER FOUR

Zofia

What am I doing? There is no excuse for such recklessness. My parents would be rightfully appalled if they knew. What parent wouldn't be? I'm appalled with myself, risking my life for love. Benjamin and I are carrying on a clandestine affair of the heart. If circumstances were different, our love would be a rare blessing. But the world around us is exploding with hatred and violence, every day more and more Jews attacked, murdered, or disappearing. Benjamin is risking his life to complete medical school, and I'm risking mine to be with him. Can our love, or any love, survive under such conditions, and to what end? What kind of future can we hope to share? Dare I trust in the inconceivable possibility that all will work out? Father, forgive me. If it were my own daughter putting herself in harm's way for no better reason than love, I would be remiss to not do everything in my power to dissuade her. Forgive me father, for I cannot stop myself from loving this man.

Benjamin

Countless times I vow to end our relationship, begging her to pull away, to fall in love with anybody but me. Rationality has not yet prevailed, but it must prevail. I cannot profess to love her and continue to put her at risk. Such foolishness is reprehensible. I must complete medical school before the window of opportunity closes for Jews. Stay alive, care for my family, these must be my only priorities right now, and yet the desire to be with Zofia is unrelenting. Zofia, I should be protecting you and not endangering you. My actions are wrong, selfish, and yet you collude with me in perpetuating this madness, and I must be strong enough to stand up for both of us. My dearest Zofia, forgive what I must now do.

Bartel

Benjamin's spirit uplifts me, as does his music, and that is a rare gift in this world. I have many friends in low and high places, and many favors due me. Benjamin has no idea how many favors I've called upon to ensure his enrollment in medical school, and he never needs to know. What I do for him is my own business. Our world is rapidly declining. My friends in high places know some, but my friends in low places know a lot more. Benjamin might be able to hold on if he and his delicious sweetheart do nothing to attract attention. Being the hopeless romantic that I am, I occasionally offer them my home all the while knowing that I'm abetting two people who, for the sake of all of us, must soon part ways.

CHAPTER FIVE

1938

Benjamin

Our doorbell never rings on *Shabbat*. Peering down from the second floor window, I spot my uncle and his two sons waiting on the stoop. In stunned silence, we receive their news. The factory was torched during the night, the damage too extensive for repair. Thankfully, being *Shabbat*, everybody had left early so no lives were lost. My uncle's face is frighteningly pale. He is swaying unsteadily on his feet. I lead him to a chair.

"We've been up all night," his son, my cousin, Mordecai, blurts in breathless tones. "They burned the factory and then threw stones into our windows the entire night. We were terrified."

"My whole life went into that business. My whole life! Now it's gone. How will any of us make a living?"

Mordecai, a tediously neat accountant, is completely disheveled. Gently patting his father's balding head, he tries to offer reassurance. "We'll find a way, *abba*. Nobody was hurt. That is a blessing."

"A blessing," my father nods in agreement. "We'll find a way."

We do find a way, but barely. My mother takes in more sewing, and my brother is hired as a day laborer. I treat a few patients who barter what they can. Once a well-respected scholar and teacher, my father finds little use of his skills in the world we now inhabit. Defeated, my father withdraws. My cherished sister, Channah, sings to him in a voice that warbles like a tiny bird, making up fantasy tales to try and lift his mood. He offers her a fleeting smile, and then sinks into his chair and disappears.

Opening a bottle of vodka, Bartel pours us both a shot. He has attended the graduation in my stead, the president of the university having forbidden me to be present at the ceremony for fear of attracting violence. This moment of celebration is tinged with sorrow. Tomorrow, in the privacy of Bartel's home, Zofia and I must find the courage to bid each other farewell. We now have no choice.

Tonight, however, Bartel and I toast our victory, for truly it is a shared victory. He has made this moment possible, and my debt to him can never be repaid. All I can offer him is the delight of our music making. Our two violas, the sound smooth and rich and velvety, are like inky black waters of a river swiftly flowing, reflecting the shimmering light of the moon. I will remember this moment and Bartel's face, flushed from vodka and inspiration, and love, his eyes illuminated, his body dancing as bow slides across strings, laughing with joy.

CHAPTER SIX

1939

Zofia

Bartel offers us his apartment. We speak little, for there is everything and nothing to say, and what there is to say, neither of us chooses to speak aloud. We lie together, my heart beating wildly, my arms encircling him, my legs wrapped around his body. His tears wet my cheeks, merging with my own.

"You must promise to let me go, Zofia," he whispers. "Promise me you'll not wait for my return. Please don't make me bear the thought of your unhappiness. If the rumors are true, I may not survive."

I offer only silence.

"Say the words, Zofia. Please, if you love me, say the words to me."

"Then I release you, Benjamin. I release you." The words draw us closer. "Make love to me, Benjamin. I want you to be my first love."

His body leans into me and then pulls away. "Don't ask that of me. I've desired you for so long, but how can I make love to you and then leave you here alone? I don't want to hurt you any more than I have already."

"My heart knows only this moment with you. I can't imagine a deeper love with anybody. Leave me with the gift of first love."

Our bodies move naturally together, the poignant pleasure of crescendo and release, a few precious moments of quiet bliss, the illusion of timelessness dispelled when we hear the sound of Bartel's voice announcing his presence. Moving out of his embrace, my body shudders, the pain of first lovemaking overshadowed by the pain in my heart. We dare not risk even a glance as I gather myself and close the door softly behind me.

Bartel respects my solitude as he accompanies me across town. Soldiers with bayonets draped over their shoulders patrol the streets. Catching an occasional glimpse, I note the hollow faces of young boys trying to look brave, inducted into this madness. Go home, go home and find love, I whisper. Lowering my head, I hasten past.

Inevitably the euphoria of lovemaking descends into the dreaded reality of loss. My body aches and bleeds, but worse than that my heart plunges into agonizing grief. Nobody can offer solace or understanding because nobody, except Bartel, knows about our relationship. He parts ways with me at the corner of my street. My family is waiting for me, concerned that I've stayed out so late. I apologize, feigning some good excuse about helping a friend, feigning happiness about graduation.

My sister, Sija, knows me well. Her sharp, discerning steel gray eyes miss little. Her thin lips are pressed so tight together that the edges dimple. There is no room for fantasy or probability in her world. We thought she would enter the world of scientific research, but my sister became a teacher of young children. That evening as we prepare for bed, I receive the full force of her determined investigation. Her eyes meet mine and refuse to turn away.

"Zofia, do you think us all foolish and blind? Do you think our parents don't know about your secret relationship?"

The shock of her assertion leaves me confused, ashamed, and speechless.

"They worry all the time, as I do. Why have you not told us?"

"It's over now." I stumble for words, the words themselves making the ending real.

"It has to be over, Zofia. It has to be over. Promise me you're telling the truth."

"I'm telling the truth, Sija, it is definitely over." Sija hugs me tightly, rubs my back, crawls into bed next to me and holds me while I sob. What I don't know is that in the midst of my grief, in the midst of death, new life is springing forth inside me.

CHAPTER SEVEN

Benjamin

Every thought of her, every sweet remembrance is an anguished groan, a paralyzing sorrow, but I know her well. The ending had to be complete. She is loyal and would have held on waiting for my return, and given the circumstances, I can never impose such a condition on her.

Perhaps it is fortunate to have so little time for feelings to surface. The dread of violence and death pervade every moment of our lives. Nobody is safe, but just how endangered we are will soon be revealed. Warsaw is receiving a steady influx of Jews fleeing Germany, speaking in terrified whispers about what they have seen and heard: mass murders, deportations, forced labor camps, and worse. The rumors are so outrageous that it is almost possible to dismiss them as mass paranoia. We do know, however, that German occupation is close at hand. Anyone with means is fleeing. Bartel is furiously imploring favors to procure visas and safe passage for my family. Given the horrifying rumors, the market for illegal visas is tight. There is not a moment to waste. Once the city is occupied, escape will be virtually impossible.

We spend our days anxiously packing and repacking, seeking places to hide our few remaining valuables. The army is less than two days away when we receive word that Bartel has procured visas. I plan to meet him in the basement of the conservatory. Viola tucked under my arm, the Cup of Fortunes wrapped in paper and tied with twine, I sprint through the streets, oblivious to possible attackers. Every moment saved means a greater chance of escape. Bartel is waiting, his face taut.

"They were promised for today, Benjamin, but they won't arrive until tomorrow morning. I'm sorry." He notices the viola and the bag. Fighting tears, I thrust them into his arms, and reluctantly he receives them.

"Keep these safe for me, Bartel. I feel better knowing it will be well used should I not return."

We embrace spontaneously. "I'll see you tomorrow. God willing I will have your visas."

Sharing the devastating news with my family, we sit down to a bleak, tense dinner of potatoes and cabbage, and a stale loaf of bread. My father offers a prayer that night, his voice soft and melodious. He sings for a long time, his eyes closed, his body rocking back and forth. The food is ready, and we are hungry, but still he sings, and we wait, his prayer opening all of us to the love we feel for each other in this moment. My mother, who seldom cries any more, holds her face in her hands and weeps. Channah anxiously clutches the doll my mother made for her years ago. Auburn curls frame her face, her beauty just starting to blossom.

Finally my father stops singing. The food is cold, but we have food to eat, and for this we give thanks. In the still hour before dawn we hastily consume the rest of the potatoes, and wait anxiously for the time to pass. If everything goes as planned, Bartel will be standing on a corner several blocks from the train station, and we'll run to catch the late morning train.

There is little we can carry with us: a change of clothes, a bar of soap, a loaf of bread, a valued book, a set of *Shabbat* candlesticks, coins sewn into the lining of our clothing, a few family photographs. The hour finally arrives, and we leave the house, a solemn procession walking in awkward and encumbered haste toward our one chance of freedom. The streets are eerily empty for this time of day. We spot only Natan, our elderly neighbor, striding toward us.

"Have you heard the news? The Germans are close. They'll reach the city sometime today."

We run to meet Bartel, our bags thumping our sides. He is pacing nervously at the corner perpendicular to the train station. Shoving the visas and train tickets into my hand, he waves us on. "Last train out of here. Run!"

The train hisses and screeches with agitated impatience as passengers disembark, while a long line of new passengers waits to board. We are almost across the square when a loud explosion rocks the ground beneath us. People scream and disperse in all directions. The sound of a machine gun rips through the air. We stand frozen in horror as bodies drop to the ground, and the train closes its doors and pulls away. My brother's voice breaks through our shock.

"Follow me," he shouts above the clamor.

We sprint to an alley leading to a door that is locked. Lining up against the wall, we huddle in terrified silence all day, legs cramping, stomachs growling, hearts beating, and minds contemplating a bleak future, if any future at all. In the cover of darkness we return home, hope lost, and the long siege of fear and hunger and despair just beginning.

German tanks roll down narrow, deserted streets. The ugly blare of megaphones, the biting staccato of bayonets, and the command on threat of death to register by noon to hand over all valuables. We gather heirlooms and stand in line, watching in bewildered horror as a child escapes his mother's arms and is perfunctorily hit over the head with the butt of a rifle. Reflexively I rush to help and receive the same punishment. The child bleeds to death. The deep gash to my head bleeds profusely. Someone hands me a handkerchief. Pressing it onto the wound, I stumble back into line. Our possessions are marked, inspected, and confiscated. The helmeted German sitting behind the makeshift table is expressionless as he fires questions at me. "Is this all you have, Jew? If we find anything not reported, you and your family will be shot."

"We have nothing else to report."

My head is spinning, and I fear fainting from loss of blood.

"Jew, pay attention. Name."

"Benjamin Janowicz."

"Age?"

"Twenty-one."

"Occupation?"

"Physician and musician."

"Instrument?"

"Viola."

"Where is your viola if you are a musician?"

"I donated it to the musical society."

"If you are lying to me, you and your family will be shot."

"It is the truth."

"Here are your work papers. Carry them with you at all times. If you are found without them, you will be shot. Line up for work tomorrow."

My father is relieved, almost ebullient, his eyes wide and innocent.

"We're a good work force for them. As long as we produce, we'll be fine."

Avi starts to protest, but I stop him. "Let him have his delusions. What harm is there in hope? What will happen will happen regardless."

My brother nods his understanding. The pain in my head is so intense, I fear my skull has been fractured. It makes no difference. I'll be murdered if I fail to report to work.

"Who is Zofia?" Avi questions me the next morning. "You were moaning in your sleep all night, and calling out her name."

Tears threaten to erupt. Avi does not press me. Then there are no more tears, only a thickening deadness. I'm a body of flesh with no heart. I do what I'm ordered to do: erect an impenetrable wall around the ghetto, build the prison that will become our coffin. Brick by brick, stone by stone, barbed wire and broken glass make escape impossible. Every day more Jews are forced inside these prison walls. We are overcrowded, lice-infested, subsisting on rations smuggled in through secret tunnels. Our own home is now home to three more families. Winter arrives, and there is no heat. We huddle together in one room. We sleep with children and elderly in the middle. The weaker ones sicken and die. We say prayers for them, but perhaps they are the lucky ones. We hear rumors. There is worse to come.

CHAPTER EIGHT

Benjamin

When a soldier shouts orders at me to leave my assigned work of mixing concrete, I'm resigned to death. It happens all the time, people murdered randomly. A rifle is held to my back, and I'm ordered to march until I'm facing a thick wooden door with ornate carvings and a brass knocker. The guard opens the door without taking his eyes off me. I enter a hall with rose-colored velvet walls, tall ceilings, and priceless artwork. A fleeting memory of Bartel flashes through my mind and then is gone. Uniformed soldiers lounge on couches and chairs, drinking vodka. Why have they brought me here? A viola is thrust into my hands.

"You better have told the truth. Perform."

My hands are shaking so badly I can hardly grip the instrument, but I must play, and I must play well. Closing my eyes, I sweep bow across strings, and the sound that emerges soothes my terror, and I play. And I play well.

A voice interrupts me. "Enough for now. Go back to work."

I'm summoned now on a daily basis. The officers feast, and I play, the aroma of seared meat making me weak-kneed with hunger. An officer tosses a scrap of meat onto the floor beneath my feet.

"Go ahead, Jew-dog."

I'm on my knees, oblivious to the laughter. I'm also laughing. If they want a Jew-dog, then a Jew-dog I will be. Starvation transcends pride.

Our elderly downstairs neighbors are beaten to death. Their screams of agony are excruciating, but we must remain silent or suffer the same fate. Finally the screaming ceases, and we breathe a unified sigh of relief. The next day new families move into their apartment. I dream of escape, but the price of escape is the torture and murder of one's family. It is only a matter of time before all of us die of starvation or disease. Even the black market is drying up.

Hearing about the deportations, we are initially relieved. The trains, we are told, will take us to work farms with clean air and ample sustenance. I've been told the truth by one of the friendlier officers, who hands me a letter to use when I'm deported. It will keep me alive, initially. I know the truth, but I tell nobody. They will all find out soon enough.

My brother arrives home shaken. He was almost caught smuggling a sack of potatoes and ammunition. He's a member of the resistance movement, and was betrayed by another member who took a bribe. The situation is under control, he assures us in a shaky voice.

My father asks to talk with me in private. We carry two straight-backed chairs into the hallway. The hallway, once attractively decorated, is stripped down to pocked plaster, the wallpaper boiled for food and the wood burned for warmth. We sit by the one window with broken panes. The cold yellow-grey light from the nearly full moon illuminates my father's face. His tears, like falling stars, land in his beard.

"Avi is not telling the truth. We will pay a price. He should not blame himself. He is being courageous, but there is no way to fight this evil." He pauses. I wait for him to continue. "Benjamin, you are a mission keeper. Do not forget. If you don't survive, there is nobody to follow you."

"I won't forget, *abba*, but I want us all to survive."

He shakes his head slowly. "We will not."

"How do you know that?"

"Do you remember when I consulted the Cup the night before we left the *shtetl*? What I saw was death, and death, and death."

The next day my father is shot in the back, his body tossed into the back of a truck and carted off to the mass grave in the field beyond the city. My mother's eyes are red and wild, the look of an animal right before slaughter. She releases one high-pitched, inhuman wail, and then she is silent. My sister is curled in a corner clutching her doll.

The following day the officers keep me later than usual. I'm so tired I can barely hold the viola, but it is this or death. Finally they are done with me. I drag myself home. Opening the door I'm greeted by a chilling silence, a frightening emptiness. They have all been taken. On the table sits one boiled potato. The animal of my body pounces on the potato, consuming it in one swift bite. I curl up in a corner and tremble.

CHAPTER NINE

Avi had also been away when our family was taken. Now that nobody will suffer the consequence, we put all our energy into the resistance movement, and into seeking an escape route. Crawling under the wall is easy, but the forests are well patrolled. We decide to chance it, but my fate is determined by the most minute of mishaps: the breaking of a string in the middle of a sonata. Enraged at the audacity of the disruption, an inebriated officer flings a shot glass at my face. Instinctively I use the viola as a shield, the force of the glass cracking the body of the instrument. In recourse, I'm hauled off for deportation.

Loudspeakers shout commands into the terrified crowd. I'm shivering, my blood cold, even on this warm, cloudless day. Mothers console children, fathers console mothers, or try, but there is no consolation. We know what awaits us. Immediate death or slow, torturous death; these are the options. Children, mothers, the elderly and infirm will most certainly be murdered. The rest of us might be spared for a while to act as a work force, but in the end, there is little hope. My mind wanders elsewhere: Zofia, Laiah, Bartel, and those glorious weeks of stardom, my family laughing and bickering.

Present reality rushes back as the train arrives, the squeal of brakes, the clanking of metal, the staccato voice behind the megaphone, the wails, the screams, the prayers, a gunshot stunning my ears. And then silence, the silence of terror. It is my turn to board. My heart freezes, my breath stops, my stomach sickens, a flash of fear, a momentary urge to run, squelched until I feel nothing but dull blankness. I close my eyes. The door clanks shut. The train lurches forward. I fall into the man in front of me and apologize. The shrill voice of a woman shouting commands: make sitting room for the pregnant, the sick, the elderly. Defecate in the far corner. Sing for the children. We sing that first tedious day but only that first day, for we have no food, no water, and our mouths are parched, our voices raspy. No air, the stench of excrement disgusting, the heat unbearable. An old man dies of a heart attack. A woman becomes psychotic, screaming that the devil is choking her. A young boy sobs. I pick him up, hold him, and stroke his soft hair. His little hands cling to me. "I'm scared," he whispers. "I will hold you," I tell him. He relaxes.

The hours are excruciatingly long, filled with the pain of standing, hunger and thirst, dread and confinement, and monotony. The boy clings to me. He will die. I might survive initially. The letter is stuffed inside my pocket. Perhaps it means nothing, or perhaps it affords me life. Evening again. Total darkness. We take turns leaning against the walls to sleep, and I dream of flying. My body lurches forward. The train halts, and we are flooded with light as the doors open. A momentary breathless pause, a brief suspension of reality and then the agony of children wrenched from mothers' arms, thrust into the arms of the elderly, that the young and able-bodied women might survive. For the ancestors, for the lineage, for the sake of life, they must relinquish their children.

The crazy woman shrieks and is shot. A child breaks away and runs toward his mother. He is shot, not yet dead he lays moaning until another shot puts an end to his life. A volcano of energy rises up my spine, the urge to kill, to mangle, to destroy, and the squelching of that urge, the contraction of muscles, the lock of the jaw, the holding of breath, the withdrawal deep, deep within. The grim parade of naked people, flesh hanging loosely from limbs, heads down, weeping or praying or singing still for the children who need not know that they are about to die. All the while an orchestra plays a lyrical, whimsical waltz. The sky above is transparent, luminous, and exquisitely vast.

The inquisitors read the note. I'm kept alive. Head shaved, numbers tattooed on my arm, attired in a striped prisoner's uniform several sizes too large, I'm handed a dirty tin cup and spoon and marched to the barracks filled with row upon row of stacked wooden planks. A thin, greyish green blanket is folded neatly on each bunk. That night I meet the other two men with whom I share the narrow wooden mattress-less bunk. Mendel greets me with a puckered frown and promptly tells me that I will be sleeping in the middle.

Karl is a soft-spoken man with hanging jowls and sad eyes who wears a pink triangle instead of a star. Karl, being homosexual, is also an apparent blight to the human race. Karl and I bond instantly. Quickly discerning that I need his help, he imparts his wealth of accrued knowledge on the fine art and science of survival in the camps. Rules of camp etiquette, he calls them.

"Don't incite the guards by intervening on anybody's behalf. Invisibility is essential. Do whatever it takes to survive, one moment at a time. Don't trust anybody, for even the most noble among us will betray you under threat of torture or death. That is human nature, Benjamin. I was lucky enough to have drunks for parents. They taught me how to survive in extraordinary circumstances. It serves me well here. Guard your cup as if it is your lover. Never put it down or lend it. If you lose it, you don't get your ration of soup, and you die. Learn to eat the maggots in the soup.

Keep your shoes and jacket under your head when you sleep, or they will be gone in the morning, and you will freeze to death come winter. Look for stray pieces of paper or anything else to shove into your shoes to prevent blisters. Blisters mean infection, and infection means death. When walking in the yard, no sudden moves and don't wander too close to the fence. The guards will not hesitate to use you for target practice. Eat quickly, or it might get snatched. You get it, Benjamin? Wake up my friend. You do have a chance. You might just make it out. Don't waste it through ignorance or pride or high moral principles."

Karl is a true friend to me. He watches over me like a mother bear guards her cub. Karl knows he won't survive long. His body is weakening rapidly. He doesn't have a strong enough constitution to endure starvation and hard labor. The thought of losing him terrifies me. I beg him to take my rations, hoping his strength will return.

"Don't waste your rations on a homosexual," Mendel says.

"You piece of shit, Mendel!"

The next week Karl fails inspection. I have no chance to say goodbye. He is sent directly to the gas chamber. I stifle a scream of horror, a wail of grief. I cannot afford to feel, for it will weaken me. I am alone, so excruciatingly alone. I want to die, but I need to live for everybody who will not survive.

CHAPTER TEN

1941

Zofia

Each day more and more planes drone overhead, dropping bombs on our city, indiscriminately killing innocent citizens. There is no safety anywhere. We are trapped and constantly scared, and perpetually hungry and cold. And yet life keeps moving. Children attend school where Sija teaches. People come for treatment to my father's clinic where we both work long hours for little or no payment. We have no medicine and few supplies, but we offer what solace we can.

My baby is growing, enveloped in his or her own private, safe haven, oblivious to the state of the outer world. During the days, I'm too busy to reflect, but at night my heart aches for Benjamin. There are hushed whispers of deportations and death camps, and genocide being the intention. Nobody wants to talk. Nobody wants to face the truth. Everyday survival is hard enough. The plight of others is too much to bear.

Even my own family seems reluctant to speak about my half-Jewish unborn baby. My parents are not prejudiced people, but these are extreme times, dangerous times. The walls listen, or so it seems. But this particular morning my father embraces me and tells me how much he already loves this baby. I'm on a brief excursion to treat an infirm elderly woman, and on the way back my baby moves inside me for the first time.

I turn the corner anticipating the sheltered warmth of my family. It is then that I spot it. Painted in the center of our front door is an ugly yellow Star of David, still wet and dripping onto the step. My breath catches in my throat. My body freezes. My legs almost collapse under me. Slowly I back away from the door and scuttle to the rear of the house. Listening acutely for voices, footsteps, weapons, I hear nothing but the relentless ticking of the clock. Taking a breath, I venture inside, creeping through the dining room, cutting my hand on a shard of glass. Food, bottles, broken dishes clutter the floor. My limbs tremble. My heart is racing. I fight the urge to bolt and keep crawling, vigilant, hugging the wall for safety. Hearing a noise, the creak of floorboards, I stop, wait, breathe, and then proceed.

Their bodies lie sprawled out on the floor of the parlor, expanding pools of blood encircling them. Neither moves. They are close to each other, their hands touching. Perhaps they had survived for a few moments, long enough to find each other. I'm shivering with cold, with fear, with grief. I recognize the signs of shock, but I cannot afford to become immobilized. Danger lurks close by. They have only recently been murdered. The murderers will likely return. Forcing myself to move, crawling back through the kitchen, I bolt out the back door.

The school where Sija teaches is an old building, with bricks missing from the side and crumbling stonework around the windows. I'd attended this same school. My legs shaky, I barely manage to make it to the steps. Feeling the urge to vomit, I lower my head into my hands and wait, noting the clang of the bell, the cacophonous shouting of children piling out of classes. I'm crumbling inside, my bones turning to dust. I wait until the rush of children passes. Rising slowly, my body moving with its own volition, I must warn Sija of the grave danger we are now facing. Walking briskly down the dark hallway, I take minimal comfort in the familiar musty odor, the well-worn dark wooden floors that need polishing, the long cracks in the plastered walls. Sija is sitting at her desk, head down, grading papers. She looks up, surprised to see me.

"You look terrible, Zofia. What's wrong?"

Tears gush forward rendering me speechless.

"What is wrong?" she insists, coming over to hug me.

Her embrace brings on more tears. Sparing her nothing, I describe every detail.

"Oh my God, oh my God," she wails softly, gripping her stomach. "They knew it could happen. They knew the danger, but still they kept on doing what they had to do. Someone must have betrayed them."

"I betrayed them, Sija. Someone knew of my relationship with Benjamin."

My secret fear has been spoken, and I now await Sija's warranted wrath. Instead she looks at me, her eyes wide with incredulity.

"My dear sister, you didn't know that our parents were part of an underground organization called *Zegota*. They were trying to find escape routes for Jewish children. Only recently did they confide in me, but they wanted to spare you the worry. Don't burden yourself with guilt, but it's true we are in real danger. They murder family members affiliated with *Zegota* as a way to retaliate. We cannot return home."

"What can we do? Where can we go?"

"Father gave me instructions. We are to go directly to the Sisters of Mercy Convent. They are part of the same organization. They will shelter us by making us members of the Order."

I pat my belly. "I will not present very well as a nun."

"You are a widow, my dear sister, cared for by the charitable nuns."

My sister guides us to the convent, located on the east end of the city. The high brick wall surrounding it is interrupted by one wrought iron gate. Ringing the bell, we wait nervously. A young nun with a soft, round face finally arrives. Wordlessly she lets us in, seemingly knowing without any exchange of words why we are here.

"I will show you to your room. After supper, Mother Superior will meet with you."

The soft clank of iron meeting iron, the turn of the key in the lock means that for the moment I've stepped out of the mundane world and into a world of the sacred, the holy, the pure, the protected. My body instinctively relaxes. A statue of Mother Mary holding the dying Jesus offers a vestige of comfort. We are led into a small, windowless study with a simple wooden desk, several straight-backed wooden chairs, a Bible, and a crucifix on the wall. The door opens and a woman with an air of composure and authority enters. We rise in deference, but she quickly motions for us to sit. She is dressed in full, black habit, as are all the nuns here. It lends her face a sharp angularity and accentuates her penetrating eyes. Nothing escapes Mother Superior's gaze, and yet behind the serious intensity of her gaze, I catch a glimpse of someone who knows delight and mirth.

"My dear children," she says, reaching out to take our hands in her own. "I assume that your being here means that your parents have been murdered."

Sija and I simultaneously break down into tears.

"I knew your parents very well. I loved them as dear friends. They were most devout Christians, in the best sense of the word."

The memory of my parents reaching out to each other, sprawled in pools of blood evokes a silent scream of horror.

"We are battling Satan," she says. "The evil descended upon us is beyond comprehension. Your parents were well aware of the danger, but they chose to fight evil. We have that in common. Every day I risk my life for the sake of decency, for the sake of what is good and right about being human." Sija and I nod our understanding. "You need to remain in seclusion until the war is over, God willing. Everyone here is at risk, but I do all I can to keep us safe. Every moment I pray for the help and guidance of Our Lord Jesus Christ."

She rises and beckons for us to follow, but I hesitate. As my protector, she needs to know my story. Mother Superior listens intently and reaches for my hand.

"We shall take good care of you, and this very special child."

As if in response, the little being moves in my belly, kicking the side of my womb. At dinner we meet the other "nuns," most of them young Jewish women, recent converts to the way of Jesus, fast learning to genuflect, recite the rosary in their sleep, and quote the New Testament word and verse. They have new names, new identities, and our safety depends on their unflinching consistency under the scrutiny of interrogation, the first of which occurs only days after our entering the convent.

Two bayonet-wielding soldiers in full uniform rattle the gate shouting to be let in. Dropping our tasks, we run to the garden, lining up with heads bowed and rosaries clicking. Mother Superior accompanies Sija and me, whispering that this will be quick since the men have been drinking and will easily accept a bribe.

"Sirs, we are all here," proclaims Mother Superior. "There are two new faces among us," she says, pointing to Sija and me. "One is here because she has a calling. The other is here for shelter because her husband has deserted her, and she is with child. They have been members of the Church for many years."

"Where are you hiding the Jews?" the soldier demands as he fondles the breasts of one of the nuns. Expressionless, she lets his hands go where they will.

"We are hiding no Jews here," Mother Superior responds. "I would like to make an offering to you. We are in possession of some very excellent vodka, and since we cannot partake in such pleasures, we offer it to you so that we may resist temptation."

The soldiers glance at each other and nod. "Do you swear that you are not hiding Jews here?"

"Yes, sirs. The only thing we are hiding is the vodka, and we are hiding that from ourselves lest we fail to resist temptation."

Mother Superior disappears and returns holding two bottles. The men remove the caps, and each takes a swig. Satisfied of its quality, they promptly depart.

"Back to work, Sisters," she commands. "The Lord Jesus Christ has watched over us today. We must give thanks."

Motioning for Sija and me to remain, we sit on a stone bench facing a statue of the crucified Jesus. Mother Superior sighs, her face pale, her small, thin mouth is puckered and tight.

"It is not always this easy," she says. "Every time they leave, I retreat to my room and pray for our safe passage through these terrible times. He understands suffering and injustice," she says, pointing to the body of Jesus. "Do you know that he is a Jew?"

"Yes, Mother," Sija replies.

"Nobody thinks about such things," she says. "How we really all come from the same source. And when we die, everybody returns to the same earth."

Rising from the bench, she rearranges the flowers left at the bottom of the statue.

"How are you doing, Zofia?"

"I'm four months along. I'm well enough, Mother."

Mother Superior laughs, but her laugh is more like a cry.

"Remain courageous, Zofia. This baby is here for a reason."

"Thank you, Mother. Thank you for risking your life for all of us."

Yes, this baby is clearly meant to come into this world. That night I have a strong premonition that this little soul is destined to be the next mission keeper.

CHAPTER ELEVEN

Benjamin

Even Mendel, with all his sourness and disdain, misses Karl.

"For a homosexual, he wasn't a bad person," he remarks.

It is enough for me to warm to Mendel, so that when Mendel is taken two weeks later, I grieve the loss of him as well. That same day I'm assigned to a barrack that houses musicians who play in the orchestras and marching bands. Apparently the note was read.

My bunkmate is a bassoon player from Amsterdam with watery dark eyes. He is part of an orchestral ensemble that the players aptly named the Tonal Travesty. I'm here because the viola player died from dysentery. What it means on a practical level is that two days a week I'm spared from hard labor in order to practice and perform. Calculating the speed of my body's deterioration, this may give me a survival edge otherwise impossible.

The music is a poignantly painful remembrance of life's beauty and goodness and the harmony and order of a world that feels devoid of it all. The music is a temporary unity, a fragile bridge, an intimate space within and among the performers, the audience and the Divine. It is so fragile and so temporary that even as the last notes are issued, the spell is broken, and the world slips back into darkness.

Hans unobtrusively enters this timeless, transcendent space beyond, or beneath, or perhaps buried within this world gone mad. He appears and disappears, an apparition of sorts, and yet not an apparition, for he is most definitely an officer. He appears at our rehearsals, standing, never sitting, gloved hands folded across his chest, listening with poised attention. We pretend not to notice his presence, for noticing would make us equals, make us human to each other, and that is not tolerated. Paradoxically, the tension of being observed, scrutinized, expendable, brings forth from within us a measured abandon, the last brilliant gasp of life's longing to express its effulgence.

I sneak an occasional, carefully calculated glance in his direction, noting the usual distinguished mode of officer's attire, from the sheen of well-polished boots to the perfectly fitted uniform. He is handsome except for a bulbous nose made more prominent by spectacles sitting atop and a dark, clipped moustache beneath. Hans becomes the subject of endless conjecture. Is he listening for inferior performance, dispensing with those who don't measure up to standard? It never occurs to us that he is enjoying the music, but as weeks wear on and no action is taken, we concede to that possibility.

At first I attribute his attention to my imagination, the combination of increasing starvation, exhaustion, and fear playing tricks with my mind. But the other musicians confirm it. Hans is paying a lot of attention to me. Does his attentiveness increase or decrease my chance of survival? In this bizarre reality it can mean anything or nothing, the uncertainty greatly adding to my distress. I try to block it out, to focus only on the music. The day he commands me to remain behind after the rehearsal, I break into a cold sweat. He stands as he always does, feet set apart, planted firmly, hands folded across his chest. In comparison to his perfectly fitted uniform I stand before him in a striped prison uniform knotted at the waist lest the pants fall down around what is left of my shoes. I've become adept at supplication, shoulders stooped, head slightly bowed, hands held together in front. Hans does not speak. I pray.

"You play well. Keep playing."

"Keep playing now, sir?"

"Yes, now."

"What do you want me to play, sir?"

"I want to hear you improvise."

I play with frenzy and fervor fueled by terror. I play until Hans signals for me to stop and a guard appears. I'm certain that this means the gas chamber, but instead I'm led to my barracks. I've missed my serving of soup and bread. The same ritual goes on for weeks. Hands folded across his chest, he listens intently. Everybody is gone, and it is the two of us and the music, and an uncomfortable intimate silence. I continue to miss "dinner." I feel it happening. My body is entering the state of starvation. I'm weakening and will soon cross the line where recovery is not possible.

Zofia

The labor pains begin innocuously, a rhythmic squeezing of my abdomen, not nearly as bad as I'd anticipated. I can do this, I affirm to myself, as if I have a choice. Thankfully the pregnancy has gone reasonably well, and to term. I've palpated my own abdomen, and the fetus seems to be in the right position. Many complications can still arise—and being a physician, I know them all—but I sense that all will go well. Without warning the pain intensifies, and all I can do is breathe through each contraction, and try not to panic. Breathe and rest, breathe and rest, moment after moment, hour after hour. Sija and Mother Superior are here with me, holding my hand, wiping my brow, speaking encouraging words, their presence helping me stay calm. Does every mother endure this agony to bring life into the world? Breathe and rest, breathe and rest, the high whistle of an air raid warning, another contraction. "Run for shelter," I implore them in between contractions, but they remain by my side. I breathe and rest, and then no rest, just intensifying contractions. Exhaustion, alarm, burning, burning, and an uncontrollable urge to push and push, and though my strength is waning, I must push this baby out.

"I see the head! Good work, Zofia, your baby is almost born."

One final push, and I feel the fetus slip out of my body. Sija cries out in joy, and the tiny, slippery bundle of life is placed on my breast.

"Welcome your son, Zofia. Welcome Rafal into the world."

The pain of only a moment ago is a memory. I'm flooded with love for my baby. My son, Benjamin's son is here. Sija cuts the cord and attends to me while Mother Superior cradles Rafal. Only now do I see the faint figure of light hovering above me. She is with me, beholding perhaps her next mission keeper. Rafal, named for the archangel of healing, is born. He is the miracle of life, in the midst of so much death.

Benjamin

Deprived of one meal a day, regardless of how meager, means that I'm walking the razor's edge between subsistence and starvation, and soon between starvation and death. I must risk telling him, or I won't pass the next inspection. I wait until I'm done performing, but I wait a moment too long, and he is already walking away.

"Sir?" He ignores me. "Sir," I repeat, louder. He stops and turns to face me, standing with arms crossed, waiting.

"Sir, this is the time that evening rations are served." He offers no response. "If I don't eat, I will not survive."

"Is that all?"

"That is all."

He turns and walks away, as if my words are annoyances to be brushed off like flies. Terrified of being punished for speaking out, I dread being sent to the gas chamber, but nothing happens. Two days later we have another rehearsal. Hans stands in the back of the room. He gestures for me to remain behind. My bunkmate, knowing the situation, meets my gaze and silently wishes me well and farewell. I play for a long time and the music is surprisingly sweet. When I'm done, Hans disappears into another room, and returns with a small package wrapped in brown paper.

"Open it."

The package contains cheese and sausage and fresh rye bread. I'm overwhelmed, unable to move. Hans orders me to eat, and he looks on while I ravish the food. His attention frightens me.

"In my youth I played the violin." He holds up his left hand and removes his white glove. Part of one finger is missing.

"My father's punishment. He judged my passion for music to be a weakness."

"I'm sorry," I say, and then regret it.

"My father was right. Life had other, better plans for me."

A confusing and terrifying shift is happening. Hans is becoming a real person to me.

"Better plans, yes, of course," I stammer.

Hans turns crisply on his heel, and then turns again to face me.

"Your records say that you are trained as a physician. Did you tell the truth?"

"I graduated medical school, but I haven't yet practiced medicine."

"That is good," he says. "I also have other, better plans for you."

⚮

Zofia

My son is an astonishing miracle. His perfect hands and feet, the silky smoothness of skin, his changing expressions, his gurgles and cries, he is my world now. Perhaps it is natural for a mother to be still enjoined with the little being who has lived within her for many months. But here it is even more so. Rafal is a reprieve from the terror that infiltrates every moment of our lives. Reality returns three weeks after his birth when I'm forced to hand over Rafal to an inebriated soldier during an inspection. He must check for circumcision, a procedure ritually performed on Jewish babies. The man is rough with him. Rafal wails. I'm utterly helpless to protect my baby.

We are forty women, most of whom recently entered the convent presumably by way of Calling. The others are self-proclaimed servants or brides of Our Lord. Or so the soldiers are told and so this charade must be upheld with absolute impeccability. The past is gone, wiped out of memory, and a new name and history is instilled so deeply that even in terrifying moments of harassment nothing is revealed. One slip—a word of Yiddish, a discrepancy in story—and we all suffer torture and death. Days are spent studying the Bible, doing routine chores, and performing endless sacraments, over and over until the mind actually believes the charade.

Mother Superior experienced a real conversion of heart that transformed her from a "wayward sinner" into Christ's beloved bride. She recounts the story to us so many times that we can recite it by heart. She does this to instill in us a nobility of purpose and credible passion. Mother Superior is short of stature, with wide set blue eyes, a sharp nose and tight thin lips that turn up at the edges. The seriousness of her demeanor is due to circumstance and not to character. She has assumed the responsibility for a group of young Jewish women hoping for a different fate than that of their families. She is a master of guile and intimidation, able to lie to the interrogators in the name of love.

"Venerable officers, we are servants of Our Lord Jesus Christ and as such we are sworn to the truth. We are virtuous Christians, every one of us, even the child. We have been called to serve Our Lord and to take the vows of obedience and chastity. Venerable officers, I offer blessings to you and to your families who, I am sure, love and also fear the great power of the Lord, as we do."

After such charades, Mother Superior retreats to the privacy of her chamber and weeps. I know this because often she asks to be in Rafal's company. Rafal is her healing balm, as he is for all of us. He grows into a healthy and robust child, with Benjamin's auburn curls and deep green eyes. The resemblance between them is comforting and disturbing. Benjamin is with me, through his son. Benjamin and the rest of his family are, from all the rumors, unlikely to survive. I cannot dwell on this horror. I turn my attention to doing whatever I can to ensure our survival, for the sake of the lineage.

CHAPTER TWELVE

Benjamin

The hospital building is a grey, cinderblock structure, more like a fortress than a place of healing. Already unnerved, I'm careful not to stumble on the cracked and uneven cement. At my back is a guard wielding a bayonet. I've witnessed a man stumble, and for this a blade pierced his heart. Rumors abound about what transpires within these austere walls, but I dare not dwell on them. My life is not my own. I do what I'm told, or I'm killed. I'm unnerved that Hans has taken such a personal interest in me. I might offer temporary amusement, but I have no doubt that I'm expendable.

The entrance to the hospital is a formidable set of rusting metal doors that the guard orders me to open. I pull hard, but either I'm very weak or the doors are very heavy. He pushes me aside and easily opens them himself. I'm weak. If nothing else, working here means that I will not be lifting any more steel beams or carting boulders from one pile to another. Men usually last three months doing such hard labor with no sustenance. If not for the music and the extra food Hans has provided, I would be dead by now. Directly inside is a nurse's station, a simple square enclosure guarded by two nurses in starched white uniforms and small, triangular caps.

"Good morning, Dr. Janovicz. Dr. Weinermann is waiting for you."

The shock of being addressed by name increases my anxiety. Why the façade? The guard accompanies me down a cheerless, windowless hall, lit by occasional flickering fluorescent lights, the reek of disinfectant, nauseating. The whitewashed cement adds a ghost-like quality. He orders me to stop in front of a door adorned by a brass placard. The guard knocks, and a voice orders us to enter. Dr. Weinermann is propped behind an immense oak desk. He gestures me to the leather armchair in front of the desk.

"Welcome to the hospital, Benjamin. Now you will learn how the science of medicine should be practiced."

Hans lights a cigar, enjoying several puffs before crushing the end of his cigar into the ashtray and rolling it fastidiously from side to side. "I will see you on the floors, Dr. Janowicz."

When the wind blows from the north, all hospital staff are given masks to filter the smoke spewing day and night from the crematorium. The stench of bone, flesh, hair permeates everything, and yet not a word is spoken. Rounds are made each day, and Dr. Weinermann imparts his profuse knowledge to the flock of new doctors. There are several other Jews in the flock, one of whom tries to impress the doctors with his medical knowledge, the other of whom, like myself, practices invisibility.

A month into my "training," I'm placed on the surgical ward and told that I will be taught basic surgical skills. The morning surgery is the removal of a large mass from the intestine of a German guard. I'm instructed to remove the mass and stitch the wound, and praised for my competence. My training will continue in the afternoon, this time with my performing the whole operation. I'm nervous, but Dr. Weinermann assures me that I will do well.

At the appointed time, I scrub up and enter the surgical room. What I see turns my stomach and confirms all the rumors I've heard. Two young girls, twin sisters I'm told, are strapped to gurneys. They lie naked, emaciated bodies exposed, heads shaven, black lines drawn on their shaved scalps, wild, terrified eyes searing my own—two little girls, somebody's precious, beloved daughters. Hans enters the room and stands next to me. A mask is placed over their faces and they are anaesthetized. He hands me a scalpel and instructs me to make deep incisions into their skulls, where the lines are drawn. I don't need to be a surgeon. This is butchery.

I'm unable to move. Hans nudges me. "This is good experience, doctor. These subjects are perfect for the work we are doing on mapping the brain. They will be giving their lives for science."

Science? Does Hans believe his own words? I glance at the face of one girl: the gaunt lines of cheekbone, the ashen color of skin, sunken eyes, mouth open. Her face morphs into the face of my sister, my mother. The scalpel drops from my hand.

"Pick up the scalpel, Benjamin, and make the incision." Hans' voice is stern, but underneath I hear his pleading. "These subjects will die either way."

I stand paralyzed, unable to move a muscle. The attack happens fast. I'm knocked to the floor, assaulted, dragged by my feet down the cement steps, hurled into a cell and beaten with rods, hands, the butts of guns, boots. The pain is excruciating. I choke on my own blood. I cannot breathe. I pray for death, but then the beating stops. I'm alone on the cold, cement floor. Instinctively I fight to stay conscious, focusing attention on one dim bulb suspended from an exposed electric wire. It casts eerie shadows swaying back and forth, the shadows lurching about like huge insects.

Footsteps, a key turns in the lock, a voice speaks in German, laughter, and then another assault begins. A boot kicks me in the eye, and I lose consciousness. When I regain consciousness, I can barely breathe or move a muscle without feeling excruciating pain. They are torturing me before the final kill. I pray to die before being beaten again. My blood runs icy in my veins. I'm shivering, and each shiver sends spasms of agony through my body. The stabbing in my head is intolerable. Hearing footsteps and the grating sound of the key in the lock, I brace, I whimper, I pray. Nothing happens.

"Benjamin, are you alive?" The voice is a raspy whisper. "Benjamin, this is Dr. Weinermann. If you are alive, I will help you."

Hans is here to help me? My thoughts are jumbled. "Answer me, Benjamin. There is little time."

"I think I'm alive, but I don't know."

"Can you stand?"

Searing pain accompanies every movement.

"Try to crawl to the infirmary. If you make it, they will help you." He pauses. "Listen to me carefully. I will say it only once, and then you are on your own. You died in the night, and your body was brought to the cremation ovens. Are you understanding me, Janowicz?"

"Yes, every word."

"You have a new identity. Your name is now Heime Heinsburg. You speak nothing of this to anybody, or you will be further tortured and killed."

The door creaks, a cool breeze reaches toward me. I manage to crawl a few paces in so much agony I almost lose consciousness.

"Come on, Benjamin, I must leave." Taking hold of my arms, he drags me out the door.

"Heime Heinsburg, remember that name."

Then he is gone. Darkness and cold enfold and infiltrate me. I must move, or I will die. The pain is too much. I yearn for death, for release from this broken body. Images of my family flash through my mind. I hear my father's words. I must survive, because I carry them inside me. Using my less damaged arm and leg, I push myself along. The infirmary is not far, but the air is frigid, and I'm losing strength fast. Then I feel it, a surge of energy streaming through me, revitalizing me and diminishing the pain. A flash of light, She is here with me. I crawl faster now, fast enough to reach the door of the infirmary before the cold paralyzes me. My voice is weak as I call out for help. Fighting to stay conscious, I try one more time. The door opens. Someone gasps, and I'm pulled inside.

Later I'm told that the coma lasted for a month. I remember only resting in the sweetness and beauty of a world that perhaps will some day be home, but not yet. When I regain consciousness I have become Heime Heinsburg.

CHAPTER THIRTEEN

1945
Zofia

Frederick, an aging priest with runny eyes and a pockmarked face, a dear friend of Mother Superior, comes regularly to deliver supplies collected from loyal church members who graciously share with us what little they have. He joins us at the long wooden dining table to share a meager portion of potatoes and turnips, and a tiny serving of canned beans from last summer's garden. He is our link to the world outside the convent walls, and his visits bring the dreaded knowledge of ever more destruction. Nobody knows what will be left of Warsaw when, or if, the war ends.

Adding to the city's woes is the brutality of winter this year. We offer shelter to a few of the homeless, but many die of exposure or starvation. Our only compensation is that we have no interrogations until the ground thaws and the tiny brave flowers in our garden timidly display their buds. We've survived another winter, but Frederick tells us that the worst is yet to come. He has news of the Polish Army preparing to fight the German stronghold in Warsaw. Neither side will be defeated easily, and Warsaw will be the battlefield.

Mother Superior decisively instructs us to prepare the basement of the convent, all of us put to work filling water barrels, taking stock of our supply of root vegetables, fruits, canned goods, and tins of dried crackers. We carry blankets and mattresses, candles and matches, and prayer books. The fighting begins and we wait, and wait, and wait, and although mid-summer blossoms above us, we barely see the light of day for two months. The cellar is dark and dusty, the bombing incessant. We live in dread that the next bomb will bury us all. We must conserve candles so there is little we can do but pray and engage Rafal in games of imagination.

Is it his imagination or Her visitation, I wonder, when he describes a meeting with a beautiful woman who has a kindly face, like the statue of Mother Mary, and whose voice is like the sweet tinkle of the bell that Mother Superior rings in the chapel. My premonition has proven itself real. Despite everything, I feel a quiet, private peace.

We feel great relief but little joy in receiving the news that the war is over. The toll of war has been too heavy for many to bear, and yet we all must leave the past behind and put all our effort into creating a new future. Buildings, homes, infrastructures, bodies, communities, families, and souls all need to be reconstructed.

Sija, Rafal, and I choose to move back to what remains of our family home. Much of it has been demolished but there are a few rooms still usable, and we'll begin with what we have. We are fortunate. Many have nothing at all. Empty glasses are strewn carelessly about the floor, most of them broken. The plastered walls have gaping holes, and the flowered wallpaper is blotched with ugly stains. The furniture is destroyed and the windows are shattered. Vestiges of mother's delicate lace curtains so lovingly created, hang tattered above the windows, like skeletons.

We remove broken windowpanes, welcoming in fresh air and sunlight. We haul broken furniture out into the street, and heave it onto the massive communal pile of debris, the alchemical pyre soon to be set ablaze. We scrub the walls and floors of the intact rooms until our knuckles bleed, cleansing and purifying all that has been defiled.

CHAPTER FOURTEEN

1945

Benjamin

Internal bleeding, high fever, and infection ravage my already weakened body. Blind in one eye, a headache that never seems to abate, likely organ damage and fractures that will never fully heal, but I'm alive. Why there is an infirmary while the gas chambers run night and day is a mystery to me, but logic here is of another order.

Conditions in the camp have deteriorated even further. Our miniscule rations are cut in half and multitudes die of starvation. My injuries are serious. I could still die of infection, or starvation, or Hans might change his mind. Will there ever be an end to this madness? There are whispered rumors of the Allies gaining strength, the Germans suffering more and more defeats. But rumors are unreliable, and here the killing machine is operating at maximum efficiency. Trains arrive daily, overflowing with people, all of whom are now sent directly to the gas chamber.

A young soldier, barely tall enough to wield his bayonet, marches into the infirmary and calls out for Heime Heinsburg. I freeze in terror. Will I be tortured or killed? If that is the choice,

I pray for death, but we walk past the gas chamber, and I feel the urge to run. Better a bayonet in my back than more torture. Instead, I keep walking until we arrive at the building where the Tonal Travesty rehearsed. The guard orders me to step inside, and locks the door as he leaves.

I am alone. The room is completely empty, devoid even of chairs. A shaft of sunlight from a high window forms a square of cold light on the cement floor. I stand within the square, invoking the light to protect me. Hearing footsteps I panic, but there is no escape. I brace for more torture, but instead, when Hans appears, I swing between relief and terror. Perhaps he will be my final torturer. Perhaps he saved me for this moment. Hans stands with hands folded tightly across his chest.

"Listen carefully," he says in a low voice. "I have no time to waste. Three days from now all surviving prisoners will be lined up and marched out of camp. It is intended as a death march. Only those too sick or too weak to march will be left behind to die. If you want to survive, do you understand what you must do?"

"I must remain behind."

"Yes. Before the camp is deserted, most of the buildings will be destroyed. The infirmary will be the safest place to hide." He turns abruptly to leave.

"Wait," I say. "Why are you doing this for me?"

He turns around, and for one brief moment our eyes meet. I glimpse in his eyes a frightening deadness of spirit.

"Why do you need a reason? Isn't it enough that you may survive?"

"I'm most grateful to you, but tell me why you are sparing me."

The stern mask of his face drops away revealing a moment of deep, deep pain.

"Because you hold what is good in me," he says, turning quickly and departing.

❧

The crematorium is still smoldering when Russian soldiers march into the camp. Corpses are strewn on the ground, naked, their clothing already claimed. Buildings smolder, set ablaze to try and hide the evidence, skeletal figures wander dazed in the netherworld between life and death. Have I survived? I'm not actually certain. Rain touches my skin. I tilt my face upward to catch drops on my tongue. I hear someone speaking to me in a foreign language. He has a young face, a kind face. He hands me a canteen and motions for me to drink. His simple gesture brings me alive. I glance at his face. He is weeping. His tears plant a seed of life in my soul. Benjamin Janowicz is once again my name, and I want to live that I may one day be able to weep again.

Survivors gather slowly, emerging like rats from the rubble, eyes dead or vacuous or terrified, many too weak to recover. Many die in those first few months. I slowly gain strength. Working with other survivors is my healing and my solace. Every wound I treat, every soul I comfort is the body and soul of my family. I search for them among the hoards of survivors shipped here from other camps, but I know that I will not find them. When I can weep again, I will mourn them. Right now I feel only a dead hollowness, and a sense of profound aloneness.

I wake up one day and feel hunger pangs. This is a good sign. Starving people do not experience hunger. My body is coming alive again. Food is reaching us now, and medical supplies, and a vestige of human concern. I function by putting myself aside and caring for others. All of us here have seen the face of evil. We know the anguish of having breathed the same air as those who delight in torturing others, and have witnessed a depth of perversion that few will even believe possible. The existence of evil means that nothing, including oneself can ever be fully trusted. Yet many are turning toward life. There is laughter and song, and when energy permits, we dance. There are marriages and mating, and even babies born in the refugee camp.

What about my own life, spared for unknown reasons? I wonder about Hans, whether he was apprehended or escaped, unsure which I would choose for him. I'm afraid to leave here, for leaving means facing the acute aloneness of knowing that my entire family is gone. It means facing a world that even now is rampant with anti-Semitism. It means reckoning with questions of direction and purpose, and in particular my relationship to Her, and a mission that seems part of another lifetime. It means facing the truth about Zofia. Should I even be able to locate her, I don't have the courage to face her kind and loving eyes knowing what she might see in my own. Having been intimate with evil has changed me in disturbing ways that I cannot yet fully comprehend.

But one thing is clear to me, the promise I made to my beloved grandmother, the promise that I will keep. I must return to the *shtetl* to retrieve the manuscript, if it has survived the war. Most Polish *shtetls* have been "liquidated," all their inhabitants murdered, *Shtetl Bedzew* likely among them. In this moment my promise feels as flimsy as life itself, but I must go, if not for myself, then for my ancestors. The manuscript might be all that is left of our family. This is all I know of my future until I meet Aaron Goldschmidt.

CHAPTER FIFTEEN

Mother Superior

Throughout those horrible years, I lay awake every night, begging God for the strength and courage to follow through with my mission. I've never been outspoken or courageous. When I chose to enter the Order, I envisioned a life of quiet inner contemplation, serving through prayer and devotion. I was certainly no Joan of Arc marching into battle to right the wrongs of this world. Little Sarah, however, made my heart fierce. Sarah was a twelve-year old Jewess whose desperate parents plotted her escape from the ghetto by stuffing her into a sack of burlap being loaded onto a truck. She had the good fortune to meet up with sympathetic folks from our church who brought her to the convent. This was a sign from God that I was being called to a mission. I joined the vast underground network of courageous people risking their lives to save Jews by hiding them or helping them escape the Nazi death machine. We were waging silent battle with the anti-Christ.

I hid as many young Jewesses as the convent would hold, praying that not a word of Yiddish or Hebrew would escape their lips even under great duress. One slip during an inspection meant we would all be murdered, or worse. It had happened in other convents. It could have been our fate. I lived in stark terror. We all did, but what choice did we have? Would I abandon my girls? Never. Like My Lord Jesus Christ I had a mission, and I would fulfill it to my last dying breath.

Although we had no room to spare, Zofia and Sija were welcomed into the Order. And when dear precious Rafal was born, he too became my special child. How he made me laugh, that child! He was a ray of sunshine in the darkest of storms.

I was not predisposed to wage battle with the Lord of Darkness. I was not born to be a martyr or a heroine. I simply wanted to engage in prayer and contemplation, but the Father had other plans for me. I developed courage and fortitude. I learned to wage battle through deception, lie to protect the truth. When it was over, my name was placed on a plaque, honoring those who had risked their lives for the sake of others. The righteous ones, they called us. My convent was given a small donation. I didn't need honoring. I was simply serving My Lord. As He sacrificed His life for us, so I was willing to sacrifice mine for the Good.

I breathe a sigh of relief. My children are saved, and this is all that matters to me. I've had more than enough of this world. Free now to do what I've always wanted to do, I retreat to an inner sanctum of prayer and contemplation.

CHAPTER SIXTEEN

Benjamin

I've observed him meandering around the camp. He is bald, with thick eyebrows that meet at his nose, making him appear more serious than he actually might be. He approaches me while I rest from the long hours of attending the myriad of people needing medical help or a sympathetic ear.

"I can offer you the chance to emigrate to America."

"America? I have no idea where I'm going. Who are you?"

"I apologize," he says. "My wife used to accuse me of being too abrupt. My name is Aaron Goldschmidt. Before the war, I owned a clothing store to help people dress. Now I help people relocate. You're a doctor?"

"Yes, I'm a doctor. Why do you ask?" My head is pounding. I wonder if I will ever again have a day without pain.

"America is the land of freedom and opportunity. What is your name? I forgot to ask for your name."

"Benjamin Janowicz."

"Benjamin, I've selected you because you have a profession, and that makes it easier to find a sponsor. Are you interested?"

I shrug. "Why not? I have no other plans. But first, who are you, Aaron Goldschmidt?"

Aaron smiles. "I think what you want to know is whether you can trust me." I nod, and he continues. "Benjamin, I'm doing this as a way to find meaning for myself. My family was deported while I was away. After they were taken, I found a place to hide for the duration of the war. They did not. I live with that sorrow, and the guilt, although rationally I know there was nothing I could have done to save them. If I can help other people, then there is reason for me to stay alive." We both look away not wanting to see the mirror of sorrow in the other. "I'm good at business, and this is a business. I match people in need of a place to go, and sponsors with means and compassion for those who were less fortunate. If you are interested, I believe I can find you a sponsor."

"What is the payment, Aaron? I own nothing but the clothes I'm wearing."

"Of course," he says. "Your sponsor and the Red Cross pay your relocation expenses. When you are settled, you send me whatever you feel is fair payment. Nothing expected up front."

"Fair enough. What is the next step?"

"You complete your business here. I secure a sponsor for you, and we arrange a time and place to meet."

"America. I never thought of emigrating there."

"Life occasionally offers pleasant surprises," he says. "If all goes well, you will soon be on a steamer that carries you across the ocean to your new life in the land of opportunity."

Zofia

I'm grateful that we have a home. So many people have lost everything to this war, and yet this home is haunted by memory. I choose my father's study for my office. I need to feel his loving and supportive presence and to remember the generosity of his heart, the soft cherishing twinkle in his eye. I look around this room and catch an occasional glimpse of the books that used to line the wall, the scent of his pipe tobacco and rubbing alcohol, the over-stuffed chair large enough for my sister and me to crawl into his lap. I don't wallow in regret, but I do often feel bouts of sadness. I wish that Rafal could have known his grandparents. But everybody has regret and loss, and there is no sense in dwelling on the unchangeable past. Life must move forward.

Sija has miraculously fallen in love. Stanislaw—a soft-spoken man with soulful eyes and a carpenter by trade—returned from the front to discover that his wife and young daughter were killed in a missile attack. His daughter had been Sija's student. They now find comfort and happiness with each other. I watch them holding hands, laughing, and I miss being close to someone in that way. The war has been over for a year, and Benjamin hasn't returned. Likely he is dead, and if it were not for my son, I could grieve, let go, and perhaps move on. Rafal, however, insists that his father is alive. He keeps dreaming of a man reaching out to him, trying to make contact. Were it not for the fact that my son is from a lineage of mystics and seers, I would interpret his dreams in a different way. I cannot simply overlook his intuitions.

I'm delighted and relieved to receive a note from Bartel Barzowski. I've been to his apartment several times, but it appeared deserted. He writes that after the house was damaged in a missile attack, he took refuge in the country at the invitation of a friend. He has now returned, and is in the process of renovation. He also writes that Benjamin left two objects in his safekeeping that he wishes to turn over to me, and is eager to make contact as soon as possible. Bartel's note fills me with a joy I haven't experienced for a long time. How surprised he will be to know that his complicity in my relationship with Benjamin resulted in the birth of Rafal. I look forward to their meeting.

Bartel greets me at the door of his apartment with a warm embrace. He has lost so much weight that the skin on his face sags as if it is clothing that is far too large. Upon hearing about

Rafal, Bartel laughs with joyful abandon and insists on meeting this miracle child as soon as possible.

"If he were older," he says, "I would share with him the strange and unlikely circumstance of his conception."

"Rafal persists in believing that his father is still alive."

"Then why would Benjamin not return to the people who cherish him?"

My heart is heavy. I don't want to talk about it, not now. "Rafal would love to hear about your memories of his father. He is hungry for contact."

"Then stories I will offer him, and to both of you I offer the heirlooms that Benjamin entrusted to me."

"What did he leave with you? One of them must be the viola."

"Yes, that priceless viola, which I confess I've played numerous times. The other heirloom is a strange looking and, honestly, rather ugly cup. Why he chose this, I have no idea."

I laugh. "I know exactly why he chose the cup. His relatives used it as an oracle, a way to receive answers to questions. It has a bit of magic in it, at least according to Benjamin."

Bartel nods. "I must share a very strange story with you. When a missile struck this building, everybody fled the building to escape the fire and the smoke. I sprinted out to the street, but suddenly remembered that the viola and this cup were in my study. Ignoring the voice of sanity, I rushed back inside to retrieve them. Surely I would have died of smoke inhalation, but this is the truth, Zofia. As I fought my way to the door, the smoke cleared just long enough for me to escape. The cup has definite magic."

Bartel disappears momentarily to retrieve the viola and the cup.

"My dearest Zofia, is there a question you would like to ask the cup?"

The question is so obvious that I almost laugh aloud.

"Please let me know what answer you receive. I love him as well."

CHAPTER SEVENTEEN

Benjamin

I'm told that the area where *Schtetl Bedzew* once thrived is now a land of ghosts, where the souls of the murdered wander about trying to comprehend what evil befell them. It is a land where the few remaining Jews are still unwelcome, and the property of the murdered, callously confiscated. I'm advised to leave the poisoned ground of Poland and not look back. Soon, I will do just that, but first I will keep my promise to Laiah.

I'm given a small donation, and a Red Cross truck carrying supplies to the eastern border offers me a ride part of the way. The young man driving is American. He doesn't speak Polish or Yiddish, but he tries to be friendly. I try to return his friendliness, but I'm weary and preoccupied. He drops me in a town with a partially working rail line, and hands me a tin of condensed milk, all he has to give. Shaking my hand, he says something that I infer means "best of luck."

The train is crowded, almost every seat taken. I sit next to a large woman who reeks of perspiration and garlic, and close my eyes as the train bumps along the tracks. The woman reaches inside her bag, retrieves two eggs and offers one to me.

I'm famished and therefore grateful. I'm getting used to her odor and wonder now about my own. I have nothing, not even a change of clothing. Finally I doze and awaken to the screech of brakes. This is the last stop, the next stretch of train tracks having been damaged and not yet repaired. It is late in the day. I'm not sure how long a walk I have, likely quite a few hours. My body is not yet fully healed and may never be. I walk with a limp, and with shooting pain, but I can walk, and I will walk as far as I need to walk.

The world I once knew has radically changed. War is written in mounds of rubble, untended fields going to seed, roads and railways destroyed. I cannot see into people's hearts and minds, or know their suffering, losses, anger, kindness. Nor can they see into mine. That is the problem. If only we knew one another, we would understand how similar we all are.

How do I know if I'm safe here, or if it is possible to feel safe anywhere ever again? As a child, I always knew that danger was immanent, but my family and community held me. Now I have nobody. My injuries are visible, and therefore draw unwanted attention. An eye patch, a marked limp, but so many are maimed and simply grateful to have survived the war.

The doors open and everybody disembarks. Wagons and a few cars, and even bicycles with carts line up at the station, ready for hire to transport people further. All the vehicles are taken, but one young man in a wagon promises to return for me. This town, I notice, is coming to life again. Window boxes display colorful flowers, and the streets are clean. I'm famished. I have little money to squander, but even a baguette would do nicely. Spotting a bakery, I hurry across the road. I find a small, cramped space with one set of shelves for baked goods, almost empty, an open kitchen in the rear, and one aproned, buxom young woman working in the back who comes quickly when she sees me.

"There is not much left at this time of day," she tells me.

"I would like one roll."

She removes a roll off the shelf. "It is stale, but it is all that is left."

I take it, and she doesn't charge me. "Thank you," I say. "Do you know how far a walk it is to *Stare Bedzew?*"

Her face has a look of contained incredulity. "There is no more *Stare Bedzew.*"

"Are the buildings gone, or just the people?"

She looks away. "The buildings are there. Just the people are gone."

I ask again for directions. She doesn't know, but she will ask her father. I panic. What have I done? I'm about to leave when a large man appears with an apron tied under his potbelly. He is unshaven, giving him a gruff appearance, but his eyes seem kind.

"My daughter says you want to walk to *Stare Bedzew?*"

"Yes, if possible. Is it possible?"

"You mean is it close enough to walk?"

"Yes, is it close enough?"

"You know what has happened."

"I know that most of the *shtetls* were liquidated, if that is what you mean." Liquidated: a more sanitized word than massacred or ravaged.

He averts his eyes. "All of the *shtetls* were liquidated, at least all the ones in this proximity. Why do you want to go there, if I may ask?"

I decide to be honest. "It was my home until I moved to Warsaw. I need to see it."

The man's face softens. "If you wait until early morning, I'll take you there. I can borrow my brother's truck, and you can sleep here. I'll bring you dinner." He pauses. "I'm sympathetic to Jews. The ones I knew were good enough people. My wife feels differently. Her father influenced her. We don't talk about it."

"I appreciate your kindness, and your honesty."

He shows me to the back of the bakery. The walls are bare and cracked. There is a small desk covered with papers, and a lamp with no shade, only a bulb. The floor is covered with a frayed rug that was once attractive. He returns in an hour, with a plate of food. There is a small portion of green beans, and a potato. He places it on the desk and hands me a blanket.

"This is all I have," he says.

"Thank you. I've slept on planks. I can sleep on a rug." I feel his urge to linger, to talk, but he does not.

"There is water in the tap," he says. "And an outhouse in the back. I'm closing the shop now. We have no more to sell. I'll come early. It's not a long drive, but better you don't walk."

I hear his warning. He leaves, and it takes me little time to consume every morsel of food. I use the blanket as a pillow, and within moments I'm asleep.

Zofia

The Cup is as Benjamin described it: thick walls, misshapen and awkward to hold. Benjamin spoke about his lineage and the mission, and I'm filled with awe in remembrance of those who have held this Cup before me. Performing the ritual, I peer inside the Cup, allowing my mind to gaze and wander in response to my question. *Is Benjamin alive?* Scenarios rise and fall, like waves upon the ocean, but nothing is solid or definite. I'm disappointed. If Benjamin is dead, I can grieve and move on. Perhaps I'll find love again and a suitable father for Rafal. If he is alive and has not returned to me, then I must still accept and move on. But I need to know.

Is Benjamin alive? Again I peer into the Cup. Nothing has changed. I'm about to toss the tea, but feel a pull to look again. Have the leaves shifted, or is it my mind that is shifting? A word is spoken directly into my heart: *manuscript.* Benjamin spoke about the manuscript, and the mission, and his grandmother, Laiah. I recall the name of his childhood *shtetl,* and his promise to his grandmother to return and retrieve the manuscript. It is a complete gamble, but I chose to consult the Cup and it has spoken.

Benjamin

Marcel is the baker's name. Waking me before dawn, he hands me a burlap sack with two loaves of bread, a jar of water, and a slice of hot bread with butter and jam. He has his brother's truck and will take me now. I clamber into the seat next to him. The truck reeks of tobacco and wet fur. I thank him for his generosity. I hope his wife is not upset with him. He shrugs.

"I saw the number on your arm," he says. Were you in a camp?"

"Auschwitz. I survived."

"Was it as bad as rumors say?"

My stomach seizes. I swallow hard. "How bad are the rumors?"

"Never mind," he says. "What's done is done." He shakes his head, lights a cigarette. "Why?"

"Why what?"

He shrugs. "Never mind," he repeats. "Better not to talk about it." We are heading due east. A slip of light ahead of us announces the new day.

"Have you been there?" I ask.

"No reason," he says. "Most locals looted everything they could get their hands on, and some moved into the empty houses. I'd rather starve. Why are you going back?"

"I promised my grandmother I would retrieve a family heirloom." The closer we get the more nauseated I feel. I force myself to eat bread, chewing methodically. "I was born and raised there. Generations of my family lived there." The words stick in my throat, making it hard to swallow.

The sun has broken open the sky. I recognize the road, and

in the distance I catch a glimpse of the barn. My breath catches, and terror grips me.

"You all right?" Marcel asks. "We can turn around if you like. Or wait for a while." He puffs nervously on a cigarette, and then stubs it out in an overflowing tin can.

"My sister once broke her arm playing in that barn. My mother blamed my brother and me. She was feisty, my sister."

Marcel listens. "How can people be so cruel? I'll never understand what happened."

His kindness helps. "I think I can keep going now. You can leave me at the barn."

"How about I come and pick you up tomorrow night. Will that be enough time to do what you need to do here?"

I glance at Marcel, but he does not look back. He stares out the window, and lights another cigarette.

"Thank you. I'll be here waiting."

The truck pulls away. I'm standing at the edge of an abyss. It threatens to swallow me. I sit down at the edge of the abyss, and for the first time in many years, I pray.

I'm wandering in a world between worlds. The streets, the houses are empty, and yet I sense the presence of everybody who has ever lived here. I'm seeing this world through the eyes of a young boy who remembers. I walk toward Slavitzky Bakery, owned by the same family for generations. Mr. Slavitsky is a rotund bald man who always has a plate of sweets for the children, so they should remember the sweetness in life. It is as if he is here now, greeting me, welcoming me home. *Aren't you Shimon's boy? Here, have a sweet I saved for you.* The tailor shop is next door, the tailor shop where my grandparents worked at their sewing machines for countless hours. The big glass windows are in memory made whole again, the sign above their shop is still there with yellow ribbons woven through the holes. Two stores away is Abramowitz General Store. The door is open. The uneven wooden floor creaks as I step over the threshold. I smell the pickle brine, and fish for the largest pickle in the barrel. Mr. Abramowitz scratches his balding head, knocking off his yarmulke that falls to the floor, just missing the pickle barrel. He places an arm over my shoulders and remarks how much I resemble my great-grandfather, Jaakov.

Suddenly a man appears and scowls at me, informing me that I should not be here. The magic ends abruptly. I feel the urge to flee from the emptiness, the pain, the silent terror still pervading everything. I will do what I came to do, and then never again return to this poisoned ground.

My feet remember the way to Laiah's house. I simply follow their guidance. The streets are meticulously clean, all evidence of former inhabitants removed. The house is still intact, and in fact the porch has been repaired. There are a pair of boots on the porch, and a bouquet of dried flowers. Somebody is living here. I take a breath to calm my fear, and I knock. An elderly woman with sallow skin and a stooped back answers, and eyes me suspiciously. I'm having a hard time finding words.

"I grew up in this house," I say, and then regret it. "I know it is your home now, but it has memories for me, and I wish to ask one favor of you."

The woman listens, expressionless. My throat tightens. I cannot speak.

"Who are you?" she asks guardedly. "What do you want?"

"I came to retrieve one family heirloom that has no value, except the personal value it has for me, a manuscript that my grandmother and I hid in the root cellar before my family moved away."

"Why did you hide it, if it has no value?"

"What I mean to say is that it has no monetary value, but it has great value to me. If you allow me to retrieve it, I promise never to return for any reason."

"You have not told me your name."

"My name is Benjamin Janowicz."

"What is your grandmother's name?"

"Her name is Laiah."

The old woman examines me closely. "What happened to your eye?"

"I was badly beaten. I'm lucky to be alive."

The woman softens, opens the door for me to enter, and then closes it abruptly. "I know your grandmother. Laiah saved the life of my infant grandson."

I feel dizzy, faint. The woman notices and points to a chair. She brings water and a hard biscuit.

"Your grandmother is alive."

"Laiah survived?"

"Yes, Laiah is on her way to Palestine, or at least that was her plan. My husband and I hid her in a shed behind the barn. In winter she slept in the root cellar. Laiah saved the life of my grandson. We lived in terror for our own lives, but we could not allow her to be slaughtered along with the rest."

"My grandmother is alive." I repeat the words over and over, making them real to myself.

"She waited for you as long as she could tolerate being here, but it was too much to ask of anybody. I told her that I would stay in the house for at least a year in case anybody returned. She left a note for you."

My body is trembling. My head is pounding. My throat is tight with unshed tears waiting for permission to release. The woman retrieves the note and hands it to me.

My dearest grandson,
God willing, you are reading this letter now. I must remain hopeful that you and possibly others of our family have survived, but I am also realistic enough to know that it might not be so. I am one of the few who survived and that is only because of the courage

*and kindness of my dear friends. I do not need to
share the details of what happened here. It is best left
unspoken that you might remember the good. Forgive
me for leaving, but I had sleepless night after sleepless
night as the dead cried out to me. I could not take any
more suffering upon myself. I am so grateful that some
of our family made aliyah long before this horror. It
is time now that I, too, make aliyah, as I should have
done many years ago when I had the opportunity. Join
me, dear Benjamin. G-d willing, you will find me at
the kibbutz started by your great uncle Josef Janovicz.
It will not be difficult to locate. I have given my friend
the collection of letters sent to me from Laura and Josef,
and these include all the information you need to locate
the settlement.
With great love to you,
Laiah*

I am in stunned silence. The woman reaches and out clasps
my hand.

"Go retrieve what you came for," she says softly.

"What is your name?" I ask.

"Janina," she answers.

"Janina, you are an angel."

Janina places the manuscript and the letters, and a jar of cabbage
stew all in a burlap sack. I'm more than ready to leave, but Marcel
is not coming until tomorrow. I make my way to the barn, walking past the stone building that was the *mikvah*, the ritual baths.
Sitting on the stoop is a man whose face I remotely recognize.
This is Eli, the grandson of Zalman, the *mikvah* master. I remember Eli being close to my age, though at the moment he looks like

a much older man. He is disheveled and makes no contact with me as I approach.

"Is this you, Eli? I'm Benjamin Janowicz. Do you remember me?"

Eli gives me a blank stare.

"Do you remember me, Eli? I am Shimon's son."

Eli looks down at his feet and mumbles incomprehensibly."

"What are you saying, Eli? Do you know who I am?"

"I am the only one alive. I should not be alive." His hands are trembling. "I am sorry. I should have let them find me. I should have let them shoot me."

"Eli, your family needs you to live, to remember them."

"Everybody was screaming, and there was so much shooting, and I was so scared that I hid in the crawlspace under the bath, and they did not find me. Everybody else was murdered. I should not be alive."

"Eli, do you know who I am?"

"You are Benjamin, Shimon's son."

"Eli, do you want to come with me? I can get you help."

He shakes his head. "I must tend to the *mikvah*."

His mind is gone. His soul is gone. He is as good as dead. I wish him well and keep moving. Reaching the barn, I consume the cabbage stew and find a grassy spot to sleep. I'm awakened by the sound of an engine. Marcel is leaning against the truck, smoking a cigarette.

"You came early. How did you know?"

"I know things," he says. "Get in. Tomorrow you will step on that train and never return here."

I thank him, and agree. My life in Poland has now come to an end.

CHAPTER EIGHTEEN

Zofia

"Talk me out of it," I implore Bartel as he relaxes in my study sipping cognac. "I know it's a flimsy plan at best."

Bartel smiles. "I'm the last person in the world to try and talk you out of a fantastical plan, my dear, and I think it makes sense, given that you have no other options. The worst that can happen is you take a miserable and frustrating journey, and end up where you are now. But I will certainly not let a woman travel alone."

"You're willing to go with me?"

"I'm an honorable man, Zofia, and you are a woman in need of an honorable man. Besides, I feel personally responsible that you got involved with Benjamin, for better and for worse. Of course I will go. And since Rafal will insist on coming, let's invite him along."

Train tracks and stations blown up during the war are slowly being rebuilt, but we are constantly shuffled from one train to another. It is late in the day by the time we arrive at the town closest to the site of the *shtetl*. From here we will need to ask for directions and find transportation. But first we must find food and lodging. Across the street from the station is a bakery. A young woman is just about to close, but seeing me running toward her, she holds the door.

"We have no fresh bread," she says. "If you want fresh, come back in the morning, but if you are hungry, I have one loaf left over from the day."

"We are hungry. I will take it." She hands me the loaf, likely baked this morning and now rock hard, but hunger is hunger. She refuses payment. "Do you know if there is lodging in town?"

She points to the left. "Walk down that way. There are several places that offer lodging. Because the trains can only go this far, my bakery sells out every day and the rooming houses are often full, but you should be able to find a room."

"Thank you. We'll come back in the morning for fresh bread."

"And cheese," she adds. "Very soft, very tasty."

On an impulse, I ask if she knows the location of *Stare Bedzew,* and where I might hire someone to take us there. The question evokes uneasy silence. I apologize, and tell her I'll be back in the morning.

"No, stay," she says. "My father can help you."

The girl disappears into the back as Bartel and Rafal join me. The young woman and her father return. He is covered in flour, and I apologize again for the interruption.

"What is your business in *Stare Bedzew*?" he asks.

Rafal answers. "We are looking for my father."

The baker looks to me for confirmation. "We don't know if his father is still alive, but his family was from *Stare Bedzew*. It is all we know to do."

The baker's face softens. He removes his apron, and carefully sits himself down in a chair with a broken back. He looks forlorn.

"What is your name, young man?" Rafal responds. "Come here." Rafal goes to stand next to him. The baker places a hand on his shoulder. "What is your father's name?"

"Benjamin Janowicz is his name."

The man sighs deeply. "I met your father, Rafal, just a month ago. He was looking to retrieve some sort of family heirloom. I gave him a ride there and then picked him up. It turns out his grandmother is also alive, hidden by a local family, but she has moved to Palestine. Benjamin is going to live in America. I can tell you he will not be returning here. That is all I know. If you still want to go there, I will take you in the morning."

Rafal is beside himself with excitement and asks the baker to describe every detail of his visit with Benjamin. The baker is patient with him. I do my best to swallow my tears. Benjamin is alive, but chose not to return to me. Bartel feels my pain and takes my hand.

The baker repeats his question. "I will take you to what used to be *Stare Bedzew* if you still want to go."

Bartel shakes his head. "Thank you. You've given us exactly what we came for."

"God bless," he says, and reties his apron. "Come back in the morning for fresh bread and cheese, my gift for your journey."

CHAPTER NINETEEN

1946

Benjamin

New York City

Besides a small haggle with an impatient young officer who cannot pronounce my surname and changes it to "James," all goes smoothly at immigration. I find myself standing alone amidst a chaotic crowd of people, holding tight to my one suitcase, seeking my sponsor, or more accurately hoping my sponsor is seeking me. I'm tall, and I have a conspicuous eye patch. That should make me easy to find. It does. I wait only for a short time before a man approaches me and asks me in Yiddish if I'm Benjamin Janowicz. I nod, and he greets me with a warm hug.

"I'm Hal Rose, your sponsor. Welcome to America."

He is handsome, with intense brown eyes that dart nervously from side to side, and a broad smile. He is clean-shaven and smells of cologne and cigars. I like him.

"Irma and I are so happy you are here. We hope to help you establish a wonderful life for yourself."

I follow him to his waiting car. Irma steps gracefully out of the car and greets me with a warm hug. She is a petite woman with thick glasses, a crooked nose, and bright red lipstick. Her features are homely, but her warmth lends her radiance. Reaching into a huge bag resembling a carpet she offers me a sandwich.

"You must be starving."

Opening the front door of the car, Hal motions for me to climb inside. Irma hoists herself into the back seat.

"His driving makes me nervous," she remarks. "Better you sit up there than me."

I've ridden plenty in army jeeps, but this is my first ride in a real car.

"Like it?" Hal asks. I nod appreciatively. "I'll start teaching you to drive right away, and we will start speaking English soon so you learn quickly. What languages do you speak now?"

"Polish, Yiddish, and Hebrew."

"I'm impressed, Benjamin. Once you learn English, you will know four languages."

"I learned the others when I was a child. I hope English comes as easily."

Irma leans forward and touches my shoulder. "You'll do fine, Benjamin. Tonight we will have a wonderful meal to celebrate your arrival."

"You're both so kind. I have no words to thank you enough for sponsoring me."

"We were among the fortunate ones, Benjamin. We want to do anything we can to help."

We reach the entrance of their apartment, a multi-storied brick building with a wrought iron fence in front. A uniformed man emerges to park the car, and nods a greeting to me.

"This is Charlie," Hal remarks. "He works for us. I've instructed him to make himself available to drive you wherever you want to go."

"That is very kind of you, Hal."

"Aaron wrote to me that you're a physician. We'll discuss your future once you've learned English and feel comfortable with American culture."

"I graduated from medical school in Warsaw just before the German Occupation, but I have no proof of being a physician. I wasn't even allowed to attend the graduation ceremony."

Hal massages his chin while pondering my words. "I have connections, Benjamin. The cardiac wing of the hospital was built largely from our donation. Work you will have."

The apartment smells like Hal, with the addition of spicy aromas emanating from the kitchen. The parlor is spacious, but warmly decorated with floral wallpaper and matching upholstery. Adorning the walls are large oil portraits in gold-plated frames. Irma hooks her arm through mine.

"Benjamin, we want you to feel at home here. I will show you to your room, and you can rest until dinner."

Setting aside my travel-worn clothing, I fill the deep cast iron tub with steaming water and immerse my body, making this my first "*mikvah*" on American soil. The next day I begin my immersion into learning English, imbibing the culture of New York City, and studying medicine. Hal is astounded at how quickly I learn, but this is an opportunity I do not intend to squander.

I've been on American soil for a year. I've become relatively proficient in English, passed the medical boards, and now work in the emergency ward of the hospital where Hal sits on the board. Soon I will begin a residency specializing in cardiology. Specializing is what doctors do in America, he informs me. It is far more lucrative, and being lucrative is part of the American dream.

Occasionally at the end of a very long day, I contemplate the ironies of life. Less than three years ago, I was in a concentration camp. I am now Dr. Benjamin James, a bright young professional moving up the American ladder of success.

CHAPTER TWENTY

1948

Zofia

Dr. Esher Klein, a balding man with rimmed glasses and sad eyes singlehandedly runs an office in Warsaw to help refugees find places to settle and rebuild their lives. He is among the small group of psychoanalysts who studied with Freud before the war. He tells me that he escaped deportation by obtaining counterfeit identity papers. I tell him that I need his help in immigrating to Palestine.

"You are neither Jewish, nor a refugee, so why are you choosing Palestine?"

"My son is half Jewish, and his grandmother and other surviving relatives live on a kibbutz in Israel. He comes from a lineage of kabbalists and Zionists, and he needs family. My own parents were members of the *Zegota* organization and were murdered for helping Jewish children. It's time for us to have a new beginning. I'm also a physician and have skills to contribute."

"You've chosen an auspicious time to make *aliyah*. Palestine is about to be given statehood by the League of Nations and will become the new state of Israel. This gives all Jews the right of return, meaning that every Jew or every person with Jewish ancestry will be allowed to come home. The Zionist dream has finally come to fruition."

"But I'm not Jewish, Dr. Klein."

"Are you willing to convert to Judaism?"

"My son needs his family. I will do whatever is needed to make this happen for him."

Dr. Klein listens carefully. "Your reason for conversion may not be a heartfelt love for the Jewish religion and way of life, but it is selfless and compassionate. I will give you the name of a rebbe, and he will provide instruction for your conversion. After that, return here, and I will help you and your son make *aliyah*.

Rafal and I meet with Rebbe Horowitz, a young American Jew who is here to help with relief efforts. He is sympathetic to my reasons for wanting conversion, explaining that my maternal devotion demonstrates Jewish values. We begin several months of intensive study. Rafal also chooses to establish himself as a Jew, and changes his name to Raphael. He also courageously chooses to be circumcised. When we've both successfully converted, I return to Dr. Klein.

"You say your son has relatives in Israel. Do you know how to locate them?"

"I have only the name of his great uncle, the founder of one of the first settlements at the turn of the century. It is not a lot of information."

"But it may be enough," he says. "If you are tenacious, I believe you will be able to locate the settlement. Israel is a small country, but I have another idea for you to consider, Zofia. When my work is done here, I will make *aliyah*. I wish to open a psychoanalytic institute in Jerusalem, to help traumatized people recover. Would you be interested in participating?"

"Yes, I'm very interested."

He gives me the name of the hospital as well as his contacts. "And your son's father?" he asks. "I assume he did not survive."

I try to hide the pain that his question evokes. "He survived, but he chose not to return to me. He doesn't know that he has a son. I believe he is living in America."

"Is that hard for you?"

I nod, my eyes welling up with uninvited tears.

"I'm sorry. Surviving trauma changes people in unpredictable, and often disturbing ways. But you and Raphael are now entitled to become citizens of Israel. You and Israel will share a new beginning.

CHAPTER TWENTY-ONE

Benjamin

Hal and Irma introduce me to eligible young women of character and intelligence. I am, in their words, a "good catch." Indeed, the "eligible" women are plentiful, and I enjoy their company, but soon enough, I fall in rank from being known as a good catch to being a "heart breaker." Hal and Irma are concerned, and I become concerned as well. I can enjoy female companionship and even physical intimacy, but my heart simply refuses to engage.

"Don't you want to be married and have children?" Irma asks. "Hal and I don't know what we'd do without each other."

Hal and Rose love each other intensely, and their love spills over into generosity.

"Yes, I want to be married and have a family."

"Then what's the problem, Benjamin? Look at all you have going for you."

I do have a lot "going for me." Irma suggests that I might benefit from psychoanalysis to discover why my unconscious keeps sabotaging me. It is a new and growing profession. I thank them for their concern, but I have no interest in delving into my past. My kindly benefactors understand, but in their earnest attempt to help me, they convince me to have dinner with the son of a friend, who happens to be a psychoanalyst. His name is Morris, and given our different proclivities, he is a most unlikely person to end up being my most intimate and trusted friend.

Morris was born in Long Island, New York, and is a practicing, but mostly secular Jew. I am a *shtetl*-born non-practicing kabbalist. He is short, stocky, and prematurely balding. I'm tall, decidedly handsome, and have a head of thick, curly auburn hair. Morris is a psychoanalyst, and I prefer to pretend that I have no past. Yet our interchanges are lively, and our fondness for one another keeps deepening. We meet for dinner and drinks at least once a week, and discuss everything from politics to our personal lives, with the one caveat that my past is not to be discussed without my permission.

"But you've had such a fascinating life, Benjamin." Tonight I order an expensive bottle of champagne. It is a special night of celebration. Palestine has been voted into the League of Nations and is now the sovereign state of Israel. Even to us American Jews living on the other side of the world, this event is profoundly significant.

Morris raises his glass for a toast. "Here is to your grandmother. May she be happily settled in the new state of Israel."

I'm touched by his recognition of her and share the story of my Zionist relatives. For the first time I acknowledge to myself that I do have family ties in Israel.

"Let's make *aliyah* together," he says, as if reading my mind. "I want to meet your relatives."

"Would you seriously want to do that?"

He nods vehemently. "All my life I've been a fat Jewish boy from New York City. I know that my life is meant to be more than that."

I laugh. "Here I am trying to fit into the urban life of New York and you want to leave."

Morris doesn't return the jest. "Having an easy life is not necessarily a meaningful life, Benjamin."

Refilling his glass with champagne, I apologize. "I didn't mean to hurt you, Morris."

Morris meets my eyes. "Let me know you, Benjamin. Stop keeping me and everybody else at a distance."

I shrug off his words. We are both drunk on champagne and celebration. "I certainly don't feel that I'm keeping anybody at a distance. I'm proud of who I've become. I landed here with nothing, and now I'm realizing the American dream."

His words, however, linger inside me. When Susan shares a similar complaint, I'm not completely surprised. Susan is an attractive nurse whom I've met at the hospital. Our mutual interest is obvious, and we begin dating each other. For a few months I think I've finally stepped out of my pattern. I don't exactly love her, but I respect her, and I find her interesting. This time, however, it is Susan who breaks off the relationship.

"Benjamin, I like you and can even see myself falling in love with you, but you're not available. You seem preoccupied with other matters, and I deserve better."

Until now, I've always been the one to end my relationships. I've never intended to cause pain to any woman, but the fact is that the moment a woman expects me to become serious I lose interest. My heart is never engaged enough for me to suffer. Or so I thought. Susan's words hurt, because they are true. It is that simple. She and Morris are pointing to the same problem, and that problem is within me.

"Then the solution is also within you," Morris points out at our next dinner meeting.

"Morris, you sound way too much like a psychoanalyst. Let me pour you another glass of wine."

Morris places his hand over the top of his glass and looks at me directly. "I am a psychoanalyst, and you're my best friend who needs some direct advice. Look, Benjamin, if I had a heart condition, wouldn't it make sense that I come to you for help? Wouldn't you insist that I do so?"

"Of course, I would insist. I would stalk you until you came in to talk with me about it."

"Exactly my point. I see you in trouble, but you won't let me help you."

"This is different, Morris."

"It's not any different from my point of view. Talk to me, Benjamin. It hurts me when you shut me out."

Susan's rejection still stings. "All right, Morris. I'll give it a try, because I'm not feeling very happy with myself right now."

"What happened, Benjamin?"

"Susan broke it off with me."

"Are you upset because you love her? Do you want to be with her?"

"No, I'm upset because I don't love her. I respect her and I like her. I find her extremely attractive. I should be able to love her. I should be able to love any of the women I've dated, but I've not let myself fall in love with any of them. Not one. Susan is probably the closest, but I can't say that I love her, and she feels it, and that is why she ended it."

"She did the right thing, Benjamin."

"Of course she did, Morris. I know that. I don't want to keep hurting women like this, even if I don't intend to hurt them. I want to change, Morris. I want to be able to feel again."

"Was it this way before, Benjamin?"

"You mean before the war, before spending time in hell?"

"Yes," he says gently. "Before hell."

I shake my head. I am deep in now. I have little choice but to continue. "Before the war I was in love with a woman. We met the first day of medical school. When anti-Semitic hoodlums assaulted me, this beautiful angel came and wiped the blood off my face. From that moment on we were very much in love with each other."

Morris draws closer to me. "What happened, Benjamin?"

I throw my hands up. "The war happened, Morris. I was a Jew and she was not. We hung on for as long as we could, but I became a liability to her and her family. Breaking it off took all the strength I had, but I couldn't live with myself knowing I might be the cause of harm to her or her family. And it was that crazy, Morris. The night I broke it off, she begged me to make love with her so that I would be her first lover. We made love for the first and only time, and then I never saw her again. The Germans invaded, we were imprisoned in the ghetto, and I was deported. The last time I saw her, I begged her to move on, to forget me, to not wait for my return. I truly thought I wouldn't survive, and believe me, I nearly didn't survive."

Morris is crying, and his tears touch me.

"Now that we've opened this, I'll tell you the truth. I feel so much remorse that I never even tried to contact her. I was just so afraid that the pain from all the losses I'd suffered, all the atrocities I'd witnessed, all the anguish I'd absorbed, all the rage I'd swallowed, would rise up and overwhelm me. I was afraid that if I had allowed her tender and compassionate heart to reach me, I would have fallen apart. I was terrified of drowning in an ocean of sorrow. I feel tainted, Morris. I feel as if the evil left its mark on me, as if I have some horrible disease that I don't want to pass on to anybody else."

Morris is crying so hard I'm afraid we will be asked to leave the restaurant, but he doesn't stop. He tells me he is feeling the pain that I cannot feel.

"Zofia," I cry aloud as I lay in my bed that night unable to sleep. "Zofia, can you hear me? Please, forgive me. I wish for you only happiness, my dear, sweet, precious Zofia. You, of all people, I didn't want to hurt. Should I have never loved you? And yet what choice did we have? I hope that you have found love, Zofia. I have not. My heart has been loyal to you, my dearest Zofia. You are the only woman I've ever loved. Please, forgive me. That is all I ask of you. Maybe that is too much to ask, but I ask it of you now."

Nightmares overwhelm me that night: the faces of my family emerging and then disappearing into a black hole, Bartel playing the viola, his face morphing into the face of Hans. Finally I give in to a sleepless night and wander aimlessly into my office seeking a distraction. Instead I see Hebrew letters dancing in my mind's eye. Sleep deprivation can produce hallucinatory states, or it can cut through resistance to the truth of any matter. I know the truth here. I've spent years pushing away everything I love, everything that could penetrate the wall of protection that has kept me safe from myself.

Reaching down into the bottom drawer of my desk, I retrieve the manuscript, ready now to open to Her guidance and to fulfill the promise made to Her, and to my lineage. Tomorrow I will contact a Jewish resettlement organization that helps survivors reconnect. Laiah is calling out to me, or am I calling out to her, or is the Shekinah calling out to both of us?

CHAPTER TWENTY-TWO

1950
Laiah

I notice the woman first. She is dressed in dark European clothing, too heavy for this climate. Her blonde hair is braided down
her back. She looks tired, distressed. Her eyes alternate between
hope and fear. She is holding the hand of a young boy, whose
large eyes meet my own. He smiles, unafraid. He looks familiar to
me, but I cannot find a place for him in memory.

"Are you Laiah?" he asks in Polish.

"I am Laiah, and who are you?"

He is about to speak, but his mother stops him. "I'm sorry to
impose without invitation, but we've come from Poland to meet you."

"I hope I can offer you what you are seeking."

The boy steps forward, and this time the mother does not
stop him. "My name is Raphael. This is my mother, Zofia. I'm
your great-grandson, and we've come here because I'm a mission
keeper, and I need you to teach me."

I gaze into his face, noting his auburn curls, the deep sea
green eyes—Benjamin's eyes— and then I receive the full impact

of this moment. My body trembles, and I cry out in sorrow and joy. The boy rushes into my arms and neither of us can let go, having found a missing part of ourselves. In one instant the three of us are bonded, no history needed, the present moment the first in a lifetime to follow.

"We had to find you," she says. "My son needs you. We both need you."

"We are family now," I say, my words inadequate to the joy I feel.

"Benjamin is alive," I tell her. "He made a trip to the *shtetl* and retrieved the manuscript before emigrating to America."

The mother's eyes are sad. She must love Benjamin still.

"He will find us," I say. "We are his family. He needs us."

"He doesn't know about Raphael. We were together, and then he was deported, and he never returned to find us."

I feel her pain and take her hand in my own. "Zofia, we often know what we don't know we know. He will find us when he is ready to find himself."

1951

Benjamin

I press my nose firmly into the tiny window of the airplane. I don't know whether my fear is of flying or the anticipation of what awaits me at the end of the journey. Right now I'm distracted by the bustle of activity as the plane is prepared for a long flight. The stewardess announces in a cheery voice that it's time to fasten our seatbelts. Since receiving Laiah's response to my letter, I alternate between shock and wonder. Not only for having found her, but also because she enclosed two other letters in her response to me, two letters that have changed the course of my life.

The engine roar sends tiny vibrations up through my feet.

The plane crawls forward and then suddenly whooshes skyward. The man sitting next to me asks to turn on the light. Wearing the collar of a priest, he looks barely old enough to shave, but as we converse, I discover that he is a few years my senior. His name is Daniel Connelly, and he is on a pilgrimage to the Holy Land. Daniel asks me my reason for this journey, and to my surprise, I tell him everything, and he listens.

"Has it strengthened your faith?" he asks.

"If faith means faith in God, then no, Daniel, I have no faith. I believe in the existence of good and of evil. I believe that the world swings between both those polarities."

Father Daniel listens carefully. "I agree with you, but faith is of a different order. Faith transcends the good and evil of this world. That is the message of Jesus Christ."

"I don't understand, Father. How does faith transcend good and evil?"

"This faith is beyond understanding, Benjamin. It comes with a conversion of the heart. It comes when the burning passion of Christ love consumes everything, and you can walk into the flames laughing knowing that what is real is eternal and indestructible."

I remember Karl, and his nightly prayers to his Savior. I asked him once how he could rely on Jesus as his savior when clearly he was not saved. Karl's eyes filled with tears. "My body will soon die, but my soul is cleansed. I have forgiven all as my Savior forgave those who betrayed him."

I share this now with Father Daniel who nods his understanding. "Offer forgiveness to those who have hurt you, and ask forgiveness from those you've hurt. This is how your heart will be made pure that you can receive His love."

"I'm not sure I want to receive Him. Remember I'm a Jew."

Daniel chuckles. "Jesus was a Jew as well."

He shuts the light and closes his eyes. I listen to the whirr of the engines and contemplate the fact that nothing but air is

holding us up. And yet it is holding us up. Perhaps this knowledge is as close to faith as I will ever experience. I drift into sleep
and dream of my son, and in my dream I am clutching him to my
heart and weeping.

Zofia

I arrive at the airport several hours before his flight is due to land.
Raphael begs to come with me, but on this I hold firm. I need
time alone with Benjamin. The book I brought to distract myself
from racing anxiety lays inert in my lap, unread. Better to lose
myself in observing the people tugging suitcases and children,
weary, irritated, excited, all anticipating tearful farewells or joyful
reunions. I take comfort in being part of this timeless stream of
people, all with their own dreams, disappointments, and blessings. Whatever occurs in the next few hours, my experience is but
one expression of the collective human heart.

The gate attendant, a man with thinning hair and thick
glasses, patiently responds to my frequent inquiries, as if he
understands my vulnerability. When he informs me that the
plane has landed, I feel a disturbing ambivalence and curb the
impulse to run, to hide, and this after years of searching for the
man I'm about to meet. This is for Raphael, I tell myself. Benjamin begged me to let go, and if I haven't done so, I have nobody
to blame but myself. Will he recognize me? My hair is now styled
instead of long, and my body more filled out since the days of
scarcity. And I'm older, more than a decade older.

Travelers trickle through the gate of customs, most looking dazed and fatigued, and then the trickle turns into a flood of
faces. Benjamin is not among them, and my ambivalence quickly
turns to disappointment. Has something gone wrong? Have I been
deceived? The rush of people again becomes a trickle. Swallowing

hard against the upsurge of tears, I prepare to leave when a tall man with an eye patch emerges through the door. My heart is beating so fast I don't trust myself to stand. He is taller than I remember, and his auburn hair is closely cropped. He walks with an air of confidence even as his face expresses unease. Breathing deeply, I call his name. He turns toward me, and a look of recognition passes between us, a palpable current of energy. The moment seems outside place or time. He moves toward me, and my well-rehearsed handshake seems absurd as he wraps his arms around me and buries his face in my hair. His body is trembling and mine as well. My breathing is shallow with anxiety and excitement. We could be back in time, embracing in Bartel's apartment. No time has passed and lifetimes have passed.

"Zofia, you are more beautiful than I remember." He kisses the top of my head. "You have no idea how much I've longed for you."

My body stiffens, pulls back. *If you missed me so much, then why didn't you return?* He feels my withdrawal and lets go. We look away. The magic of the moment has dissipated.

"I'm sorry to be late. They detained me at customs."

"I was worried you missed your flight."

He laughs. "I was sitting at the airport four hours ahead of time." He pauses, and I wait. "Zofia, I didn't know about Raphael."

"Is that an excuse for not trying to find me?" I feel angry, hurt, but I wish to retract my words. "I'm sorry, Benjamin. Seeing you after so much time brings up such confusion."

He sighs. "I was wrong, Zofia. There are reasons I didn't return to you, but they are not the reasons you might be imagining. I know I don't deserve your understanding or forgiveness, but I will ask that you listen."

"I will listen, Benjamin. That much I can promise."

"Zofia, if you are married, I will respect your life. I will not interfere."

"And if I'm not?"

"If you are not, then I want you to give me a chance to know you as you are now. I want you to know who I am now. If possible, I want to begin again."

Am I dreaming or is this really happening? I stutter, stumble. He takes my hand. My legs wobble underneath me. "Yes, I mean no. I'm not married, and yes, I will listen."

He laughs and I laugh, and it seems that everybody is laughing with us. He holds me to his chest, kisses my neck, and then he finds my lips. There is no sense in fighting this. I will lose. I may be hurt again. I may regret all of it, but I don't think so. I'm a woman again, and for the first time in a very long time, I feel passionately alive.

"I offer no excuses, Zofia, but I can tell you that you are the only woman I've ever loved. I thought myself incapable of love, but instead I realized that I was denying my love for you. I was too broken to risk it, Zofia."

Oblivious to the bustle of people moving purposefully around us, I stop walking and meet his gaze. "Risk it all now, Benjamin, for this is the only chance for happiness that we'll get."

Benjamin

The next day I meet one of my relatives, a young man named Yuli who will drive us to the kibbutz. He hardly looks old enough to be driving, but he makes weekly trips between the kibbutz and Jerusalem.

"Welcome to Israel," he says. "You'll not regret making *aliyah*. We're all family here."

Yuli tosses my suitcase in the back, and we slide into the front seat of the truck. Zofia squeezes my hand as we hit a pothole and Yuri curses.

"I hope I didn't blow a tire again. I make that same mistake every time."

"How far is it to the kibbutz?" I ask.

"Not more than two hours, maybe less if the truck behaves. This is a small country. Nothing is really very far away."

The road cuts through jagged hills with steep buttes, dotted with strands of greenery but mostly barren red earth. Passing through villages with children and dogs playing in the streets, Yuli slows down and makes ample use of the horn. He talks about the history of the kibbutz and about his great-grandmother who was one of the founders of the settlement. "You'll be happy to know that your grandmother and Laura, my great-grandmother, were reunited for several years before Laura passed away."

Heading up an incline, the truck lurches backward and then digs in for the ascent. Groaning, it reaches the top. Yuli turns off the engine in front of a simple concrete block, one-story building painted mustard yellow with a faded red door.

"Welcome to the kibbutz," he exclaims, turning off the engine. A young woman with a long ponytail and khaki shorts emerges from the building, kisses Yuli on both cheeks, warmly acknowledges Zofia, and greets me with a hug.

"Welcome to our kibbutz," she says. "We are so happy to have you here with us, Benjamin Janowicz. Remember to visit the grave where Goldie Janowicz is buried. I believe she is your great-grandmother, yes?"

Yuli accompanies us to the living quarters, an octagonal shaped layout of buildings consisting of eight long row houses with a playground set in the enclosure. The buildings are all painted the same yellow, but many are decorated with children's murals. Raphael must have seen us approaching, for he throws open the door the moment we arrive, a burst of bright energy meeting me. He is taller than I'd envisioned him, and lanky. His clothes hang loosely on his frame, as if waiting for him to grow into them. What catches my attention most are his eyes, large, round, slightly wide set, the same dark green color as mine, and awake. He engages me with a barrage of questions as if I'd just stepped out of his life for a short time.

"Do you want to see my room?" he asks. "What happened to your eye? What was it like flying in an airplane?"

Zofia motions for him to slow down. "Benjamin, this is your son, Raphael, and Raphael, this is your father."

"What do I call you?" he asks with a directness that I soon learn is his nature.

"I have not yet earned the title of father, so call me what is comfortable for you, Raphael."

He shrugs. "You're my father, so I'll call you father, *abba*."

"Then *abba* it is."

My fears dissipate in the face of Raphael's exuberance.

"We are a family now," he says with no hesitation.

My tongue feels stuck to the back of my throat. I cannot speak, for any utterance would diminish my joy in coming home after a very long exile. Zofia calls to us from the kitchen. "Before the two of you disappear, let's share some tea and sandwiches."

Raphael looks disappointed, but obediently takes his place at the kitchen table.

Zofia places three delicate teacups on the table, and some crispy biscuits from a tin.

"I'm a mission keeper," he says. "Like you."

"Like me, yes."

"I play the viola, like you. Bartel was my teacher, like you."

Raphael taps my arm. "I want to see the manuscript."

"This moment, Raphael? We've only just met."

"Yes, this moment, "Raphael insists. "Great-grandmother, Laiah, has been teaching me *gamatria*."

"You are already learning decoding?"

"Yes, and she told me everything she remembers about you, and she tells me we are very much alike."

Zofia laughs. "Meet your son, Benjamin."

That night I dream about Bartel. He is smiling and reaches out to take my hand. I'm a youth again riding the waves of hope and pride. I'm again a rising star.

Laiah

He stands at the threshold, both of us mute, and seeking the way to close the gap that time and trauma and sorrow have created. He had been an innocent boy filled with optimism when last I saw him. My hands are shaking, tears begging for permission to release. He looks uncertain, not quite believing this moment of meeting to be real. I reach out and touch his cheek with the tips of my fingers, moving them across the surface of skin, rough from a day's growth of beard, across the fabric of the eye patch. He flinches only slightly, but I catch it and withdraw my hand. We have so much to share, ten years of living through our own unique versions of hell, and many loved ones to grieve. He reaches out and pulls me toward him, and he holds me tight against his chest, his breathing shallow, quickened, his heart beating against my cheek. Silently he shares his story, and my tears find their release, and he holds me tight while I sob, and he tenses, winces, contracts, let's go.

"You are home now, Benjamin," I whisper. "You are safe."

"I couldn't return until now. I'm so sorry I hurt you and my family."

"You needed time to heal."

"Yes, but I'm still not healed, Laiah."

"I know."

"Evil exists, and I live in dread of being like them."

"To know this truth is wise, my grandson. But wiser still is to know the power of love."

"Will that heal me?"

"Words will not heal, but when you experience certainty in your heart, then you will be healed."

"How do I find that, Laiah?"

"I don't know how it will come to you, Benjamin, but I know that it will."

"Until then?"

"Live your life. Love your family, and receive the love they have for you. Work with the manuscript, for that is how She guides you."

"I don't deserve all that I'm being given."

"Perhaps not, but you are being offered it. Now use it wisely, my grandson. You are Her mission keeper, and for the sake of this broken and beautiful world, heal yourself that you may heal others."

CHAPTER TWENTY-THREE

1955

Benjamin

The elevator groans its way up to the seventh floor, the keys entrusted to the doorman dangling in my hand. I've returned to complete the life of Benjamin James. The space I'm about to enter has been empty for nearly three years. On this late summer day, the apartment is hot and stuffy, but the play of light and shadow, and the eerie silence evokes a sense of timeless purity, as if all movement has paused, awaited this moment of return. Everything is imbued with memory. Soon all will be gone, like the backdrop on a stage.

Morris and I meet for dinner at our favorite hole-in-the-wall restaurant, seated at our special table beside the window. We order wine from a handsome young man with a crew cut and goatee. Morris holds his glass up for a toast.

"To our friendship."

"You are irreplaceable, Morris. I hope you, and Julie, and the twins can visit soon. Our home is always open to you."

"Thank you, Benjamin. What kind of a Jew would I be if I didn't pray at the Wailing Wall at least once in my life?"

I laugh. "It is every Jew's responsibility, especially if that Jew is my best friend."

The waiter interrupts to take our order. Morris remembers my favorite appetizers, fish in cream sauce, and a thin broth soup flavored with thyme and rosemary.

"Morris, I miss a lot about New York."

Morris nods. "And yet, oddly enough, Julie and I have been discussing the possibility of moving to Israel, making *aliyah* as the real Jews would say."

I almost choke on a cracker. "You what?"

Morris smiles. "I was going to wait and let Julie break the news to you, but here it is. I couldn't wait to tell you."

"What is this about, Morris? If you're serious, Zofia and I will be elated."

"Please don't be upset with me, but Zofia already knows. In fact she initiated the contact and asked if I would be interested in working at her clinic."

"This has all been happening behind my back?"

"I'm so sorry, Benjamin. I didn't mean to offend you."

"I'm just teasing you, my friend. I'm shocked and elated."

"I'm so relieved. We wanted to have it be more definite before telling you."

"And so, is it definite?"

Morris nods. "Julie is totally behind the move. She feels it's right for our family."

"What is prompting your decision?"

Morris shrugs. "Do you remember when we heard the news about Israel gaining statehood? I'm an American secular Jew, and hearing about Israel's birth, I wept like a baby. That tells me something about what is meaningful to me."

"My relatives were part of the first wave of Zionists. There were seers among them, who predicted the holocaust. Decades later their predictions came true. Six million lives sacrificed, and the phoenix rising from the ashes of six million incinerated bodies has been the world granting Israel statehood."

Morris and I part ways, and I'm buoyant with the joy of

knowing that we will soon be reunited. So many blessings are coming to me. Perhaps this is the phoenix rising from the ashes of my own shattered life.

Slowly I walk the streets, still vibrant at this time of night. People clustered outside bars, music streaming from doorways and spilling onto the streets, taxis and police sirens and the rumble of streetcars, I feel it pulsing through me, the sheer thrill of life effulging. Sweet memories waft to the surface of my mind: Hal and Irma, Susan, dinners with Morris, the wounded survivor who became the confident Dr. Benjamin James. I feel gratitude for all of them, and a willingness to let them all go.

CHAPTER TWENTY-FOUR

Zofia

Rebbe Moshkovitz resides in the Hasidic section of East Jerusalem. Mothers dressed in black toting Bibles and children, men with beards and ringlets praying as they walk, oblivious to my presence, absorbed perhaps in unearthly realms. I've memorized the rebbe's address, the most important detail being that it is above Disraeli's falafel stand. I order several falafels and then push open the rusted metal door leading upstairs to his apartment. The stairs are steep and not well lit, and exude the sour odor of mildew. Were it not for my trust in Laiah, I would be hastily turning the other way. But Laiah insists that Rebbe Moshkovitz is a man I must meet.

The hallway leading to his door is also dimly lit. I pause a moment to catch my breath and then knock assertively. His quick response takes me by surprise, as does his appearance. He is handsome, his strong features accentuated by his almost emaciated leanness. The skin on his face appears translucent, his temples pulsating visibly as if tiny vibrators are inserted underneath. Pale gray, his eyes seem to stare right through me, as if I'm some interesting alien creature. Being quite tall, he has a slight stoop to his shoulders, likely from years of having to take care not to bump his head. All in one motion, he opens the door and gracefully steps aside to allow me entrance.

"I'm happy to meet you, Zofia. Laiah is a dear friend and has spoken very highly of you."

"Thank you for seeing me, rebbe. I know you don't ordinarily accept new students." I remember the falafels in my bag. "I brought these for you."

He smiles graciously. "That is so thoughtful of you, Zofia. Let me find some plates, and we shall share them. As it is, we need to meet in my kitchen. My office is currently under water."

"Under water?"

He laughs. "A broken pipe in the apartment above me, or a faucet that one of the children left running. Thankfully most of my books and papers were spared."

He leads me into his kitchen, a tiny windowless space large enough only for the stove, a small refrigerator, a sink, and a grey Formica table covered in books and papers. Motioning me to one of the chairs, he makes a half-hearted effort to push back the books to make space for the plates.

"These are the best falafels in Jerusalem," he says, handing me a plate. "I tell them so at Disraeli's all the time. I apologize for using the table as my desk. My wife would have been appalled by my poor attempt at housekeeping. She kept order for all of us."

I look at him and then away, not wanting to pose the question.

"My wife and children are no longer alive," he says in response to my unasked inquiry. "I am the only survivor."

"I'm sorry, rebbe."

"I don't think I can say that I'm sorry or not sorry. Such a tragedy is beyond comprehension. My wife was a beautiful soul and my children . . . they were children."

He moves to the stove to prepare a pot of tea. The silence is heavy, but when he turns to pour the tea, his face is serene.

"How do you cope with such a loss, rebbe?"

"The only way to cope is to fully embrace it. Otherwise it doesn't leave you alone. It begs for its voice to be heard; it begs to be dignified."

"Forgive me rebbe, but can you explain how conducting pilgrimages in the sites of concentration camps dignifies anything?"

He chuckles. "So Laiah told you already. Let me try and explain. In the science of alchemy there is a principle stating that any poison or enemy, no matter how toxic, once transmuted, releases its power to us and becomes our greatest ally. To transmute a poison we must embrace it fully. We must conquer it by understanding its truth. I invite people who attend the pilgrimages to embrace and confront their particular poisons, and in doing so to take back their lives."

"That sounds a lot like psychoanalysis, rebbe."

He smiles warmly. "Exactly so. Psychoanalysis is a form of alchemy. Now tell me, why are you here, Zofia? How I can serve you that you may serve the heart of humanity?"

"I wish I could claim such nobility of purpose, but the truth is that I feel a great emptiness in my marriage, and I want it to change. I feel such guilt in my discontent since Benjamin did survive and we were eventually reunited, even if I had to wait ten years for it to happen."

"No need for guilt, Zofia. You deserve a fulfilling marriage. Laiah and I have spoken about Benjamin. She is concerned for different reasons, although both arise from the same cause."

"I recognize trauma, rebbe. I work with people incapacitated by trauma, but I can't reach my husband, and therefore I can't help him."

"I know personally the nature of his suffering. How do we reconcile love and hate, goodness and evil, faith and doubt? Something happens to one who witnesses, or participates in, or is victim to those who can murder and torture children, women, with cold indifference or vengeful pleasure. One either imbibes the poison, or escapes into the light, but our task here is far more challenging. Our task is to reject neither, but to bring the light of truth into the darkness, to metaphorically die and be reborn."

"Benjamin is still grappling with this polarity?"

"Yes, I believe so. In a sense I was fortunate to be forced into descending into the heart of darkness. Benjamin is rightfully scared to do so. And being a mission keeper means that he is doing the work of purification and alchemy for many souls. That makes his task even more challenging. Does any of this make sense to you, Zofia?"

"All of it makes complete sense, rebbe."

His warm smile invites my tears. "And with all that said, you deserve a fulfilling marriage."

"Can you help him, rebbe?"

"I can offer him the help he needs when he is ready."

For the first time in a long while, I feel hope. "Thank you, rebbe. Laiah was right in bringing us together. You are a very wise man."

"I'm wise only in that I've used the tragedies of my life to become a person who can guide others. As have you, Zofia. That makes an ordinary person a wise person."

Rebbe Moshkovitz

I experienced the most unexpected awakening during the darkest moment of my life. Near death at the time—emaciated, forced into hard labor and beaten if I failed to perform—I could imagine no deeper hell until a guard blithely informed me that my wife and two children had been gassed. My anguish was beyond description, and yet a voice arose from deep within. *Who would honor their memory if I died?* I must survive for them. Their deaths became my reason to live.

That night I had a dream. In the dream I was thrown into a pit of snakes, their mouths wide open, their tongues darting in and out, jabbing me with poison. My only defense was to consume them, and that is what happened in the dream. Overcoming my own revulsion and terror, I kept swallowing them until the pit was empty of snakes. Then an immense energy rose up inside me, as if all the power in the universe was surging through me, there at my discretion to create and to destroy. I knew then that I would survive, and that I would use this power to help others transmute the toxic poisons of evil into the power of love.

CHAPTER TWENTY-FIVE

1957

Benjamin

I'm gazing into the luminous face of an angel, softly enfolded in her presence. Her mouth moves and song emerges, and I know that she is blessing me. Reaching out to touch her, I see her dissolve into the light. I wake with a jolt. I know what just happened. Checking my watch, I note the time as three thirty in the morning. Zofia doesn't stir as I dress and quietly shut the door behind me. It is dark, but already the birds are chirping, and someone in the distance is chanting a prayer. I walk unhurriedly, stopping to breathe in the coolness of the night air. I need not rush. Laiah needs time alone.

In the hushed silence my footsteps echo as I ascend the metal stairwell. Her door is unlocked, and I'm greeted by the unerring ticking of the wall clock. Her bedroom door is open, but her bed is empty. I find her on the balcony lying face up on her favorite lounge chair, her mouth agape, arms hanging by her sides. There is no sign of struggle. Hesitantly, not wanting to disturb her, I approach. I feel her neck for a pulse, knowing I will not find one. My body shudders. I stroke her face with my hand, kiss her forehead, wipe the drool from her mouth, and lay my head on her breast. I feel the urge to cry, but no tears arise. I notice an envelope on the floor beneath her chair. A piece of paper, poorly folded, is inside.

My dearest Benjamin,
I write to you in the weeks before my death. Forgive me, my beloved grandson, that I share these last words in this way. I wish not to be overtaken by sorrow even knowing that we are never truly apart. I have been blessed with a rich and fulfilling life. I have known cruelty, but also immense compassion and selflessness. I have experienced divine love and imperfect human love. I have grappled with my own weaknesses and tried for justice, even in the face of injustice. My grandson, the difficulties of life mature and ripen our hearts, bringing us ever closer to divine perfection. We have both had our share.

Even so, goodness is the nature of the world, Benjamin. I know it does not always appear to be so, particularly when we have suffered greatly. But as death approaches the veils thin, and I glimpse the glorious light of perfection. Healing is possible, because everything in its purity is perfect and good.

I love you, dear grandson, with all my heart. It is a great privilege to know you. Make peace with yourself and with life, Benjamin. This is my parting wish for you and my parting blessing.

Laiah comes to me now as the light she has always been. She is loving but stern.

You have work to do, Benjamin. Your heart calls out for healing.

I kneel in front of her body and speak aloud. "Rest in peace, dear Laiah. You have been true to Her and to the mission. I know your concern that the mission will fail if my heart does not heal. Dear Laiah, I make a promise to you, Zofia and Raphael, the Shekinah, and myself, that I will heal my heart. Whatever it takes, I will not fail this mission. I love you, Laiah, and knowing you in this lifetime has been the greatest of blessings."

CHAPTER TWENTY-SIX

Benjamin

Stepping tentatively into the dull gray van pocked with dents, I hide an unnerving sense of dread with bouts of forced frivolity. I have no reason to be afraid, or so I tell myself. Rebbe Moshkovitz has impressed on me the fact that recovery is not about forgetting, but about remembering fully and consciously. I haven't forgotten, but neither have I chosen to consciously remember. When was the last time I wept? Maybe I shed a few tears when Karl was taken. I can't recall. My heart weeps, but my eyes are dry. To be fully human again, I must recover my ability to cry.

Seated in the van are all the people who love me and want nothing more than to support me. I trust them all: Raphael seated to my left, Zofia to my right, Morris and Julie, Sija and her husband, Stanislaw, all seated across from me, and riding in the front with the driver of the van is Bartel Barzowski! He surprised us with a visit a year ago. If I could weep, then that would have been the occasion. Or perhaps it might have been the year that Morris and Julie, and their twin girls, made *aliyah*. I've been so blessed in this life. I yearn to give myself fully to the people who deserve so much more from me.

Why then, am I feeling so unnerved? Nothing on display in the Auschwitz museum will surprise me. I was there. I know what it was like. I will not be shocked or horrified by the photographs of walking skeletons, the mountains of shoes and clothing left by those who were forced to walk naked and terrified to the gas chambers, the remains of the crematoriums, the torture chambers. Another wave of dread passes through me. What am I doing here? What are any of us doing here? Why not all go on a pleasant vacation together and recount the good times we've all experienced. Why this? What does the rebbe mean when he says we are here to consciously remember? The van comes to a halt. I look through the windshield. We have arrived at Auschwitz. I'm about to find out for myself.

Zofia

We meet in the basement of a local church. Bins of toys are stashed in the corners of the room, used by the children who attend school here. The gurgling of a percolator and the pleasant smell of brewing coffee waft through the room promising refreshment, comfort, familiarity, safety. An elderly woman, pleasantly obese with bright red cheeks, hobbles around the circle holding a platter of pastries covered in powdered sugar, almost pleading with us to take a pastry or two, her contribution to making the world right again. The disappointment on her face as I decline her offer makes me reach for two, and the man to my left is happy to consume my portion; all these ordinary, comforting rituals of life. The rebbe appears just as the woman with the pastries is departing. They exchange knowing smiles, and the rebbe accepts a pastry.

"Welcome to all of you," he says, lowering himself into his seat in the circle of metal folding chairs, scanning the faces and nodding to each. "We shall begin this retreat with a prayer and an intention. May we receive the healing we need, and may our work contribute to the healing of those that preceded us, and those that will follow us."

My parents are with me now, reaching out to make contact, their faces radiant with love. How I long for them to know their grandson, and my husband, and to thank them for the courage it took for them to sacrifice their lives to preserve what is good in this world. Tears cleanse my heart, and someone silently passes me a tissue. My eyes meet the soft, compassionate gaze of Rebbe Moshkovitz, who nods to me and continues to speak.

"Our pilgrimage has begun. This is the first of many gatherings. We will meet at the beginning and end of each day. We will learn to listen to each other, to bear witness to the stories, emotions, and thoughts that arise in the course of this retreat. I promise you that what you thought was unbearable will become bearable. What needs telling will be heard, what needs forgiving will be forgiven, what needs kindness will receive kindness. Our wounds heal when we acknowledge them, accept them, and offer them what they truly need. I know you are all committed to being here. Nobody would choose to participate in a pilgrimage to Auschwitz without a sincere intention. Some of us, including myself, are survivors. My wife and children were among the six million murdered. At least one of you spent time in a concentration camp as a guard. The particulars of our involvement matter only in that our stories matter to us. Anybody on any side of this tragedy has suffered and continues to suffer. I ask that we be open to each other without blame or condemnation. It is a lot to ask, but it is what I'm asking of you. I discovered the greatest freedom and the greatest compassion in the depths of my despair. I'm asking you to demonstrate the best face of our humanity. Otherwise there is no reason for us to meet."

I'm moved by his words particularly knowing that his life is a clear demonstration of his message.

"I want you to take a few moments now to find words for why you are here. What is it that you hope you will receive from this experience? Please take out your journal and write whatever comes to you." He waits a few moments and then asks if anybody is willing to share. Bartel is the first to raise his hand.

"My name is Bartel Barzowski, and I'm here to make peace with myself."

"Why are you not at peace?

Bartel begins to sob. "I'm sorry," he says. "I didn't expect this to happen." I hand him the tissue box.

"Don't be sorry, Bartel. We're all here to bear witness to each other. You are courageous to share the intensity of your feelings. I'll repeat my question to you. Why are you not at peace?"

"Because I failed to rescue Benjamin's family. If I'd been able to obtain visas in the time they were promised me, his family would have escaped. My mind goes over and over that time, and I cannot rest even after all these years. I should have started searching for visas earlier than I did. I should not have entrusted such an important task to only one source. I should have somehow found a way to save them."

"You are a deeply compassionate man," says the rebbe, "but you are wrong to think that any of us can decide the fate of others. We do our best, but there are forces greater than us over which we have no control. Our human limitations we must accept with grace and humility."

The next person to speak is a wispy young woman, her hair tied back with a red scarf that accentuates her pallid complexion.

"This is very hard for me to talk about, but I'm not here to waste my time, or yours. Recently I discovered evidence that confirmed my suspicions. My father was a Nazi officer, and knowing I am his offspring is devastating to me. I've tried so hard to live a good and moral life, and now it all feels like a travesty."

"You are not your father, Gloria. Who you are is not determined by his actions. That is true for all of us. Children are born into particular families for many complex reasons. Perhaps the unconscious knowledge of your father's transgressions caused you to become dedicated to living an ethical life."

I'm startled by the piercing scream of a woman dressed in black, sitting across the circle from me. She pounds her fists into her thighs. Bolting up from his chair, the rebbe kneels beside her, holding her hands firmly in his own.

"What is wrong, Selma?"

"I'm as evil as the Nazis. I deserve to die, but I have one living daughter and three grandchildren. If I take my life, they will suffer."

"You came here to be healed. What makes you believe you deserve to die?"

Selma suddenly dashes from her chair into the bathroom. The noise of her distressed vomiting sends shivers up my spine. The rebbe sits in calm attention waiting for her return.

"What is it, Selma?"

"I was in this camp," she whispers. "My baby was murdered right away, but my older daughter passed the first inspection. They lied to me. They said if I became a guard, a *kapo* as we were called, then the life of this daughter would be spared. If I followed their orders, they would return her to me and if not, she would be killed. I had to believe them. What choice did I have? They ordered me to do terrible things to other prisoners. I did whatever they ordered me to do thinking I was saving my child. They lied to me. My daughter was sent to the gas chamber, and I sacrificed my soul."

The rebbe kneels in front of her. "Look at me, Selma. Any mother would have done the same thing. You acted out of love for your daughter. All parents will do what they can to protect their young ones. That is what makes us human."

The rebbe returns to his seat. We sit in shocked silence. Already I'm exhausted, overwhelmed by the depth of suffering. I feel the urge to leave it all behind. Was it a mistake to come here and invite everybody else to join me? It is all too much. I long to return to the moment when life is simply about choosing a pastry, or not.

Benjamin

The rebbe tells us that we are here to consciously remember. I have no problem remembering. In fact, as I wander the remains of the camp, I remember every detail with photographic clarity. I can almost conjure up the nauseating stench of excrement, rotting flesh, and burning bodies. I can almost feel the rawness of skin from the relentless assault of lice and all manner of nasty creatures. Yet, none of it feels real to me. I am an actor on the stage of a movie set. A terrifying sense of unreality is taking me over. Where have I gone? Who is this person who has accidentally wandered into someone's crazed mind? I've come here to be healed, and instead, I'm sinking deeper and deeper into a cavernous hole of emptiness.

Raphael's usual buoyant mood is gone. His face reflects a state of shock. He tells me that he understands now why I didn't return, why I fled to America. It is his way of offering forgiveness. I accept it with quiet dispassion. I'm anxious to leave. We are here for seven nights, and this is only the fourth. I feel Zofia's concern. She has come with hopes for me, for us, but in this moment, I have nothing to offer anybody.

The rebbe has advised all of us to observe silence at night. Zofia and I hug briefly, and she falls easily asleep. I lay awake agitated. Finally, I slip on clothes and step out into the cool night air, feeling the relief of open space. I pace the length of the main street before remembering the warning about covert anti-Semitism. Returning to the rooming house, still agitated, I crawl back into bed trying hard not to disturb Zofia.

My mind is racing with thoughts and images, uncontrollable and dangerous, like a train without brakes ready to go off the rails. The memories arise in a disorganized jumble, with no sense of time or place. An image appears of my mother canning green beans, and in the next image she and Channah are on the train to Auschwitz, my terrified sister clutching her doll. I see my father deep in prayer, and then his body is being thrown into the back of a truck onto a pile of corpses. Where am I? Have I fallen through some time machine that is jumbling up eras? I try taking long, deep breaths to calm myself, and it works somewhat, until the image of the two little girls on the gurneys arises from the jumbled time machine, their eyes staring up at me, terrified, imploring me to help them. "I can't help you," I shout aloud, the face of Hans, my own voice screaming as my head crashes into each step. "Get away from me!" I scream. Hans returns. *Make the cut, Benjamin. It is your life or theirs and they will die either way.* My body is trembling so hard I fear falling onto the floor. I'm in a cold sweat even as a surge of heat rises up my spine, even as an annihilating force overtakes me. "Give me the scalpel, so I can stab you a thousand times right through your evil heart. Give me the scalpel, give it to me!"

Zofia bolts out of bed. "Benjamin, are you all right? Do you know where you are?"

"I'm in Auschwitz," I shout. "I'm in hell. I'm in hell. I'm in hell."

My body is now being held down against the mattress. Rebbe Moshkovitz is leaning over me.

"Kill them, Benjamin. Let it all out come out of you. Your friends will hold you and keep you safe. Let the energy move through and out. Annihilate the evil ones. Go ahead and defeat them until they are no more."

I fight and scream and thrash and punch until every last bit of strength is gone, and I fall back on the bed, exhausted, my mind totally still and empty. My body shudders like an animal come close to death, and then the miracle happens. My eyes, both eyes are wet, my cheeks are wet, and I taste the salty stream of tears. I hold myself as I rock back and forth, back and forth, the pain intense and relentless, but I welcome the pain, because I'm feeling again. I'm feeling again, and the tears keep flowing, and waves of sorrow wash over me and through me, and I'm human again. I'm human again, what joyful sorrow to feel human. From the depth of my heart, love emerges that pervades and accepts everything, exactly as it is. I know beyond any doubt that this love is real and pure and indestructibly good, eternally innocent, and beyond defiling. And I too, am made of this love.

CHAPTER TWENTY-SEVEN

1985

Benjamin

Dov Hendelbaum enters my office as a prospective patient. My first impressions are scanning for signs of pathology, and with Dov the signs are easy to find. His gait is stiff, wooden, his shoulders bend forward, his complexion is pallid, one eyelid droops, his nose is irregular, likely broken at least once, and he wears a poorly fitted toupee. Even so, he is not unattractive and might have at one time been handsome. His demeanor, however, concerns me the most, for he conveys a sense that life is a burden that he wants to soon put aside, like a boxer tired of the fight. Gesturing for him to take a seat, I initiate a few casual inquiries. He shares that he is a retired businessman who made *aliyah* right after the war. He didn't offer, and I didn't press for more personal details.

"What brings you to see me, Mr. Handelbaum?"

He hesitates, coughs, and evades my gaze. "Let me be clear, I'm not here as a patient. I'm a very wealthy man, and I want to make a substantial donation to your hospital."

His response is surprising and off-putting. We can certainly use donations, but there are channels and protocols for such offerings.

208 LIGHT RADIANCE SPLENDOR

"On behalf of the hospital, I'm grateful to you, Mr. Handelbaum, but I'm not the right person to handle such matters."

"You may not be the right person, Dr. Janowicz, but if you want my money—and I assure you it is a substantial sum—then you're the only person I'll speak with about this matter. Is that clear?"

"Very clear."

"I have reasons, but my reasons are not relevant. You either accept my offer, or lose the opportunity. Only you can make that decision."

He mentions an impressive amount of money. The donation, should it be real, would be more than enough to complete the cardiac unit we've been struggling to fund. I'm on the hospital board of directors. This is not the usual protocol, but there is nothing unethical about it. If he wants to donate his money, my only course of action is to receive his offer with gratitude.

"Then I accept your offer, Mr. Hendelbaum. The hospital will be grateful to you for such generosity."

"The hospital is not to know the source of the donation," he states succinctly. "My only stipulation is that it be an anonymous donation. If you can make that guarantee to me, I'll write you a check in a matter of weeks."

I nod my agreement. "Would you accept an invitation to dinner at my house as a way for me to show my appreciation?"

He shakes his head. "How about instead we dine at my favorite restaurant?"

The restaurant is one of the most exclusive in Jerusalem. The hostess greets him by name and leads us to a private room with an expansive view of the city. When the waiter comes to take our order, Dov takes charge and arranges the whole dinner for both of us.

"I know the chef personally," he says. "He'll take good care of us."

The waiter returns with two bottles of wine and an expansive cheese platter. Dov gestures for him to fill our glasses. "I suggest starting with the red, and try this outstanding cheese imported from a farm in Denmark." The waiter leaves the room, closing the door behind him.

"I'm grateful for your donation, Mr. Hendelbaum."

"Please call me Dov, and if you don't mind, I will call you Benjamin."

"Agreed," I say, warming to him.

"The money is useless to me. I derive some comfort in knowing it will be used well."

"It will allow us to save many lives."

"That is exactly what I want."

"Do you have family?"

"I'm divorced now for many years. I have a son who will not speak with me. He has children that I've never met."

"I'm sorry."

"I'm not," he says perfunctorily. "Why would I want anything to do with people like that?"

"Where are you from, Dov?" I ask, hoping to find something more neutral to discuss.

"There is no need to talk about the past. I'm more interested in what future I have left."

Dov has secrets, but everybody who survived the craziness of the last half-century has secrets. I'm not here to befriend him, and he is entitled to his privacy.

"What brought you to Israel?"

Dov fills both our wine glasses. "It served my purpose. And you, Benjamin, what brought you here?"

I share my story, filling in as much detail as possible to avoid the uncomfortable silences.

"Then you are happy, and your family is happy?"

"For the most part, yes, we're happy." The main course is delivered, and we spend a few moments savoring the pungently flavored lamb stew, and the hot, buttery pastries.

"Benjamin, let me ask you another question." Dov finishes

his third glass of wine and calls the waiter over to order a shot of vodka. "Care to join me?"

I laugh. "Is that your question?"

For a brief moment, I catch him smiling. I realize how seldom he smiles.

"No, I'm afraid my question is more philosophical, or perhaps even existential." Curving his neck back, he holds the glass to his lips, and in one deft move, swallows the entire shot. "Benjamin, are you afraid of death?"

Like everything about Dov, his question is disconcerting.

"No, death doesn't scare me. I believe death to be a transition to other possibilities, and that the soul continues to exist after death. What makes you ask?"

He ignores my question. "Do you believe that people are held accountable at death for their actions in this life?"

"I don't know, but I would hope that there is both accountability and mercy for all of us."

"Then you believe that sins will be punished."

"I don't know what happens after death, but I myself try to live according to the simple morality of treating others the way I want to be treated. How about you? Are you scared of death?"

"Yes, very scared," he says without hesitation. "That is why I choose to make this donation." He slides an envelope across the table. "Go ahead and open it." Inside is a check whose value is far more than I will earn in my entire lifetime. "It is real," he says, "but untraceable."

"I don't know what to say to you, except thank you. Is there anything we can offer you in return?"

"There may be something," he says, "but now is not the time."

Dov calls a ride for me and leaves me at the door. "We hardly made it through two bottles. I can't let such expensive wine go to waste."

"Will I hear from you again, Dov?"

"You will likely hear from me, but it may be a while. Please use the gift wisely. It is all I have left to offer on behalf of my soul."

CHAPTER TWENTY-EIGHT

1990
Zofia

My grandson, Aviel, recently told his parents about his encounter with a woman who was made of light. Her shimmering body reminded him of the iridescent underwater creatures he had seen in the aquarium. I'm now the wife, mother, and grandmother to three generations of mission keepers, and I myself have never met Her. It shouldn't matter to me. In retrospect I know that I made the choice to serve Her the moment I said "yes" to Benjamin on that first day of medical school. And I have said "yes" ever since. It shouldn't matter to me. My life is deeply fulfilling, and my troubles now are few. But it does matter to me. I yearn for one glimpse of Her beauty, one taste of Her nectar.

I'm keenly aware of the passing of time. It is the eve of my seventieth birthday, a day of sweet and joyous celebration. Benjamin surprises me with soft pink roses, a quiet dinner on the patio of our favorite restaurant, love poems read aloud to me with our fingers entwined. Later we behold the sun disappearing into the bosom of the mountains behind our home. We dance and make love, and hold each other close for a long time. Benjamin falls asleep in my arms, and I lie awake feeling blissful and alive.

Drifting into sleep, I notice a flicker of light. Is something wrong with my vision—cataracts perhaps—or is it the effect of the wine? The light flickers again, like a firefly appearing and disappearing, until the light becomes a steady glow that transforms into a sphere that then morphs into the shape of a luminous body. Her face appears, no more than the intimation of features within the radiance. Her body is filaments of light that sparkle like jewels and move with the fluidity of water. And then Her face appears as a face resembling my own.

"*I have heard your call, my dearest Zofia, and I have responded.*" Her voice is as melodic as wind chimes.

"Thank you, Goddess," I whisper.

"*The mission you and I serve is a mission of love for a world in such need. You have listened and responded to My call. You have trusted a journey that cannot be understood except with the heart.*"

"It is my greatest honor to serve You."

The light fades until there is no trace of Her. She has dissolved into the darkness from which She emerged. My body vibrates with bliss, my heart is melting in gratitude, and my mind is at peace. She has gifted me with Her presence, and this one moment will sustain me for the rest of my days.

CHAPTER TWENTY-NINE

2000

Benjamin

Morris and I both turn eighty this year. We've been meeting for breakfast every week since he and his family moved here many years ago. We share the noteworthy events of our lives—news of our families, his work at the clinic, my directorship of the new cardiac wing of the hospital, and a myriad of old-age difficulties.

We speak about the painful and complex issues facing our little country. Israel was birthed from two thousand years of a diaspora in which Jews were continually persecuted and oppressed. It was birthed from an almost-successful attempt at genocide. We fought hard to create a nation that would offer us safety and freedom. But our pain and determination blinded us to the plight of another people, for the land of Israel is also home to the Palestinians. To the many Palestinian people that have been displaced, we are occupying land that is rightfully theirs. To those people we are now the enemy, to be fought and overcome. The fighting is escalating, and there is no plan or moral leadership to find a resolution. It is cause for deep concern both pragmatically and morally, and this is the legacy that our children and children's children will need to resolve.

Morris and I meet at the same café every week. The café is owned by an American named Steve, a young man with an unkempt beard and the beginning of a potbelly, likely from his talent as a pastry chef. Each week he offers us his latest creations, this week's being a thick *rugallah*—rolled pastry dough layered with fig jam and almond paste. Next week, he tells us, he will surprise us with lemon filled tarts. Today Morris has an early appointment with a patient.

It is a gorgeous sunny day, and I enjoy the walk to my car, despite the chronic pain in my body, the legacy from my time in Auschwitz. I've had my share of challenges and blessings, and I feel strangely grateful for it all. Zofia is not home when I arrive. She still works almost full time at her clinic. She, Esher, Morris, and Rebbe Moshkovitz have created a world-renowned educational center for the treatment of trauma. Walking into my house, I'm now curious to see who came all the way to my house in order to slip a letter under my door.

Dr. Benjamin Janowicz,
It has been many years now since our last meeting. I am sure, however, that you remember who I am. Does the name Dr. Weinermann mean anything to you? If you recall, I abetted your escape from torture and certain death. In other words, I saved your life, not once, but several times. I ask you to consider that in the light of why I am writing to you.

I have lived far longer than predicted by all your esteemed colleagues, but now I really am at the end of my life. I wish to meet with you. That is the reason for this letter. I am a wanted war criminal as you know, but at this age, I will take the chance. If you meet with me and wish to turn me over to the authorities for trial, then that is your prerogative. If they wish to give me the death penalty, I will spare them the trouble. Do you have any idea why I am reaching out to you now, why I feel the need to meet with you before I die? Let me simply tell you. I have few regrets and even less remorse. The world condemns me, or at least pretends to condemn me. You would be surprised how many people still believe we were doing the right thing, that our actions were pure and courageous, and that had we succeeded the world would be a better place. I believed it at the time. Given that, it is still a mystery to me why I put myself at risk to save your life. But life without some illogic would be infinitely boring.

On the other hand, I am admittedly not without doubt. Particularly as I face death, I wonder how I will be judged, assuming of course that there is the possibility of life continuing in some form after death. All those notions of heaven and hell that were taught me as a child weigh heavily these days. Will there be consequences for my actions, even if my actions at the time made complete moral sense? Will I be punished or glorified? Either is possible. Perhaps that is why I chose to save your life. I split the odds down the middle.

I will make this letter brief. You will either agree or not agree to meet. Included are instructions for how to respond to me. I have little time left to live. I await your response.

CHAPTER THIRTY

Benjamin

The doorbell rings exactly at noon. Nobody knows about this meeting, a condition ensuring privacy that in this moment I regret. I'm scared to see him, scared of the memories that may surface, and even knowing they are memories does not alleviate the fear. Courage arises and fizzles, and then rises again, and I open the door. But it is not Hans standing in front of me. Disoriented, confused, I search for words.

"Dov, what are you doing here? I haven't seen you for years." Dov has aged considerably, his face drawn, tired, his jaws drooping, his body shrunken and lost inside his clothing.

"It's been many years, I agree. May I come in?"

"It's not a good time. I'm expecting another guest. Perhaps we can get together later for dinner?"

"By my watch it is now noon. Isn't that the time you told me to come?"

Is my mind playing tricks on me? Am I hallucinating?

"I do have a meeting at noon, but it is not with you."

"Are you sure? How do you know that Dov and Hans are not the same person?"

"Wait a moment, Dov. Are you saying you know Hans? Hans Weinermann?"

"Of course I know Hans. I am Hans Weinermann, or I was Hans Weinermann in another life."

I laugh involuntarily at the absurdity of what I'm hearing. "Your face is not that of Hans."

"If you look closely you can see scars from the plastic surgeries. With money, anything can be done. I was given a living mask and a different voice. But let me offer you final proof." Lifting his hand, he peels off a layer of what looks like skin. Underneath is a hand missing part of a finger.

"I don't understand. Is this a trick?"

"It is not a trick, and I will explain, but first I would ask for permission to enter. As I told you in my letter, I'm a dying man."

I step aside and lead him to my study. His breath is shallow and labored. He is accurate about the seriousness of his condition. He sinks down into the chair, a dying old man who once used his power to sentence hundreds of thousands of people to death.

"I will explain it all to you, Benjamin, and then present the reason I asked you to meet with me, but first let me know if you intend to hand me over to the authorities."

I stare at him for a long time, a fallible human being who committed the most heinous crimes against humanity, against my people. He will be dead in less than six months. What would be the use of turning him into the authorities? Israel has enough problems to contend with.

"No, there is nothing to be gained."

I see tears forming in his eyes. He begins to speak, but his voice is quivering. "May I have some water?" he asks.

I'm grateful for his request. It gives us both the time to gather ourselves. When I return, he is ready to talk.

"I know you must think it strange that I'm an Israeli citizen, but this is where I came to live after the war."

"I think it strange that you would want to live here of all places, and incredulous that you found a way to do it."

"Let me respond to both questions. As for the first, I surmised that this would be the last place anybody would think of searching for me. And I was right. I've lived a long and relatively unimpeded life here."

"How did you obtain citizenship?"

Hans offers a half smile. "I'm not sure you want to hear the story."

"I want to hear it, Hans."

"Very well, I will tell you the truth. While I was an officer, I used women prisoners to satisfy my male urges. Most of them I had no feeling toward, and when I tired of them, they were disposed of. But I developed a preference for one of them, or at least enough of a preference that when she became pregnant, I allowed the baby to be born, and both of them were allowed to survive. The boy was born before the dissolution of the camps. When it was clear that we had lost the war, the plan came to me. She and the child became my cover. When Israel became a country, we were all allowed entrance. Nobody had any clue of my real identity."

"Did you stay married to her?"

"I had no use for her, nor the child once I was settled here. Out of curiosity I did keep track of the child. Ironically, the boy became a rebbe."

"Does he know about you?"

Hans shakes his head. "He never met Hans, but he did meet Dov."

"What is his name?"

"Rebbe Yitzhak Ben Yehuda. But all those details are not why I've asked to meet with you. Let's get to the point of this meeting."

"I'm listening."

"It has to do with the question I posed to you when we met some years ago, the question about what happens after death."

"Yes, I remember you asking that question. You said that you were afraid of death."

"That has not changed, and I'm close to death. My hope is that death is the end of it all, that nothing happens except that we cease, but what if there is a heaven and a hell? Was my life a glorious, if failed, contribution to the betterment of humanity, or was I the deluded disciple of the wrong god? Can you tell me? Can anybody tell me?"

My muscles are taut with rage. I've imagined ripping him apart many times, and now I feel the barely controllable urge to do it for real. "What do you want from me, Hans?"

His body is trembling. He coughs, wheezes. I'm afraid he will die in this moment, but he pulls himself together.

"I'm dying. I don't know where I'm going, or where I've been. I don't know what or who will meet me. I need the forgiveness of one person, at least one person. I'm asking you to be the one person who forgives me."

The truth is I have a strong sense that justice exists in this universe. People who commit egregious crimes do suffer, not in the old eye-for-an-eye way, but because at some point they begin to wake up. They will feel the agony of the people they harmed. Hans will feel the anguish of those twin girls strapped to the gurneys, of their parents and grandparents, and the suffering of the millions and millions of people whose lives were extinguished by the Nazi death machine. Hans has reason to fear death. If indeed our souls continue on, then he will be held accountable not by an external authority, but rather as he evolves, he will hold himself accountable. He will want to see through his delusions and embrace the truth.

His eyes are already dead, his soul parched, empty, hungry for life, for love. His pain calls forth from me a wellspring of compassion, an exquisite, soothing tenderness that holds the whole world in its embrace. I reach for his hand, the hand with the missing finger violently severed by his own father. It does not excuse his actions, but it explains them. His hand quivers, his whole body begins to quiver, to come alive to his own suffering and his own need for love. He fights the grief and the terror, but he is losing the fight. He is moving out of his delusions. He is waking up.

Hans has been my savior and the incarnation of evil. He is the victim of abuse and a psychopathic perpetrator. He has been someone's darling infant, and now a tortured old man about to die. As I behold him now, he is no longer the face of evil, but the indivisible face of God.

"Yes Hans, Dov," I whisper. "I forgive you."

One single tear rolls down his cheek that he deftly rubs away. Rising slowly to his feet, he moves awkwardly toward the door, hesitates, and turns around. It is then I spot it; the radiant spark of light, the initiatory light, Her gift to humanity, has now been awakened in him, and it will ultimately guide him home.

"May I ask one last favor of you?" Reaching into his pocket, he pulls out an envelope. "Would you give this to my son? It's a check for a large sum of money, the rest of my savings. He has children. I know he can use it. His name and address are written inside. Give him any story you want, but make sure he receives it."

Hans leaves without looking back. Placing the envelope on my desk, I feel restless, agitated, disoriented. I feel the urge to call to him, the urge to retrieve my viola and play for him. I hate him, and I love him. I sit down in my favorite lounge chair and sob. That is all I can do. A memory enters my mind. Some years ago, I walked the ancient path, known as the Stations of the Cross, where Jesus, weak from torture, had been forced to drag the cross to the place where he would be crucified. Walking that same path today one encounters trashcans, children playing, graffiti, booths selling cheap plastic souvenirs, and even a pizza stand. Tourists by the busload walk this narrow, crowded passageway, some bored and others weeping in empathic sorrow for the Savior's suffering.

It symbolizes the constant change in life. Everything falls away and is replaced by new creation. Our most sacred loves, our most anguished wounds, our most compelling stories all pass, like the ocean that remains the ocean, even as the waves rise and fall upon the surface. My heart is so open in this moment, so light and free, as if all the burdens of this lifetime have been released. I want to cry out in ecstasy: all is right with the world. See what I see right now. All is right with the world. And in this moment I know that I have finally achieved the state of consciousness I need to complete the mission. I feel Her presence descend, a radiant, blissful light that makes the world appear in all its splendor, luminous golden filaments interpenetrating and binding all together. I am now Her eyes and Her hands, and Her radiant presence in the world. I sit at my desk and receive Her words. When my task is done, I close my eyes to rest.

"*You have served Me well, Benjamin.*" Her voice is as soft as wind chimes dancing in the breeze. Enfolded in Her love, I fly like an angel into the light.

Second Decoding

> *Hear me now,*
> *You have reconciled the sons of darkness and light in the divine act of forgiveness. You who forgive are forgiven and the perceived sins of the past transformed into wisdom. In the true condition, You and I are not separate. The hierarchy of self and God no longer exists, and that which has been projected outward no longer transcends the flesh of humanity, but dwells within the body of humanity. We enter a new harmonic. Your body has become My tabernacle.*

BOOK THREE

RAPHAEL / IBRAHIM

Peace does not descend on us from the outside. Peace arises from within us, arises in the midst of our conflicts. Peace arises as we are about to strike the enemy only to discover that the enemy has the same face as our own. Peace is not simply the absence of conflict. It is the exquisite vastness of the night sky. It is the eternal silence discovered within.

—the Great Rebbe

CHAPTER ONE

Jerusalem, Israel, 2012
Raphael Janowicz

Yitzhak Ben Yehuda, my teacher and friend, appears at my door, and with hardly a greeting hands me an envelope.

"What's this?"

He shrugs. "I'm only the messenger, Raphael. Read it and see for yourself." His face is taut with unexpressed emotion. "Try and read it with an open heart."

An odd thing to say, even for Ben-Yehuda, known for his circuitous but impeccable logic. One glance at the envelope, however, and I know the meaning of his words. I've always admired Ibrahim's sprawling calligraphic handwriting, with letters resembling musical notes, or poetry. How audacious of him to write me now, and how insensitive. Ibrahim knows me well, or knew me well, as I knew him. But it's been some time since we've seen each other. What do we know of each other now? Does he expect understanding, forgiveness, compassion? My hands are shaking as I grasp the letter, curbing the impulse to rip it into pieces: such a pathetically insignificant gesture of defiance. Inhale deeply, exhale slowly; I know the method well. Calmer now, I open the envelope, liberating the letter from its sheath, noting its insubstantiality, one thin sheet of paper folded neatly that has already caused much distress. In earlier, happier times, Ibrahim and I corresponded regularly. My excitement at receiving his letter flares and fizzles. All those moments belong to the time before Aviel's murder, before my precious son became the victim of a terrorist suicide bomber who happened to be Ibrahim's son.

The letter triggers memories of that day. A year and a half later, my palms are clammy, and my breathing contracted as I recall the incessant and intentionally annoying ring of the emergency phone in my office. I'm a physician, a cardiologist also trained in emergency medicine. I'm among the list of first responders, ready at a moment's notice to rush into scenes of horror to save lives, or lessen the agony of death. The phone is set up with distinctive rings to indicate different levels of emergency. The ring I hear that day is the ring we all dread, the ring indicating a terrorist attack. Answering the call, I soon learn that it is not a call to me as a physician, but a call to me as a father. In a state of shock, I sympathize with the man making the call. I've made similar calls, and it is excruciating to feel that one's words have just shattered the lives of others. I hear the weariness, the helplessness in his voice. "Those Palestinians should all rot in hell," he exclaims sympathetically.

That afternoon an unshaven and unkempt young man is working at the morgue. He is a medical student no doubt, earning some extra income. He looks like he hasn't slept for days.

"I'm so sorry," he says. "There are no words."

"There are no words," I agree, grateful for the dissociative numbness of shock allowing me to function. He opens the refrigerated compartment and slides out the gurney holding Aviel's remains in a body bag.

"He died of a head injury," he says, studying my response, hoping his words are comfort to me. "His body is intact. I don't think he suffered much."

Likely the attendant is right, and although dead is dead, I feel an iota of relief. Dutifully, he opens the body bag. Beholding the gray lifeless face of my son brings an involuntary gasp, followed by an earthquake of grief. The attendant looks away.

"Do you want me to close it?"

"No, I want to see him."

"Take all the time you need. Call when you want me to return." He touches my shoulder, a small but genuine gesture.

Aviel's eyes are closed, and his mouth turned upward, is smiling. I know my son. He's reaching out to me, assuring me that he is at peace. When I've had as much as I can bear, I call to the young man, who promptly, as promised, returns. Leaving the windowless basement I'm grateful to feel the warm sun on my face. If not for the numbness of shock, I would be choking on the bitterness of Her betrayal. Aviel was Her mission keeper. How could She have let this happen to him?

A year and a half later, and I'm still waving my fists into the air. Aviel is dead, and righteous indignation will do nothing to change this immutable fact. Protesting is the most flimsy of defenses, but the only one I have. For the moment it serves as a buoy in a tumultuous sea that threatens to pull me into its watery underworld of grief and despair.

I'm hardly a stranger to death. Being a physician, death is my nemesis. Too often I'm the harbinger of doom, facing anxious loved ones waiting for the smallest glimmer of hope. I trained myself not to look away from those suffering faces, but rather to look directly and speak with forthright honesty. Compassionate objectivity, the experts on grief call it. I know it well. I speak the words so often that I can recite them from memory.

"Death shatters us, but it is an inevitable part of life. The shock will last for a few weeks, giving way to intense anguish. This stage will pass, and the next thing to be encountered is guilt and remorse. What could we have

done differently? Was there anything left unspoken, incomplete? After this passes there is the stage we call existential emptiness. What meaning does life have for us if death erases it in an instant? Eventually you will find acceptance, and ultimately peace."

Do I believe my own words? Aviel and I had spoken just that morning. He'd been reluctant to leave his pregnant wife, even for a few short days—a few short days that turned into forever. If our conversation had been shorter or longer, the timing of his day would have been altered by a few minutes, enough perhaps that his life would have been spared. Maybe this, maybe that; my son is dead. Ibrahim's son is also dead, blown into a million pieces by the explosives strapped to his body. I become aware again of Ibrahim's letter. Another hour has been lost in replaying a past that will never change. I unfold the letter.

My friend,
I am inconsolable in my grief for you, for me, for Aviel and Sayyim, for all affected by this tragedy. How could I have failed to see the signs, failed to see the suffering of my own son? I have no answer, only profound regret. Only profound regret and a burning desire to make right the wrongs that have been done to you, to your family, to my family, and to all of us caught in this terrible cycle of vengeance and violence. Can we redeem the lives of our sons, and transmute the poisons of fear, anger, hatred into something worthy of our humanity? I want to work with you, Raphael, to complete the mission of which you spoke many times. In the name of our sons I ask that we, the fathers, let this not tear us apart but rather, unite us in a mission of peace.
Ibrahim

The letter drops to the floor beneath my feet. I let it remain where it lands. My hands are shaking. Tears rush into my eyes, a momentary lapse of control. I can't allow sentiment to weaken me. I wipe the tears with a quick sweep of my hand. Folding the letter back into its envelope, I place it in a folder that also contains copies of music that Ibrahim and I composed. I feel hard, constricted, deadened, caught in an intensely uncomfortable bind. I miss him, and I never want to see him again.

CHAPTER TWO

Ibrahim

The events of that day run obsessively through my mind, a futile attempt to comprehend the incomprehensible, to wrap a layer of meaning around the meaningless. The ritual of prayer, offered at first light of dawn, our voices praising God, calling for His protection, the sharp angular light like fingers touching our bodies, our souls, blessing us with His radiance, this was how our day began, like every day without exception. Beside me on his prayer mat, Sayyim's body rose and fell in rhythmic supplication. His mind had been focused, I assumed, on Allah. Try as I might to find any hint of difference between that day and any other, I fail to do so. Ruminations haunt me. What was he contemplating that morning? Did he feel the reassuring hand of Allah reaching down to him, the smiling face of his God welcoming him into Heaven? Did he experience any fear of death, even the primordial fear that animals feel when they know death is imminent? Was he going over the details of the plan, how he had been taught to strap the explosives close to his body, the body that Amala and I created in love? What was he experiencing in those last moments? Where was his soul as his body was blown into a thousand fragments? A father should know these things about his son.

After prayer that morning we sat together, Amala, my grandson, my two unmarried daughters, and Sayyim, to share a meal of *labneh,* and pita, and olives, and tea. We were poor, and the portions were small, but I recall that on this particular morning we also shared fresh apricots from our neighbor's tree.

Amala worried obsessively about Sayyim, in retrospect, a mother's intuition. Since childhood he'd been shy, sullen at times, pulled inside himself like a turtle. The others openly vented their anger, their discontent, their frustration, but Sayyim became mute. That morning, however, he was joking and laughing with my oldest daughter's son, Ahmed, handing him olives in exchange for correctly reciting the alphabet. I loved watching Sayyim laugh, his dark eyes sparkling. At his usual time he kissed Ahmed on the head and left for work at the machine shop. He put in long hours there, and most of his wages went toward our household. That was life. Whoever could find work gave his wages to support the family.

Sayyim was a singer and a drummer, and he would play late into the night, his voice melodic and resonant. Despite our interrupted sleep, we let him go on. He gave his days to support our family. He deserved to play; he needed to play. In this way Sayyim and I were much alike. We were both musicians, and a musician needs to make music or something in his soul withers. I'd known this much of Sayyim, but I hadn't really known him at all. I hadn't known the heart of my own son. This is shameful for a father to admit. To love someone is to enter the other's world.

In my failure, someone else gained access to his world. They gained access to his secret desires, his unconscious fears, the vulnerable, weak places within him where he could most easily be manipulated, programmed, influenced, poisoned. How fervently they must have fanned the flames of his anger, dredged up his hatred and convinced him that in the eyes of Allah he would forever be a martyr, a special star in the firmament. He couldn't have known that Aviel would be among his victims. They played together as children. If he'd known that Aviel would be killed, would he still have detonated the explosives? Or had every Israeli fallen into the category of the infidel?

How do I grieve my son? How do I sorrow for the fate of his soul and feel outrage for the suffering he inflicted on others? Could they have so brainwashed him, so taken over his mind? Is a father accountable for the actions of his son? Is a son accountable for the actions of his father? Where does accountability start and end? Does it matter? Who is to blame? Am I to blame for failing him as a father? Are the terrorists to blame for distorting justice? Are the Israelis to blame for continuing to steal our land and our dignity, for keeping us oppressed and impoverished, for robbing our youth of their pride? Are the politicians to blame for all their personal agendas that sabotage the possibility of true solutions? Is the world to blame for turning their backs on suffering, or worse, for using us as pawns in their own power games?

Whoever is to blame, my family pays a steep price. We lose our son, we lose our pride, and we lose our home, the second home that my father built and lost to the Occupation. The bulldozer crawls down the road, a yellow monster with a gigantic mouth, rattling the whole neighborhood. Within an hour our precious home is reduced to rubble. People shriek obscenities, boys hurl stones, but the bulldozer keeps coming, relentless in its mission to exact revenge, and teach us a lesson. As if the terrorists would heed that lesson, as if this act of "justice" would do anything but create more hostility. Our beloved home is destroyed, and shock waves of hatred ripple out through the community.

My brother-in-law's family offers to take us in, making now twelve of us living in three small rooms, two rooms being used as sleeping rooms, and the third as the kitchen. Most other activity takes place in the dusty yard in back of the house or on the rickety set of stairs in the front. My brother-in-law, Amala's younger brother, is a rotund man with chubby, baby-like cheeks. Since being out of work, his usual soft manner has disappeared. Now he spends his time doing little other than eating dates, irritating his wife by spitting seeds onto the floor, cursing and praying.

"They treat us like prisoners," he proclaims, "when it is our land they are invading. They call themselves righteous, but they are arrogant. They call themselves victims, but they are oppressors. There is no justice being served here."

Gracious soul that she is, Amala quietly tolerates her bossy sister-in-law. My two unmarried daughters beg me to find good husbands for them. The radios of neighbors on one side of the house blare incessantly. A garage on the other side repairs motorcycles at all hours of the day or night. To keep my sanity I perch myself on the front stoop and play music for hours and hours, trying not to think of Sayyim or Aviel or Raphael, or the fact that we have no money, no home, no dignity, and likely no hope for a future beyond this living nightmare. What happened to my life, once resplendent with riches? I had five beautiful children, and a wife I'd grown to love and respect. I was a teacher and a musician and a poet. Raphael had been my dearest friend. Now it is gone, all lost to circumstances beyond my control. I'm flailing in the ocean with no shore in sight, and I feel myself sinking.

Yitzhak Ben Yehuda has the wisdom to not try and alleviate my suffering. Neither does he condemn. An unconventional kabbalist with a passion for good wine and an aversion to dogma, we had all three become friends years ago. He is an odd looking man with a bulbous nose on which he perches delicate wire-rimmed glasses. His weight fluctuates so much that his clothes are either too loose or too tight, and almost never the exact fit.

Yitzhak has mastered the art of listening with simultaneous concern and dispassion. He is principled and yet holds no ultimate positions. Life is to be taken completely seriously, and yet not seriously at all. He elicits people's trust and their secrets, and thankfully the trust is warranted, and the secrets dignified. Knowing this about him, I shouldn't be surprised by the continued regularity of his visits. He understands the web of complexities that culminated in the horrific tragedy that left his two best friends with their beloved sons dead.

Every week he arrives, bearing a pot of stew or fresh cheese and bread, or a dessert baked by his wife, and we sit on grimy plastic chairs in the back of the house, or on the rickety front step with the cacophony of noisy trucks and motorcycles. Yitzhak seems oblivious to the noise while I strain to hear his words. We speak of the practical, the philosophical and the mystical. We speak of politics and injustices, and the deep sorrows of the human heart. We speak of Sayyim and Aviel and Raphael, and the knot in my chest from which I have not one moment of relief.

"If it were you, Yitzhak, if it were your son, what would you do? How would you react?"

He studies his palms, turning them over and over. "Far be it for me to offer advice to you, my friend. Far be it for me to suggest how such a tragedy should find resolution, or even beyond resolution, become the opening for *tikkun*."

"What should I do, Yitzhak? Should I reach out to him or is it kinder for me to disappear from his life?"

He shrugs. "I can't advise you, Ibrahim, except to remind you to listen to your heart. The answer to that question is within you."

I'm hardly as confident. Buried at the bottom of a sea of grief, guilt, shame, and outrage, perhaps my heart is speaking, but for the moment, I hear nothing but sorrow and confusion.

"I will tell you one thing, my friend." Yitzhak groans as he pushes his ample body up from the low step. "Every time we move in the direction of *tikkun*, we are supported by a thousand angels. It may not be obvious right away. Likely we encounter forces of resistance, but I can tell you that the support will be there."

"The force of resistance seems immense." We witness a speeding motorcyclist run head long into a stray dog. Letting out a wail of pain, the dog limps away, the driver cursing the dog as he guns the engine. Yitzhak eases himself back down onto the step.

"Some dogs are more awake than people," he says. "Allow

me to share a parable with you before taking my leave." He pauses, studies his palms, and begins. "There was once a great forest fire, and all the animals fled to the other side of the river to contemplate what they could do to stop it. It was so big that the animals just hung their heads in defeat. All of them, that is, except one little bird. This little bird filled her beak with water from the river, and flew over the fire to deposit her few drops. Over and over she performed this action. The other animals asked, "why are you doing that? Your actions are foolish ones. Do you think your tiny drop of water does anything at all to stop that fire?" The bird paused for a moment and laughed. "You take me for a fool, but I am hardly a fool. I can see that my own efforts will do nothing to the fire, but they do everything to me, and my own consciousness is the only thing I can change."

CHAPTER THREE

Raphael

My wife, Rebecca, is an admirably and annoyingly principled woman, vehement about her version of fairness, justice, and the higher moral ground. Blame to her is as abhorrent as weakness is to me. She believes in the basic goodness of humanity, but Becky has never come face to face with evil. Her descendants stepped onto the American shore at the turn of the century with a wave of immigrants fortunate enough to reach the land of opportunity. Her family prospered when her father's small corner market expanded into a chain of supermarkets.

Although her family provided material ease and comfort, Becky made *aliyah*, seeking a life of deeper substance. The women's organization she formed is dedicated to the empowerment of women, all women no matter their race or religion. This was my wife before the murder of our son. Will the world look so benevolent and redeemable now? Part of me hopes that her idealism, like mine, will be shattered. Part of me prays fervently that it will survive.

After years of marriage, we hold few secrets. We respect each other's interiority, but loving familiarity has dissolved any vestige of boundaries. Our psyches are ordinarily open territory for each other, but not lately. We grieve in solitude, or rather I grieve in solitude, and Becky turns to her myriad of friends and colleagues. We come together, however, around our concern and care for Tziporah, Aviel's widow, our beloved daughter-in-law.

Tziporah was five months pregnant and carrying twins. We feared that the shock would trigger premature labor, and even Aviel's children would be lost to us. Tziporah's devastation transformed into dogged determination, and she held on, and the babies held on, and we had the ambivalent joy of being at the birth of Avida and Aaron, both healthy and strong.

Ibrahim's letter is poorly timed, and from my admittedly skewed perspective, insensitive. Insensitive because I'm just pulling my life back together, just gaining control of emotions that seem always ready to erupt with volcanic force. Ironically, Ibrahim is the friend I would have turned to had circumstances been different. He would have insisted that we transform grief into music, allowing our song of sorrow to touch the heart of the world. To whom could I turn? Do I simply want someone to affirm my outrage, or do I truly want to grapple with the complexities of the situation? After Aviel's death, Yitzhak cradled me in his arms, soothing my anguished moans. Yitzhak knows how to listen if truth is what I seek, but can I tolerate that his compassion extends toward Ibrahim?

We'd all been close friends, sharing impassioned conversation, and the wisdom gleaned from our different cultures and experiences. This was all before the year 2000, the year of the second Intifadah, the Palestinian uprising and the resulting Israeli security measures: concrete walls, entrenched positions, missiles, stringent checkpoints, and the ever-present threat of attack and counterattack. I could not morally condone the violence of the Palestinians. Ibrahim could not morally condone what he saw as the Jewish occupation. Yitzhak witnessed it all, shrugged his shoulders, and ignored the walls, the armies, the missiles, the cries of outrage from both sides. Yitzhak is truly an unappointed and unproclaimed spiritual ambassador.

Rebbe Yitzhak Ben Yehuda and I were brought together through a most unlikely circumstance. The day my father died, I spotted an envelope sitting conspicuously on top of his desk. The envelope contained a check for a large sum of money, and a simple note stating where and to whom the money should be delivered. The note was not signed. Dutifully I called the next day, but instead of perceiving me as the bearer of good news, the rebbe responded to me with annoyance.

"I don't want the money. Kindly give it to charity."

"The check is in your name. You'll have to donate it yourself if you don't want it." There was silence on the other end of the phone. I heard a long sigh. "I apologize. Could I ask you to be so kind as to deliver it here?"

How the check had ended up on my father's desk, I could not discern. Perhaps it was an old patient who had left it in my father's keeping, but this was a large sum of money being given to one person clearly not eager to receive it.

Aviel, at the time an adolescent, accompanied me to Ben-Yehuda's office. We found the right address and stepped into the narrow, dark hallway, locating the bell marked Yitzhak Ben Yehuda. The bell was loud, jarring, irritating, and yet it drew no response. We climbed the steep, unlit stairway to the second floor. The hall smelled musty, with a faint odor of cat urine. For the sake of this man, I hoped the check was legitimate and would afford him a better office space. Locating his door, I knocked loudly, and still there was no response.

"I'm looking for Yitzhak Ben Yehuda," I shouted.

A gruff voice admonished us for being so rude. Outraged, I retrieved the envelope from my pocket and was about to slide it under the door, but Aviel gestured for me to remain. He was obviously finding this more amusing than me.

"This is not a good beginning," Ben-Yehuda shouted through

the door. "The study of kabbalah takes patience, and you are clearly not a patient man."

Aviel and I looked at each other, baffled. Taking a breath I persevered. "I'm sorry, rebbe, but you told me to meet you at this time, and I didn't know if you were here."

"I wouldn't have told you to come at a time I wouldn't be here. How idiotic that would have been. Do you think I'm an idiot?"

"No, rebbe, I thought that I might have been the idiot who mixed up the time."

"Then if you're an idiot, why would you come here wanting to study kabbalah? Do you think kabbalah is for idiots?"

Aviel's hand was over his mouth squelching his laughter. "Rebbe, we're not here to study kabbalah. I told you that we are here to deliver you a gift."

"What you told me on the phone and the check you have in your pocket are not the real reason that you are here. Nor is it the reason that your son is here with you."

Aviel and I looked at each other in astonishment.

"How did you know that my son is with me? Did you see us from the street?"

"I saw nothing from the street. I see two auras standing outside this door."

"You're right, but will you allow me to give you the check?"

"Do you not understand even now? You are both here to study kabbalah. Are you not from a lineage of kabbalists?"

Aviel and I exchanged bewildered glances. "How did you know that?"

The door swung open. Standing before us was the rotund figure of a man, a head taller than me, with a prominent bulbous nose, that along with a beard as unkempt as his unironed khaki shirt gave him the look of a clown. He reached out and pulled me into an immense hug.

"Come in, come in, and welcome to my humble office." His office was not only humble but also tiny and disheveled.

"I think better in chaos. Too much order makes me nervous."

Aviel and I thus became students of Rebbe Yitzhak Ben Yehuda. We joined a group of other students who met every week to do the work of preparing body, heart, and mind to receive the light of divinity, in the marriage of human and divine. He proved to be a remarkable teacher and Aviel, a remarkable student. According to Rebbe Ben Yehuda, Aviel possessed the maturity of soul to become a *tzaddik,* an enlightened one.

Memory, in this moment, offers me reprieve from anguish. I will call Yitzhak and share the letter with him. I simply can't bear this alone.

CHAPTER FOUR

Ibrahim

Why would you do this, my son? Why would you take your own life in such a violent way? Why would you take the lives of others? I'm your father. Help me understand.

I will do what I have to do, Father. The glory in life is serving Allah. His people are being persecuted, oppressed, humiliated day after day, year after year, and nobody is listening to our suffering. I will make the world pay attention. I will serve Allah. I will add to His glory.

Oh my son, what you are doing is so wrong. You are being duped, brain washed, dragged in to do the dirty work for those whose hearts are hard with hatred. You will cause great suffering, my son. You will leave behind the ravaged hearts of those who love you most. Your mother will sorrow, your siblings will quarrel among themselves, some condemning you and some defending you, and I will be broken, Sayyim. All that gives meaning to my life will be taken, taken by your one act of foolish defiance.

I'm truly sorry, Father. Can you not understand that it takes sacrifice to win this Holy War? Our enemies are powerful right now, but they will be brought down by the righteous.

No, Sayyim! No!

Amala's voice breaks into my dream.

"Husband, wake up! Your shouting will rouse the whole household."

"Was I dreaming? Is Sayyim alive or dead?"

Amala sighs loudly. "He's dead, my husband. It's too late to save him. Go back to sleep."

"Hold me, Amala. Hold me while I weep for him, for you, for us, for Raphael, for Rebecca, for Tziporah. Hold me."

Amala holds me, cradling my head to her bosom, wiping my brow with her hand. Her skin is soft, smooth, warm, her touch comforting. Her voice is a low murmur, like bubbling water, lulling, soothing. Amala hurts as much as I hurt, and yet she generously offers her love. My heart softens, the tension drains away, and only the bittersweet taste of sorrow remains. She is my angel of mercy, like the man who offered Jesus a cup of water on his way to the crucifixion. A cup of water to a dying man with thirst is a true blessing.

I know what I have to do to save myself, to redeem this once precious life. I have to write Raphael. I have to risk his rejection. I must find meaning, to make sense of this senseless act of murder, this blind brutality. I must make peace with myself, and with my son, and with Raphael. My words become a fountain of sorrow pouring out onto the page.

Ben Yehuda, in offering to be the messenger embraces me. "You have now become the bird dropping her tiny beak of water onto the flames."

CHAPTER FIVE

Raphael

I was born in the midst of war. They were agonizing, fearful years, but I recall feeling loved and mostly sheltered from the terrifying world that existed just outside the walls of the convent. This other world frequently intruded into our cloistered existence, men with stern faces commanding us to line up, yanking down my pants, spanking my bottom, shouting obscenities.

I'd been told that my father had been killed in battle. It was a story not unlike so many in those wartime years, and yet when my real father returned, it was not a complete surprise to me. I'd known the truth. When we finally met, I felt as if we'd been inside each other all along. Later, my father tried to convey to me the improbable miracle of my conception, almost as if he were describing the virgin birth, but not quite. At the time, I had little context for comprehending what it had been like for my parents to risk loving each other knowing the certainty of separation and heartbreak.

My love for Rebecca Rabinovitz helped me understand more profoundly the nature of their sacrifice. When Becky made the decision to return to the States with no promise of return, I knew with painful poignancy what my mother had experienced in those lonely years of solitude. I knew that Becky was my beloved, and that whether or not she chose to return, I would be satisfied with no other. I was lucky that my conviction was never tested. Becky thankfully returned.

She was one of the young, "privileged" American Jews whom we aptly named the tree planters, those idealists who collected money in Hebrew schools to buy trees to make the "barren dessert" bloom. I was proudly fulfilling my army duty at the time, although my pride, admittedly, was not so much in serving my country as in serving myself. Never had I been so muscled, tan, masculine, and self-assured. My pride, however, was brought down a notch when my unit was stationed outside a kibbutz to protect the young idealists, hardly an esteemed assignment. Becky happened to be one of them.

Of all the attractive young women at the kibbutz, why she was the one who caught my eye remains a mystery of love. Becky donned overalls three sizes too large, while the others displayed their figures in tight fitting T-shirts and jeans. But she intrigued me. She was complex, challenging, and real.

I've never once seen Becky compromise her ideals. We haven't always agreed on matters of great importance, and we've learned to respect our disagreements and to accept each other, if not each other's positions. Becky is a fierce contender, and I love that about her, but when she softens, she is beautiful and vulnerable, with a moon shaped face and dark almond eyes that seem to perpetually fight the urge to smile.

CHAPTER SIX

Ibrahim

My father had been a devout a man, a forgiving, gentle man who, even after being forced at gunpoint out of the home built with his own hands, didn't succumb to hatred. Nor did he succumb to the humiliation of perceived defeat. Pride, freedom, joy were not a function of life's gifts, bestowed and rescinded, but a matter of devotion to Allah. And music. Music was Allah's way of expressing Himself: the musician, God's instrument. My father played the drum and the oud, and had a voice with a range and power that could bring a whole village to its knees. Music was for my father wind rustling the desert grass, voices crying or laughing or shouting. Music had the power to transform and transcend the world.

I soared with pride the day my father presented me with my own oud, a beautiful instrument with carved engravings in her voluptuous body. We performed together, and always our audience wept in felt recognition of Allah's ecstasy. Sayyim and I shared similar moments of communion. Sayyim, of all my children, had been blessed with the gift of music. For Sayyim the world was rhythm. He felt rhythm in the melodic beat of raindrops falling from the roof into the rain barrel. He heard rhythm in car engines, conversations, birdsongs, the roar of airplanes, and barking dogs. Sayyim tapped his feet, his hands, his fingers; he tapped out the rhythms of life, his own heartbeat, and even the earth spinning around the sun.

My father told me that no matter what happens in life, as long as you have music you are free. *Men cannot sing and fight at the same time. Men cannot sing and be sorrowful. Music is the language of love, and love liberates the soul. Even if the voice is lost, and all of one's limbs severed, music is never gone, because it comes from a realm beyond the limitations of body. Listen, my son, listen! If ever all seems lost, then listen for the music. It will never fail you. It will set you free.*

Doesn't every human being deserve to sing his song freely into the world? I was wrong about you, Sayyim. I thought your song was the uplifting music you created, that your destiny was to transcend the limitations of this life through music. I was wrong. The last sound you created in this life was the sound of explosion, and the agonized wails of those fated to die with you or endure life with bodies maimed. How can I hold you in my heart, my son, when everything inside me screams in horror at what you have done?

CHAPTER SEVEN

Raphael

Miracles, destiny, fate. This particular day I'm filling in for a physician whose wife is in labor. The emergency room has been busy and my lunch break postponed several times. I've just hung up my lab coat when I spot him sitting hunched in a chair in blood-stained clothes, a bloody bandage wrapped around his left hand. He is Palestinian, close to my age, a handsome man with a high forehead, sharp chiseled cheekbones, and a strong jawline accentuated by a short, groomed beard. His face is contorted with pain. The nurse notices me looking toward him.

"Take your break, Dr. Janowicz. Dr. Fischer will attend to him when he's done with the attempted suicide patient."

"But he's bleeding profusely. He'll be my last patient."

She nods, conceding to my notorious stubbornness, and motions for him to come with her into a treatment room. He follows me with his eyes, as if wanting to be sure that it will be me, and nobody else who will treat him. I enter the room with the usual posture that a physician takes toward a patient, a well-practiced mixture of concern and authority. He looks up, his face brightening, and exhales a barely audible sigh of relief.

"I see you've had an accident. May I remove the bandage and take a look?"

"Of course you may. But let me warn you that the tip of my middle finger is almost completely severed. It's hanging by a fold of skin."

"What happened?" I ask, although it really doesn't matter what has happened. A severed finger is a severed finger.

"I was careless, doctor. I was helping a friend sculpt a block of wood."

He winces and holds his breath as I remove the bandage and examine the finger. It is as he'd described. The tip of his finger is nearly severed.

"How could I have let this happen?"

"Accidents are accidents," I offer.

"Can my finger be saved, doctor?"

"I don't know. I will try reattaching it, but healing depends on how your body responds."

His jaw quivers. He holds his breath to quell the tears.

"I'll do my best, but would it be so terrible to live life with one slightly shortened finger? It would hardly interfere with anything."

He groans softly. "Would it be so, doctor, but it would interfere with everything."

"What do you mean?"

"I'm a musician, doctor. I play a stringed instrument called the oud. It takes great deftness of hand. If I were missing the top of my finger I may not be able to play, or at least my playing would be greatly compromised."

Suddenly my interest is ignited. "I'm also a musician. I play the viola."

He smiles, a beautiful and gracious smile. "The moment I saw you, I knew that you were the right doctor. Now that I know we are both musicians, I can relax. You'll save my finger, doctor. I have great faith in you."

"Thank you for your faith in me, but it will be your own body that does the healing."

"When I'm healed, I will invite you to be my honored guest at a concert."

"We're getting ahead of ourselves. Let's begin by reattaching your finger."

I pose questions about his life to distract him while I perform the procedure. I learn that he has five children, his family lives in Gaza, and he has taught music and philosophy at the conservatory in Jerusalem. He is here at the invitation of his friend, and gave a performance the night before the accident. He thanks me profusely when I'm done stitching the finger and applying the bandage. I hand him antibiotics, and uncharacteristically give him my private office address, curious about my own motivation for doing so.

"Come back and see me in two weeks."

Ibrahim's impression lingers long after he leaves. I recall the contours of his face, the concern in his eyes, the touching sincerity of his trust. When he appears in my office two weeks later, I feel an unmistakable sense of delight.

"Good to see you," I say. Ibrahim smiles warmly, his eyes averted as if following the unwritten protocol between doctor and patient, or Israeli and Palestinian. "Come into my office, and we'll remove the bandage. Have you been experiencing pain?"

He shakes his head. "A little pain at first, but it's diminishing."

I remove the bandage, and to my relief there is no sign of infection. It appears his finger will indeed heal.

"That is good news," he exclaims. "I'm grateful to you. How long until I can perform, doctor?"

"Allow two months for it to heal properly."

His face glows with satisfaction. "Will you and your family attend a concert I give in your honor?"

His innocent gratitude touches me. "I'd be honored to hear you perform, but please no mention of me. I'm simply a doctor doing my work."

He leaves and although thoughts of him linger, I'm surprised to receive an invitation to attend his next performance. Becky and I are warmly embraced as we enter the crowded café. Ibrahim is at the far end of the room, on stage with a drummer and a flute player. The moment he spots us, he makes his way through the crowd and greets us effusively, announcing that I'm the excellent doctor who saved his finger. I'm cheered and saluted. So much for anonymity! We are seated at a long table, and served more courses than I can count: pita and tabouli, olives and feta, dates and white beans, lentils and lamb.

Then the music begins with the drummer offering complex, intriguing rhythms. The wooden flute enters, adding layered counter rhythms alternating quick staccato with long drawn out curved notes. Ibrahim's melodious voice dialogues with flute and drum, and finally the oud enters with its textured richness. The music moves deep inside me, the song of divine and mysterious Eros awakening the passionate longing for an unnamable Beloved.

CHAPTER EIGHT

Ibrahim

"Did he say anything about the letter?"

Yitzhak and I sit tentatively balanced on the rickety wooden step that forms a precarious bridge between house and road, awkwardly attempting to enjoy the lemon cake, a gift from his wife. A truck filled with garbage roars by, the steps vibrate, and Yitzhak almost loses his balance. The heat of shame burns my body. A year and a half later and my family is still living in the house of our relatives. *Hamas* offered to rebuild our home for us, their way of winning support by donating help to victims of the oppressors. Resisting temptation, we refused. How can we accept help from the ones whose violence we abhor, the ones who poisoned the mind of our son? Whatever vestige of dignity my refusal offers me does nothing to change the humiliating circumstance of my life. Yitzhak finishes the cake and clears his throat.

"Raphael says he will keep an open mind."

"Yitzhak, I've known you long enough to know when you're not telling the whole truth."

He raises his hands in a weak display of self-defense. "He is struggling, Ibrahim. He is not yet ready to forgive."

His response arouses my fury. "Forgive? Have the Israelis apologized for the unconscionable ways they've treated us? Did they think we would just hand them the keys to our homes, step aside as they steal our land, and meekly accept being imprisoned in the squalor of their refuge camps?" Yitzhak nods silently, and prepares to leave. "I'm sorry, my friend. You are only the messenger and one of the few who understand."

In our many years of friendship, Raphael and I have seldom spoken directly about the Palestinian/Israeli conflict. This is known by the Palestinians as the Occupation, and by some Israelis in disparaging vernacular as "mowing down the weeds," meaning that the Palestinian "problem" can never be totally uprooted, but merely managed. In all other ways, Raphael and I are completely transparent with one another, but here we are evasive, cautious, engaging each other as though navigating a minefield. Our friendship is too precious to risk venturing into that terrain. Such is the way of fate that the night following one of our best performances, our music received with enthusiasm by Israelis and Palestinians, our music heralded as a unique synthesis of both cultures, we are out celebrating and unwisely order a second bottle of wine. Our conversation, always rich and poignant, leads that evening to a remembrance of our fathers. Anecdote after anecdote rises from memory, affection, and gratitude. Raphael recalls the first time he met his father, and how he beat him at three games of chess. I offer the memory of my father carrying me on his shoulders and walking underneath the branches of olive trees, the leaves tickling my face. Raphael recalls his father helping him learn decoding. I praise my father's design and craftsmanship in constructing our ornate tiled floors and for planting the lemon tree in front of the house that produced almost-sweet lemons.

"I miss that house," I say, the wine opening up feelings ordinarily held private. "That house was supposed to have been my father's legacy. Life was never the same for the family after we left."

"What happened to that house, Ibrahim?"

The pivotal question, the controversial question, the question that drives us deep into the minefield.

"The Zionist army forced us to leave, holding guns to our heads, shouting that we had ten minutes to gather our belongings and vacate the premises. My father protested, and they almost shot him, but my mother's pleading stopped them. It was a sad day, Raphael, a sad day for my family."

I feel Raphael's tension, the holding of breath, the slight backing away, the tense gripping of the wine glass. His words are sharp, taut, brittle.

"War is never easy."

If I hadn't been drunk, if the conversation hadn't brought up memories of my father's heartbreak, I might have nodded in agreement and ended it there. Instead, I speak the truth.

"War? We weren't at war with you. We were simple people going about our lives, farming the land, taking care of our homes as we had for the last four hundred years. Is this war?"

Raphael's jaw tightens. "Our spiritual roots have been here for thousands of years. We were expelled from the land, but we never gave up the dream of return. We resettled this land, purchasing tracts of land from landowners who gladly took our money. The world gave us the right to statehood. We tried to negotiate a fair settlement with you, but you resisted. Then, yes, it became war."

Heartbreak is fueling my outrage. I feel the ground giving way under us, but it is too late to stop the explosion.

"You talk about being expelled from this land, but this land did not lie fallow as your people would like to believe. We have been living here for over five centuries. This is our home, our land, and our spiritual roots are here as well. Our prophet, Mohammed, was born here. You try and ignore our very existence, our right to be here. Yes, you hold the power and now the authority, but that does not give you the moral authority to steal from us what is ours."

"We purchased tracts of land, legally and fairly."

"In the beginning, yes, but later you took what you wanted, stopping at nothing." Please, I pray silently, let this end now, but the line has been crossed.

Raphael bolts up, his voice raised in high staccato tones. "We tried again and again to find a peaceful solution, but you refused to compromise."

"Refused to compromise? You are occupying our land, and you refuse to see this. You offer us pittance for land that you stole from us. You use force, coercion. You bully and intimidate us by building more and more settlements. You who were persecuted, oppressed, how can you do the same thing to my people that was done to you?"

The waiter hurries over and tensely asks that we keep our voices down. We are disturbing the other customers. Would we like the check now? Raphael's body is shaking. I fear he will lose control but his outrage suddenly melts into tears.

"It was a matter of our survival, Ibrahim. There was nowhere else we could go, but back to our homeland."

His pain softens me. "I understand, Raphael, but this is our home as well, and you insist in denying the truth."

Suddenly I am returned to the present by the sound of Yitzhak's voice. "Fear makes people insensitive to the rights of others."

"Is it fear, Yitzhak, or is it lust for power that makes people trample on the rights of others who are in the unfortunate position of being in the way of what they want? Why do they not see that we are human beings? Raphael is a sensitive, caring man, but here he is blind. Israelis treat us as the enemy, and don't see that they have made us into the enemy."

"And do you not do the same?"

His words cut deep. "Perhaps it is so. Perhaps we stay entrenched in our immovable positions. Perhaps we refuse to accept defeat and compromise because of our pride, and for no other reason. Perhaps we also need to learn to soften, to forgive, and accept compromise, no matter how unfair it seems. Life is not always fair, and sometimes we must simply accept."

The traffic on the road quiets. No dogs bark. No radios blare. A plane flies overhead but it is inconsequential. The moment is a pause, an in-breath, as if when the dance of the world begins again anything may happen.

CHAPTER NINE

Raphael

Ten-year-old Mariana is my inspiration. Knowing about Aviel's death, her parents have chosen me as her physician, rightfully assuming that I will understand the anguish of losing a child. Mariana, born with numerous birth defects including an irreparable heart condition, will die young. Scrawny, gaunt-faced, she is acutely aware of her mortality.

"Not more than six months now, Dr. Janowicz," she proclaims with disturbing equanimity during her latest visit. Her eyes, once strikingly blue are now a somber grey, but her gaze is intense as she meets mine, searching not for reassurance, but for truth. I want to offer hope beyond the likely course of her condition, but I know that such empty words are disrespectful to her. Mariana's heart is failing. She is dying. Finding my own courage, I confirm what she already knows. She nods her understanding, her ponytail bobbing up and down, reminding me that despite her wisdom, she is still a child.

"I'm almost ready to die, Dr. Janowicz. I'm not sure I want to live any longer."

"Is it the pain, Mariana? There is medication that can help you experience less pain."

She shakes her head vehemently. "No, Dr. Janowicz, I'm used to living with pain." Her eyes scrutinize me. "Can I tell you a secret?"

"Of course, Mariana. You may tell me anything."

"You won't tell my parents."

"If it's a secret, I won't tell anybody."

She draws her chair closer to me, her voice dropping.

"Dr. Janowicz, I don't really live here in this body."

"What do you mean, Mariana? Where do you live?"

A giggle escapes her lips. "I live in the world of the angels. We fly, and dance, and sing, and play. When I'm with the angels, I'm so happy. I don't feel any pain in my body. I know I'll be with them when I die. That is why I'm not afraid. I'll be with them, and we'll help other children to not be afraid. When I die, I'll visit a little child, and help her feel safe and happy."

Sorrow and joy crowd my heart, each offering its own reason for tears. Mariana grins, and for a moment her eyes are bright again.

"I'm glad I can talk to you, Dr. Janowicz. I love my parents, but they are so uncomfortable when I talk about my death. I know they'll miss me, and I'll miss them, and my sister and brother. I'll be able to see them, but they won't be able to see me. I'll try very hard to make them know I'm still with them, but I think it's harder for parents." Mariana catches my gaze. "Do you ever see your son, Dr. Janowicz?"

Her question exposes raw vulnerability. "Aviel, do I see Aviel?"

Mariana nods, and attentively waits for my response. I shake my head, and I see her brow furrow. "That is very strange. I can see your son even as I speak with you."

"Aviel is here? You can see him?"

"Yes, that is what I'm trying to tell you. He is smiling, and he keeps pointing at something and saying the word, 'mission.' Do you know why he keeps saying that word?"

I nod my head through my tears.

"I wish my parents would stop feeling guilty about me," she says. "They think they did something wrong to make me have all these birth defects, but they did nothing wrong. I chose to be born this way, and they agreed to take care of me, and they have loved me so much. That is why it's so easy to let go of life. After I'm dead, Dr. Janowicz, help them understand. Help them know what good parents they were to me. Help them understand that I'm still here, that I'm with the angels, and that all I want is their happiness."

The buzzer interrupts us. Her parents have come for her, as the angels will soon come for her soul. Mariana, like Aviel, is an intense flame of love and inspiration. These wise souls are radiant shooting stars, gifting the world with their splendor before disappearing back far too soon into the infinite depth of the night sky.

CHAPTER TEN

Ibrahim

Hours, days, and years can pass with breathtaking swiftness while at other times they tarry. Some are like eddies in a flowing river where water is caught in the swirl of its own tiny orb, appearing to never move along with the rest of the river. Such are the two years following Sayyim's death: devoid of work, home, money, dignity, and Raphael. I pass agitated time playing the oud, grateful for the calming focus and the semblance of privacy it offers me. In this overcrowded, teeming household and neighborhood, where the frustration of tacit imprisonment, punitive deprivation, and unrecognized injustice threaten to poison our souls, music offers me solace.

Music is timeless and transcends all conditions, as does God, and in its purest form, love. I aspire to this kind of love, but I constantly fail, and my limitations are the source of my own suffering. If only I could love in this way, then my heart would be pure and imperturbable, and I would be at peace. I fight the urge to succumb to hatred, and the bitterness of injustice, and the sting of betrayal, and the defeat of despair. Round and round in the eddy I spin, caught in a swirling current that refuses to move forward or let me sink mercifully to the bottom.

Eventually the river of life carries our lives along with greater ease. My oldest son begins to repair and sell used engine parts. My oldest daughter will any day give birth to her third child, and my two younger daughters are married within months of each other. The river of life is flowing for us again, and Amala and I move back into our own home. The community organized to rebuild our house in its original location, and we step over the threshold to the sound of cheers. The neighborhood celebrates with a feast and music and dancing, and for the first time in a very long time, I'm happy to be alive.

We are now alone in our own home, the silence intoxicating and terrifying. We stand awkwardly together, like newlyweds, our fingers touching, offering a tentative invitation. We make love for the first time in two years. I curl up next to her, breathing in her scent, and I weep. Amala is changing. She is more confident, and less preoccupied with the opinions of others. She refuses to hide in shame, or agree with those who wish to martyr Sayyim. She speaks up for justice but not revenge. Her strength makes me oddly desirous of her.

Many years ago, Amala and I met in the aftermath of a devastating personal crisis. I'd been hired to perform at the home of a prestigious family. The moment I beheld their youngest daughter, my heart quickened with passion, for never had I seen a woman so lovely. She listened attentively to my performance, and my music became a love song to her. We dared not speak a word to each other, nor even risk a glance. Departing that evening, my brief intoxication descended into the anguish of unrequited love. Her family would never accept me. My fate was cast. The rest of my days and nights would be filled with yearning, and this would have been punishment enough, but there was greater to follow. I was invited back for several more evenings, but at the end of my last performance, her father strode angrily toward the stage, accusing me of accosting his daughter. I could hardly believe his accusations. I had uttered not one word, nor even brushed

against her beautiful skin. Adamant about the truth of his griev-
ance, his public recrimination shamed my family, and sullied my
reputation as a potential husband.

In repentance for whatever sin of desire I had committed,
I vowed to remain celibate, but my father, with greater wisdom
initiated a search for a suitable wife. Still smitten with desire for
my unattainable beloved, I was hardly interested in my father's
array of potential brides. Oddly, I was attracted to Amala because
she was as unhappy being thrust into a marriage with me as I was
with her. Thus we bonded over our disgruntlement.

Amala and I have taught each other about love, about the
practical, earthy kind of love that one needs to traverse the vicis-
situdes of life, and to grind down one's tenacious and stubborn
patterns. We help each other become better people, and this is the
real gift of our marriage. Perhaps the purpose of life is to test and
temper our lofty ideals, our dreams and fantasies, and to shape
them into the lived reality of a human life. If we succeed, then the
truth shines through us with ever more radiance. If we fail, the light
diminishes, and our spirit dies. We have only these two options.

The night we move back into our home I have a dream, a
glorious dream, perhaps a prophetic dream. An old woman
approaches me, with dark, creased skin and white bedraggled hair
that hangs limp down her face. She holds out her hand to me like
a beggar. With upturned palms, I signal my own impoverishment.
Everything has been taken from me. Pulling me toward her with
surprising strength, she shakes me hard. I watch with great astonishment as diamonds and rubies and every kind of gem pour out
of my pockets until I'm standing in a pile of glistening gemstones.

"Why do you withhold from me?" she demands.

"I'm confused. I thought my pockets were empty."

"If you reach far enough inside, this is what you find."

I implore her to say more, but she disappears. I awaken to
the moonlight cascading in through the one curtain-less window.
Amala has not stirred. In quiet haste I dress and step out to the

street. An occasional car passes, and already a vendor is setting up his wares. A pack of mangy dogs hunts for scraps of food. The moon is almost full, casting the city in a cloak of silver veneer, illuminating half-demolished buildings, piles of litter, neon signs with missing letters, cars stripped of doors and windows, rats and cats chasing each other, lovers embracing in corners, a bar playing tired music.

The dream is still alive in me, its hope infusing me with energy, vibrancy, optimism, and joy. A car rambles down the street, a loose fender scraping the pavement, music playing softly on the radio. The man in the car waves to me. In the wake of the car's passing, there is silence. In the silence I hear my own voice sing out into the night.

"I'm alive. I'm alive, in this moment. I'm alive, and it is good. It is good. It is good to be alive."

Time has slipped away from me. The first light of dawn and the muezzin calling Gaza to prayer arrive simultaneously. Being without my prayer rug, I remove my shirt and bow to the God of creation and destruction. I bow to the God of abundance and emptiness. I bow to the God of redemption. By whatever name, I pray to that God, and give thanks.

CHAPTER ELEVEN

Raphael

While our family was young, we chose to live in a crowded flat on the fourth floor of a stuffy apartment building. We sacrificed comfort to allow Becky the time and finances to build her grass roots organization, called Women for Women. Later, we satisfied our longing for serenity by moving to a home set in the Jerusalem hills, overlooking the valley and mountains beyond.

Aviel and Tziporah chose to be married here, preferring an intimate wedding ceremony, with Ben Yehuda presiding as rebbe. Among the select guests were members of Ben Yehuda's Kabbalah study group, where Tziporah and Aviel first met. I was also a member of the group, and fondly beheld their evolving relationship.

Tziporah had recently made *aliyah* from Russia, and was struggling to learn Hebrew. She was a quiet and contained young woman with a lightness of being that reminded me of a humming bird. She was brilliant and innocent, incisive and open, and moved with unselfconscious grace that accentuated her delicate, ethereal beauty. Her face had a sculpted refinement, with high, rounded cheekbones, a small but voluptuous mouth, and hazel eyes that held a steady gaze. She'd been enigmatic to me, and even more so in contrast to Becky's earthy, bold demeanor. Becky's first impression of Tziporah was of a fragile young girl who would have difficulty weathering the inevitable storms of life. Her concerns were assuaged, however, when she learned that Tziporah had left everything of her old life behind, in order to make *aliyah* and pursue her calling.

Aviel and Tziporah had shared striking similarities even in outer appearance. Aviel, like Tziporah, had been slender and graceful, with an air of unselfconscious elegance. This surprise son of our middle years had been labeled as gifted even before he entered school. Reading at the age of two, he had a photographic memory, definite psychic capacities, and seemed perpetually wise. Tziporah and Aviel knew that they were intended to be together, and their relationship blossomed and flowered with delightful ease. They harmonized and balanced each other, like practiced dancers who flow together with attuned grace.

Tziporah and our two grandchildren have moved in with us so that we can all participate in childcare. We've bonded even more deeply, and she has now become our beloved daughter. The twins, now close to two years old, are high spirited and delightfully mischievous. They display no trace of the sorrow surrounding their birth.

This day we've chosen to commemorate Aviel's death. Friends and family gather in our home, as the twins, delightfully oblivious to the solemnity of the occasion, chase each other around the living room. Tziporah, tired of admonishing them, squats down on hands and knees, and becomes a giraffe in the animal parade. Soon we are all on hands and knees, and the memorial service transforms into a hilarious cacophony of animal noises. Tziporah informs me that Aviel is clearly present with us, sending a message through his children. *Do not grieve for me any longer. Live fully and freely and joyfully. I am with all of you.*

"*Abba*," she says to me, "would you play your viola for us today? I know that Aviel would love to hear you perform again."

I hesitate. I haven't played the viola since the day of Aviel's murder.

"Please, *abba*, play for us, play for Aviel."

The room holds its breath as if awaiting my response. Even the twins have ceased their frolic. Reluctantly, I agree, leaving the gathering to retrieve the viola from my office, a spacious light-filled room in the back of the house. I remember now that the evening before the bombing, I'd been practicing for a performance that Ibrahim and I would be offering as a fundraiser for a clinic in Gaza. Becky's voice interrupts my reverie. Leaning against the wall, hands folded across her chest, she shows a strange blend of sternness and kindness.

"You don't have to perform, Raphael."

I nod my acknowledgement. "Thank you for not judging me."

"I miss the joy in your music. I miss sharing the joy of life with you."

"Have I been that hard to live with?"

Becky approaches me and wraps her arms around my waist. "I miss him as well, Raphael. I carried him in my womb, and pushed him out of my body, and nursed him. He was a gift to us, and to the world. I can only trust that he lived out his destiny."

The viola is a beautiful instrument with a long and miraculous history. As I hold her between chin and shoulder, it takes only a moment for my body to remember. Her responsiveness surprises and delights me. A fleeting memory of Ibrahim arises, and a spontaneous love for him visits my heart, a moment that lasts as long as it takes to play a single note.

CHAPTER TWELVE

Ibrahim

Raphael has offered me no response. I'm despondent, for nothing else will heal the wound in my heart. Sunrise brings hope, and sunset delivers disappointment. This is no way to live. I must stop the obsession and recover my capacity for patience.

My father had been a patient man, a man who knew how to wait with dignity. A sliver of a memory arises now, sweet and sour like the sliver of ripened orange that was handed to a seven-year-old boy accompanying his father on a journey. I am that young boy, and the man is my father, and we are on an important mission to retrieve medicinal plants in the desert. I'm plump with pride as my father hoists me up onto the back of a passing wagon. I've waited to be old enough to share this moment with my father, and now I'm here, bumping along in the dark, the scent of dried hay filling my nostrils, my father humming softly. My father hands me a flask of water and points to the horizon.

"Look, Ibrahim. We'll arrive just at dawn."

The farmer halts the wagon, and my father lifts me out of the wagon and places me deftly onto the ground. We stand alone on the side of the road, the silence so vast that I can hear the beating of my own heart. My father hands me the burlap sack while he holds the small clipper and a little spade. He starts walking, and I follow behind him, careful not to bump into him when he stops suddenly upon recognizing a plant he wants to retrieve. He shows me how to use clipper and spade, expounding on the medicinal properties of the plant that live sometimes in the root, and sometimes in leaves and flowers. Suddenly, I'm shocked by my father's forceful grip, digging into my shoulder so hard that I have the urge to cry out in pain, but terror stops any sound from emerging.

"Be still, Ibrahim," he whispers. I spot the danger. A viper is lying right in our path and could easily strike. My legs tremble.

"Concentrate all your attention on your breath. Forget everything else."

He grips my shoulder with even more firmness. Knees shaking, I cling to his words, hoping my legs will support me. My life depends on it. Each breath I follow to its pinnacle and down to its emptying, again and again until I'm so concentrated on my breath that time disappears, and even the snake disappears from my thoughts. My father's voice breaks my trance.

"You can relax now, Ibrahim. The snake is gone."

"What just happened?"

"Snakes can only see moving objects. If we had moved, the snake would have struck, but by being totally still, we became invisible to it."

The memory fades as I contemplate the circumstance of my life now. I feel surrounded by snakes ready to strike me, some external while others arise from within my own thought stream. The foundation of my life is shattered, its principles, structures, and assumed purpose gone forever. I'm spinning in circles, the noise, the chaos, the poverty, the frustration, the rage, all trapped within the tiny and overcrowded prison of Gaza. The poison is slowly seeping into my soul. I taste its bitterness, and feel Sayyim's anguish. I staunchly refuse to succumb to hatred, and vengeance, and violence. The devil stole the soul of my son, but it will not take mine. I set a firm intention to practice the stillness and patience learned in the desert at the foot of the viper. Every breath, every feeling, every impulse to act out becomes a snake, becomes the means for me to practice stillness. I become master of my own mind. They can imprison, demean, and torture my body, but inner freedom is mine to choose. I'm free to take any position or no position, a point of view, or no point of view, or all points of view. I'm free to live or die. I'm free to be mired in guilt or remorse, or to let it all go. I am free to sink or soar. The discovery is so radical that I can hardly contain my joy. I feel the urge to shout it into the streets, as a prophet might hail his revelations.

"People, we are not oppressed. No matter who or what imprisons us, if our mind is free, then we are free."

I know enough to keep silent, for others will think me a madman or a traitor to the cause of our collective injustice. There was a time I would have shared such revelations with Raphael. If he never reaches out to me, in the name of our dead sons, I wish for him this freedom.

CHAPTER THIRTEEN

Raphael

The long table running the length of the living room is lavishly decorated with flowers, fruit bowls, wine, grape juice, and little ornaments created by the children. A large silver platter holds the ritual objects used in the Passover ceremony—matzoh, horseradish, salt water, bitter herbs—all representing aspects of the Biblical story of Moses, and the liberation of the Hebrew slaves from the Egyptian Pharaohs.

My brother-in-law, Ron, stands proudly at the head of the table, gazing at the faces of our family and friends. This is his first time leading the Passover service. Ron is a handsome man with unkempt, graying eyebrows, a strong curved Semitic nose, and suntanned skin. His gaze is soft, his face relaxed. Lifting his wine glass to offer the first toast of many, he begins the traditional reading of the *Haggadah*, slowly, carefully articulating each word, glancing often at the children.

"Passover is a celebration of freedom," he explains. "A very long time ago, the cruel Egyptian Pharaoh forced the Israelites into slavery. The prophet Moses was sent by God to liberate his chosen people by performing miracles. One plague after another befell the Egyptian people until the Pharaoh relented, and the Israelites were liberated. After years of wandering in the dessert, God led His people to the Promised Land, the land of milk and honey, where they would settle and multiply. The land that we are living on is that very same land."

The children respond with exclamations, even though they heard the same story last year.

I feel an upwelling of love for Ron and Amelia. Becky and her sister, Amelia, once estranged, are now dear friends. Growing up, Amelia and Becky had little in common besides being smart, assertive, and attractive women. Amelia was ambitious, motivated by the love of power, status, and wealth with all its amenities. Becky worked tirelessly, selflessly for her ideals. Amelia became a sharp-witted corporate lawyer, married Ron, a successful stockbroker, and the two of them indulged in a hedonistic Manhattan lifestyle. Becky made *aliyah*, married me, moved to a modest apartment, and sacrificed material comforts to create an organization to empower women.

The unlikely conversion of Ron and Amelia was precipitated by the horrific terrorist attack of 9/11, and the miracle of Ron's survival. Ron's office had been located in the upper floors of the World Trade Center in New York City. The evening before, a social event had kept both of them out into the early morning hours. Rarely did Ron let himself sleep an extra half hour, but that particular morning he didn't even hear his alarm. He was almost an hour late by the time he hailed a taxi. Preoccupied with how many trades he'd already missed, he was about to admonish the cab driver for going so slowly when he noticed crowds of people sprinting down the street. He smelled the grey acrid smoke before looking up to see the Twin Towers of the World Trade Center in flames. The driver threw open the door to the taxi, and shouted for Ron to run for his life. The scene had such a sense of macabre unreality that Ron wondered if he was dreaming, but the wail of ambulances, fire trucks, horns, screams, brought him into the living nightmare of the present moment. Later, he heard the news. A plane had flown directly into the building in an act of terrorism, and every one of his colleagues had perished in the attack.

Ron had been plagued with nightmares—witnessing his friends in their last agonizing moments of life—and obsessed about why he had been spared. He'd done nothing noteworthy in his life to merit such grace. There had to be an explanation. Whatever intelligence there was in the universe, and by whatever name, it had undoubtedly spared him for a reason, and finding that reason became his personal quest. Amelia, equally stunned and sobered, uncharacteristically suggested a trip to Israel to visit her estranged sister. Ironically they ended up making *aliyah* and using their extensive knowledge and resources to expand the scope and effectiveness of Becky's organization and its mission. For Becky, the reconciliation with her sister meant that she now had an honored place in a family where she had previously been shunned.

Ron completes the formal part of the Passover ritual and leads us in a round of singing and dancing, in joyful celebration of life. Wine glasses are filled again and again, toasts generously offered, and the feast that follows leaves us all satiated and drowsy. The adults sink back in their chairs while the children entertain us with plays, and songs, and games.

Aviel is here with us, offering proof by ringing the wind chimes on a day when the air is holding its breath.

CHAPTER FOURTEEN

Ibrahim

The high-pitched whistling sound pierces the air only seconds before we hear the explosion, its impact shattering the windows, throwing us both to the floor. What follows is an eerie silence, as if the entire universe has gone into temporary shock.

"Are you hurt?" I ask Amala, scrambling to my feet, and offering her a hand. When she is standing we embrace. She is trembling.

"That missile landed in this neighborhood," she exclaims. "What are they doing bombing neighborhoods with children and families? We are caged animals with nowhere to take shelter. They are a cruel and heartless people."

I sweep the glass from the broken windows into a corner. The high-pitched wail of ambulances, the incessant blare of fire trucks, and the angry scream of police cars form a cacophony of sound that gradually dissipates. My skin feels raw, my heart numb. Amala sighs as she slowly bends down to retrieve her knitting needles. She is learning to knit, but the fact that there is no yarn compels her to use the same ball of yarn over and over, knitting and then destroying what she spends all day creating. The soft, hypnotic click of the needles fills me with exasperation and outrage. It emulates far too accurately the situation of our lives.

"Why are you knitting if there is no yarn to make anything?" I finally ask her, hardly bothering to hide my annoyance.

She doesn't look up as she answers, "Some day there will be plenty of yarn, and I want to be prepared."

"Prepared for what, Amala?"

Finally she stops knitting and pays attention to me. "I had a strange dream last night, my husband."

"What was your dream?"

"In the dream I was bitten by a poisonous spider, a black widow. Instead of dying, I became the spider, and my arms spun a huge spider's web that kept expanding until the entire world was suspended inside the web. I was frightened that I had ensnared the world in this web, but instead the world thanked me for spinning it back together."

She returns to knitting. The hypnotic sound of the needles is now tolerable, even comforting. Amala knits, and I stir the chickpea stew, our only staple. Thankfully chickpeas are dense enough to weigh heavy in the stomach, thus curbing the incessant hunger pangs.

Amala knits, and I cradle my oud and strum a song my father taught me when I was a child, a tale of two lovers dancing on a rooftop in the light of the full moon. I sing softly at first, and then the passion of music overtakes me, and transports me back to my father's home, back in time before the occupation and the violence, back before we lost our home, and the olive groves, and our dignity, and our son. Amala's voice suddenly joins my own. Her voice is beautiful and rich and melodious, like thick, raw honey.

CHAPTER FIFTEEN

Raphael

Yitzhak orders four large falafel wraps from the falafel stand right under his window. Two would have been plenty, but Yitzhak is generous. We ascend the dreary stairwell, and pace the length of the windowless hall to the same apartment he has used since I met him. I withhold my usual advice for him to find a cheerier space for his work, knowing his response will be the same as always.

"Our forefathers received their prophecies in caves or mountaintops, and they didn't do so badly."

He unlocks the door and rattles through the kitchen for plates.

"What is this meeting about?" I ask when he finally sits down.

Yitzhak bites into the falafel and wipes his face and beard with a handkerchief that he neatly folds and returns to his pocket.

"I've again been asked to deliver a message to you. This time it's from Gill, my grandson. Do you remember him?"

"Of course I remember Gill. He's the handsome, progressive young man with big visions."

"That is Gill, the son of my son, Michal, the Orthodox rebbe who reads the Torah as the literal and final word of God. Gill and his fiancé, both peace activists, are as challenging to my son as my son is to me."

"Where do I fit into this? What is the message from Gill?"

Yitzhak's smile fades. "Please remember I'm merely the messenger." Ben Yehuda opens his desk drawer, retrieves a small photograph frayed on the edges, and hands it over to me.

"This is Gill and his fiancé. They are getting married in two months."

The photograph displays an attractive young couple, the man's arm around the woman. The man's expression reflects his adoration, and the woman's smile reflects her delight in his adoration. The man is Gill, and the woman wears a Palestinian headdress.

"Her name is Baraka," Yitzhak explains. "Her family is from the West Bank. She's a lovely young woman, beautiful and brilliant. She studies international law."

"Congratulations. Am I to assume that Michal is upset about his son's choice of mate?"

"Not only does he threaten to disown Gill, but he threatens to do everything in his power to obstruct the marriage."

"And her family?"

Yitzhak shakes his head. "They're almost as unreasonable as my son. They're not making threats, but they are pressuring Baraka to change her mind."

"I assume that the threats are not deterring the young couple from their intent to marry."

"Not at all. The marriage date is set, and they've planned a wonderful event that celebrates both cultures, and I will preside at the wedding."

"What is the favor, Yitzhak?"

"Some years ago, Baraka heard you perform, and was enchanted by your music. She felt the magic of it, and is requesting that you bring the same magic to her wedding."

I suddenly feel trapped, cornered. "Be honest with me, Yitzhak. Is she plotting for me and Ibrahim to perform together?"

"She has not said so explicitly, but I assume that is her wish."

"And Ibrahim?"

"I've asked him, and he has agreed to perform no matter what your decision."

"If Baraka knows the situation, why would she do this?"

Yitzhak chuckles. "My future grand daughter-in-law is a wonderful, innocent, sweet, mischievous trouble maker who can't help but stir any pot that needs stirring."

"This pot does not need stirring," I attest with vehemence. "I respectfully decline."

Yitzhak brings his palms together as if in prayer. "I should have refused to be the messenger. I apologize if I disrespected you."

"No need to apologize. We've known each other a long time, and I trust the sincerity of your intentions."

Ben Yehuda laughs. "Which is a lot to say after considering our unusual first meeting."

"Quite the unusual meeting, indeed. I have yet to figure out how my father came to be the recipient of money meant for you to receive. Did you ever solve that mystery?"

Yitzhak, unshakable in almost any situation, looks startled. His eyes widen, his breath catches, and even his hands stop moving.

"Are you all right, Yitzhak?"

"I'm all right, yes. And no. And yes, I think I solved the mystery."

"I'd love to know what you discovered."

Never at a loss for words, Yitzhak hesitates. "If I tell you, I would need your promise to keep it strictly confidential. I would not even want Becky to know."

"Uncharacteristic of you, but of course I promise confidentiality."

Yitzhak sighs. "I don't ask for my sake, Raphael. I'm afraid it could impact my family in ways that are too unpredictable to chance. Are you sure you want to know?"

"Yes, I want to know. Whatever it is, I want to hold it with you, as you hold so much with me."

Yitzhak nods. "Think about it, Raphael. You know that my mother was a prisoner, and I was born in the camp. Why was it that we were both allowed to survive and not sent to the gas chamber?"

Suddenly the pieces begin to fall together. "Someone needed to keep both of you alive."

"Yes, and that someone had to have power and authority to make that decision. Whenever I asked my mother about my father, she looked terrified and would divulge nothing. Likely he had threatened to harm her, or me, if she ever exposed his identity. The only thing she ever divulged about him was the fact that he was a doctor." Yitzhak reaches for his handkerchief to wipe the perspiration from his brow. "Are you making the connection yet, Raphael?"

"You mean that a Nazi doctor saved my father's life? Do you think your father and this doctor are the same person?" Yitzhak nods. "Then why of all places was he in Israel?"

"I think that he had the audacity, or the genius to make Israel his home. And I surmise that he kept us alive to use us as his cover."

"Apparently he had some feeling for you if he wanted you to receive his money. He took a risk to make that happen. And he did save my father's life."

"Yes, I'm guessing he was a very conflicted man, a very tortured man."

"And you are a man of such compassion and principle, it is hard to fathom."

"I've grappled with this for some time, how to not simply reject this tortured and horrible man who sired me by using my mother. But sire me he did, and I owe him my life in that way. I've walked a fine line between compassion and revulsion, and finally I've learned to practice radical acceptance." He studies his palms carefully, turning them over and over. "I must bow to God and hope that He, or She, knows better than me. Or maybe God, like Baraka, is a very mischievous trickster."

CHAPTER SIXTEEN

Ibrahim

Amala has barely spoken to me for days. She pretends to be engrossed in her knitting—doing and undoing what she has done. I know my wife. When she is angry with me she shuts herself away like a timid mouse hiding in a corner. It would be less torturous, I tell her, if she were to explode like her sister-in-law.

"She explodes, and then her husband beats her. Is that what you want?"

"How can you compare me to her husband? I've never beaten you, and I never would even raise a hand to you. Is that not true?"

"It is true," she concedes.

"Talk to me, Amala. That is all I ask."

Amala sighs and takes her time wrapping the yarn into a ball. "Keep your voice down, husband. Everybody is eager for morsels of gossip."

"Talk to me," I repeat, but more softly. "What is the problem?"

She turns toward me, her face softening, her eyes glistening with tears. "The problem is that people are talking about you. They say you ingratiate yourself with them, and abandon the cause of our people."

I'm shocked. "What is this about, Amala?"

"People know that you've agreed to perform at an Israeli wedding, and this following the latest round of attacks."

My outrage is escalating, but it is no longer directed at Amala. "Anybody who speaks like that is ignorant. They don't even have the facts right. This is a mixed wedding, not an Israeli wedding, but even if it were an Israeli wedding, for the sake of my friend, I would perform. He's done nothing but support our people and our cause, and now they turn around and complain that I'm performing at his grandson's wedding? They speak from ignorance."

"People are saying that you are desecrating the memory of our martyred son, that you disgrace our family."

"Tell these gossipers to find the courage to talk with me directly."

Amala reaches her hands out to me. "You're right, my husband. I respect what you are doing. You are brave, and I've been the coward letting myself be swayed by petty ignorance. I want you to play, and I will support you."

The *muzzein's* megaphone intrudes on our moment of intimacy. She releases me, and without prayer rug, I supplicate myself on the floor of our home.

"I'm going to help my sister this afternoon," she says, when the prayer is complete. "The wedding is soon. I know you need time to practice."

"Thank you for understanding," I say, and then suddenly, unplanned, the words spill out. "Amala, will you come with me to the wedding?"

Her eyes meet mine and hold my gaze. For a moment, time slips into the past. Amala appears to me as a young girl of sixteen, the two of us sitting in uncomfortable silence in the parlor of her parent's home, pretending to enjoy the powdered dates and fresh squeezed fruit juice.

"Do you want to be here?" I asked her, awkward as any young man might be.

"I do not," she declared quietly, but boldly. "It is not personal to you. I simply want the right to choose my own husband."

"And I want the right to choose my own wife." We burst into spontaneous laughter, and our relieved parents entered the room to witness us agreeing to the marriage.

"Will you come with me to this wedding?" I ask again. "I want you by my side. I need you by my side."

Still holding my gaze, she nods. "Yes, I'll come with you, and now I'll leave you to practice."

The oud is resting in a corner of our sleeping room, standing upright and wrapped in a thick blanket. This oud had been my father's favorite, made from dark colored wood that reminds me of chocolate. Sitting cross-legged on the edge of our sleeping mat, I gently remove the blanket enfolding her. I feel, and then see the long crack running down the length of her spine. The violations are as if to my own body. Opening my mouth to howl in outrage, no sound emerges, and yet I know what I need to do. This instrument is badly damaged, but with highly skillful hands it can possibly be saved. Those hands belong to a man in the Old City of Jerusalem, a man who has repaired Raphael's viola. Raphael calls him a miracle worker. My oud needs a miracle worker. Reluctant as I am to ask Raphael for help, on behalf of my father's oud, I have no choice. I will need Ben Yehuda to intercede right away. The wedding is close at hand, and I can hardly imagine finding the courage to perform without the support of my father's presence through the medium of this instrument.

CHAPTER SEVENTEEN

Raphael

Cradling a bundle in his arms, a look of deep concern creasing his face, Ben Yehuda stands at my door.

"May I come in?"

I step aside. "Who, or what, are you carrying?"

He places the bundle on my dining room table, a thick grey blanket wrapped around an odd-shaped object.

"It's broken," he says, "and you are the only person I know who might be able to help."

"What is broken?"

Carefully, tenderly, Ben Yehuda removes the blanket to reveal an oud that I instantly recognize as belonging to Ibrahim. Many times I've held this instrument, and I know that it is precious and irreplaceable to Ibrahim, his last vestige of connection with his cherished father. The oud lies motionless, wounded on my kitchen table, crying out to be made whole.

"How did this happen?" I ask, carefully picking up the instrument and examining the long crack running down its spine. I'm startled for a moment as the body of the oud shape shifts in my mind's eye into Ibrahim's body. I shake my head to ward off the vision.

"Ibrahim is certain that it was done intentionally, an act of sabotage."

"Sabotage? Why would anybody want to sabotage Ibrahim?"

"Because some people feel that his agreeing to perform at the wedding is a betrayal of the Palestinian cause. They judge him to be playing into the hands of the enemy."

"The enemy?"

"Yes, Raphael, that would be you and me, and all Israeli occupiers. Do you think it is repairable?"

"You mean the oud, right?"

Yitzhak laughs. "For today, let's keep life simple. Yes, I mean the oud. Is it repairable?"

"I would trust the expertise of only one person, a man named Yael who is a master instrument maker. His violins are considered among the best quality in the world. I met him when I needed a repair to my viola. If it is repairable, he's the man who can do it."

"But will he do it?"

"I'll call him right away. He's a man who cares nothing for politics. His heart is moved by music and the quality of the instruments that produce it."

"Then I did right by bringing this to you."

I nod, understanding the implications of his question. "You did right, Yitzhak. You just about always do right, unconventional as your actions often seem."

Ben Yehuda sighs. "Thank you, Raphael. You're a good man."

"Am I a good man? Wouldn't a good man accept the invitation offered by your grandson? Wouldn't a good man shake the hand of reconciliation when offered him?"

"If you did that now, it would be a travesty, a concession to some idea of righteousness you think you should uphold. Better you do nothing than act on anything that does not come directly from your own truth."

"How did you come to be so wise, Yitzhak? Most people in this world, including myself apparently, adhere to their positions as though they are life rafts on a turbulent sea."

CHAPTER EIGHTEEN

Ibrahim

"Sakinah—radiant and splendid Goddess, spirit of tranquility—through the prophet Muhammad You have graced all true believers. You have bestowed life upon me, and for this I offer praise, for all that You have given me, great and small, sweet and bitter, pleasure and pain. Beholding the world, I behold Your face in everything and when that is so, I bow in true humility, my heart aflame with love. How can we pursue counterfeit treasures when Your splendor is everywhere? I hear You calling to me, beloved Sakinah, that I might serve You, and I am willing. I ask only that You tell me how to serve You best. If it is my voice you want, then I will sing for You. I ask only that I be allowed to serve You, for that is my true joy and delight.

CHAPTER NINETEEN

Raphael

Wearing a shimmering emerald green evening gown and matching emerald earrings, Becky dances from the bedroom, her long streaked gray hair curving gently around her neck.

"You are as alluring to me in that dress as you were in overalls."

She laughs, and moves her hips seductively. "Are you tempted?"

In response, I wrap my arms around her waist. "Is this an invitation?"

She playfully pushes me away. "It's an invitation to dance with me at the wedding."

"Are you trying to make me feel guilty?"

"Not my style, sweetheart. We've respected each other's differences for decades now. I'm simply reminding you of what you'll be missing. You could be out on that dance floor with the most beautiful older woman in the crowd."

"I hope to have other opportunities to do just that."

"Life may get very busy for me after the wedding."

"Are you disappointed that I'm not coming?"

"I respect you, and yes, I would certainly rather you be there."

She disappears into the bedroom and returns wearing jeans and a tee shirt. "Raphael, seeing Ibrahim will be no easier for me than it would be for you. I'm not doing this out of some high-minded principle."

"Then why are you attending?"

"Because I have only two choices in life. The first is to close my heart to the pain of life, but then something in me dies. The second is to open to the pain, open to the heart of this world groaning in anguish. The only way I get to love fully is to let my heart break open."

"My heart has also been broken open, Becky."

"I wasn't saying anything about you, Raphael. Every person's path is different."

Becky reaches out to me, and we embrace. The familiar feel of her body reassures me.

"You are not only beautiful, but wise, but I still want to take you dancing."

Becky's moon face softens and smiles. "You lead, and I'll follow."

"That would hardly be your nature, sweetheart."

"I know I can be a stubborn idealist."

"Such a martyr I am for putting up with it."

She laughs, and the tension between us dissipates. "I'm sure you won't be the least surprised to hear that I have a very big project on the horizon."

"What kind of project, Becky?"

"It's a knitting project."

"I didn't know you were even interested in knitting. How big could a knitting project be? A sweater, two sweaters, a hundred sweaters?"

"No, the knitting project is just one scarf."

"Rebecca Rabinovitz, you are an endless source of surprises. I would have been less shocked if you had told me you were planning to become an astronaut preparing for your voyage to the moon."

CHAPTER TWENTY

Ibrahim

Ben Yehuda uses his connections, or perhaps his magic, to move us uneventfully through the checkpoint at the border between Israel and Gaza. He is driving, with Amala and me sitting anxiously in the back seat, our hands clutching. The young soldier with a crew cut and tight-fitting uniform studies my work papers, his face blank from practiced neutrality.

"You are a musician?"

I nod.

"Where are you performing? How long will you be here? Where is your instrument? Is this your wife?"

His voice, like his face, is officially neutral and not hostile. I answer his questions succinctly, and he waves us on. Ben Yehuda steers the car into a dusty, crowded lot that serves as a meeting place for those crossing in either direction. A young woman in khakis, her hair a mass of auburn curls approaches us. Aside from the hair, she has a strong resemblance to Ben Yehuda. She deftly slides in beside Yitzhak, and places a kiss on his cheek before turning to introduce herself.

"Hi, I'm Tamar, the sister of the groom. Welcome to Jerusalem."

Tamar's features don't compose a particularly attractive face, with a nose too large and front teeth slightly protruded, but her friendliness and buoyant energy make her appealing.

"You'll be my guests," she says. "I have an extra bedroom. Ibrahim, I picked up your oud today. I've been instructed to tell you that the repair was successful, and that Yael thinks it's one of the finest sounding ouds he has ever played."

My heart leaps in hearing her words. "I'm so relieved, and thank you for retrieving it."

"Thank you both for coming. Your presence means so much to my brother and Baraka. Baraka thinks you are some kind of miracle worker."

Her words shock me. "I offer only my music. If there are miracles, they are not of my doing."

"Dubaal, the percussionist, will come over to meet you in the morning. He's the cousin of Baraka, and rumor has it he's an excellent musician. You can have the apartment to yourselves tomorrow, to practice."

She turns to Amala. "Rebecca wants to meet with you. I'd love to show you my restaurant, and then we can drive together over to her office."

Amala nods. "I'm grateful."

I'm again surprised. "Have you and Rebecca been in communication?"

"We've spoken," she says abruptly.

Ben Yehuda turns down a side street and parks the car. Tamar and Ben Yehuda insist on carrying our two bags.

"Gill and Baraka are coming over for dinner tonight," Tamar informs us.

The apartment feels spacious, furnished sparingly.

"It's kind of Zen," she remarks, noticing me looking around. "I mean Buddhist. I'm a Buddhist, and a lesbian."

Ben Yehuda's laughter puts us all at ease. "My poor son must be agonizing over his children falling so far from the tree."

Tamar is exasperated. "My father, your son, deserves all the suffering he brings upon himself, and other people. He should stop acting as if he has exclusive knowledge of God's plan."

Ben Yehuda stops laughing. "I know it's not funny for you, Tamar. It just baffles me how your mother and I could have a son who became an Orthodox rebbe."

Amala and I exchange glances, as both of us have pondered the same question about Sayyim.

Ben Yehuda leaves, and Amala and Tamar busy themselves in the kitchen. I'm happy to have time to reacquaint myself with the oud. It is now housed in a hard case with a lock to protect it from damage. Tentatively holding her, I study the body, noting the intricate detail of repair that Yael has done. He's rebuilt her entire back. Tentative at first, my fingers soon gain confidence, as sound emerges rich and resonant. My fingers dance, my feet tap the rhythm, and my voice soars. Waves of rapture pulsate through me until a voice startles me out of my transcendent state.

"Your music is beautiful."

Opening my eyes, I see her leaning in the doorway, with hands folded across her chest, her long, slender body accentuated by tight fitting jeans. Unbound, her dark hair flows down her shoulders. Her eyes are laughing. For a moment, I have the strange sense that I've met her before, but the sensation soon dissipates.

"I look forward to your performance, but at this moment I'm inviting you to join us at dinner."

"You must be Baraka."

"And you must be Ibrahim," she says, smiling. "Gill and I are so grateful that you'll be performing at our wedding. Many years ago when I was a young girl, I heard you and Raphael perform, and it was magical, transporting, intoxicating. I never forgot it." Closing her eyes for a brief moment, that young girl appears. "We need magic at this wedding, Ibrahim. That is what made me think of you and Raphael, and when I found out that Gill's father knew both of you, I took it as a sign that we would be able to transcend all the obstacles we might encounter."

"I'm humbled by your words, Baraka. I'm merely a musician, but I offer you what I can."

Baraka smiles. "Your presence and your music are a lot to offer."

Entering the room, Gill strides over to greet me with a hug. He is a man with a large presence and a surprisingly slight stature, his slim body appearing almost sculpted, his eyes a penetrating gray, his face well-proportioned and handsome.

"Thank you for coming," he says. "I'm honored that you've agreed to perform. You've made Baraka a happy woman."

Baraka's laughter is warm. "No my darling, you've made me a happy woman, and Ibrahim has made me a happier woman."

She reaches for his hand as Tamar's voice beckons us to dinner. "Tonight you are all my guests," she says emphatically, placing a soup bowl in front of each of us. "You sit, I serve. This is my famous cucumber-yogurt-mint soup with pistachios. It is a favorite at my restaurant."

"Tamar is chef and owner of what the critics consider the two top restaurants in Israel, one in Jerusalem, and the other in Tel Aviv."

Baraka is clearly proud of her sister-in-law, and for good reason if the soup is any indication. Freshly baked crusty bread dipped in spiced olive oil accompanies it.

Baraka turns to face Amala. "Thank you both for being our guests at the wedding. I'm honored and delighted to have you, and I'm most grateful for the support. Our families are anything but supportive, with the notable exception of my sister-in-law and my grandfather."

Gill interjects. "However we want to be absolutely clear with you that we don't know what to expect. Everything might go smoothly, without glitches, and we'll all just have a wonderful time, or it may not. Our families are determined to make trouble.

We've hired a dozen security guards, but things happen. If at any point you feel it is right to back out, please rest assured that we will support you in every way possible." Gill pauses, taking a long and deep breath.

"Why did you invite us?" I ask. "Knowing our presence might stir up even more trouble."

Gill takes some time before responding. "I'm sure life will call upon us to make many compromises and sacrifices, but I don't want to compromise at our wedding. At least not because of the close-minded ignorance of other people."

Tamar rises to clear the dishes, and effortlessly delivers the main course, a steaming lamb stew over rice. "This is a Moroccan dish," she explains. "I confess to having had the chef prepare this for us." For a few moments we savor the rich blend of spices and textures. "I hope you both will be guests at my restaurant before you leave."

"The food is delicious, Tamar," says Amala. "It would be my honor to dine at your restaurant."

"That's wonderful. After the wedding is over, I'll arrange for a dinner."

I look more closely at Amala. Her large dark eyes are alert but unafraid. Her mouth is soft, the rhythm of her breath relaxed. Then I see it, the one tear that travels all the way down the contour of her cheek before she wipes it away. I know that Sayyim's entire life and death are contained in that tear. The table is silent.

"I will perform at your wedding, in honor of my wife and my son, who lost his way."

Everybody exhales at once.

"*Mazeltov*," exclaims Tamar raising her wine glass. "Now to complete our meal with my fantastic flaming flan."

CHAPTER TWENTY-ONE

Raphael

The sun has barely peeked over the horizon, and Becky is already in motion.

"I have a long day of meetings before attending the wedding tonight. Don't wait up for me." Kissing me perfunctorily, she heads toward the door with several large bags hoisted on each shoulder.

"Do you want some help?"

"I'm fine," she says, hesitating as if searching for more words.

"Are you angry with me?" I ask.

"I'm not angry, Raphael. I'm just missing you, or maybe we've both been changed in different ways by everything that's happened."

Her words disturb me, because they are true. "I'm missing me as much as you are, Becky. I've lost part of myself, and I don't have any idea what to do about it."

Becky places the bags on the floor and we hug, a warm, long, soft hug that brings tears for both of us.

"Aviel wouldn't want it this way," she says.

"I know that, sweetheart. Whatever is holding me back is no longer about Aviel. It is bigger, more existential. I'm grappling with a question I don't even know how to ask."

"I understand, and of course I don't understand at all because we are different people, no matter how close we are."

She hoists her bags onto her shoulders, refusing my help. "I can do it, Raphael."

Her words again sadden me. "I know you can do it. Sometimes I just want to help."

"Do your part, Raphael. That's all I ask. Now I really have to leave."

Becky waves, smiles, and is gone, leaving me agitated. Do my part? What does she mean by that remark? Resolving to start the day on a better note, I dress in shorts and sneakers, and head out of the door to jog along the slopes and valleys of the neighborhood. The air is crisp, the sun bright on the horizon. I'm looking forward to this day of solitude and reflection, and a renewed engagement with the manuscript.

I've run my full loop just as the sun is rising fast in the eastern sky. I shower and enjoy a light breakfast of fruit and kefir. The valley is lit up, the sun is reflecting off roofs, and the birds are busily chirping. My heart feels lighter. Settling into my favorite chair on the patio and preparing to engage with the manuscript, I'm interrupted by the grating buzz of the doorbell. Dressed in a poorly fitting tuxedo, Ben Yehuda greets me with a smile.

"I apologize for the impromptu visit, but may I come in for a moment, Raphael?"

"Of course you can come in, but what are you doing here today of all days? Is anything wrong?"

"No, no, nothing has gone wrong yet, but I have concerns that I would appreciate discussing with you."

"Let's sit on the patio. Find your favorite chair, and I'll make coffee."

Yitzhak sighs. "Thank you, Raphael. I'm anticipating a stressful day, and I appreciate a few moments of respite with a good friend."

I return with a tray of coffee and fresh pastries. "This is an unexpected delight. I thought you would be preoccupied with the wedding."

Ben Yehuda chuckles. "I'm completely preoccupied with the wedding, which is why I'm here."

"Please tell me you are not here to convince me to attend."

Ben Yehuda shakes his head vehemently. "I told you once and now again, I have absolutely no position on whether or not you attend this wedding, whether or not you ever mention Ibrahim's name again."

"I appreciate hearing that from you."

"And I mean every word of it. Truthfully, I'm tired of being in the role of mediator and peacemaker. I would far prefer to celebrate my grandson's wedding than to try and appease two irate and irrational families, both of whom are so intent on maintaining their righteous positions that they are making everybody else miserable. This should be a joyful celebration of the union of two lovely people."

"You don't deserve to be stuck in the middle of this."

"None of us deserves to be handed problems we did nothing to create, but it seems that we spend most of our lives doing just that. We are handed problems, or we create problems for future generations to resolve."

I listen sympathetically, but Yitzhak isn't here simply to rant. The reason will emerge.

"Raphael, may I ask a favor of you?"

"Of course."

"Would you play the viola? I'm in need of comfort and inspiration."

I play the viola for him, and for one brief moment I remember the magic that arose when Ibrahim and I performed. Baraka was right about that. When I'm done, Yitzhak stands reluctantly, gestures his gratitude, and departs.

CHAPTER TWENTY-TWO

Ibrahim

Tamar and I have spent the afternoon loading her car with boxes of specialty foods and gifts enclosed in wrapping paper that looks more like art than a covering to be discarded. My oud, and the pillows and props for my performance, are placed last in the overly stuffed back compartment.

"Where is he?" Tamar gestures her exasperation. "The food should not be sitting in the car for this long." She glances at her watch. "I'll give him fifteen minutes, and then we are leaving."

I nod sympathetically. "I know your grandfather. None of his actions, even his lateness, are arbitrary. If he's late, he has a good reason."

"That may be true, Ibrahim, but the laws of time are immutable. As the saying goes, time waits for no man, not even my beloved grandfather."

Thankfully, Yitzhak walks through the door, winded and flustered just as Tamar is spinning alternative plans.

"Where have you been? If we don't leave this moment, we'll all be late. Amala and Becky are already at the wedding."

"I'm ready," he says. "I apologize. I had some important last minute tasks to complete."

The elevator takes its time ascending. Tamar is mumbling under her breath, counting the seconds. Ben Yehuda reaches out and places a hand gently on her shoulder.

"Trust me, we'll arrive just at the right time. As long as you are not pulled over for speeding, my dear granddaughter, we'll be fine.

"Have I ever been in an accident?"

"None that I know of."

"None, period," she asserts. "I'll be careful. This day has enough potential drama without me adding to it."

The car is parked on the curb in front of the building. Despite my offer to ride in the back, Ben Yehuda wedges himself in beside the boxes. I climb in the front and Tamar wastes no time cutting sharp corners and zooming down the highway. Finally, to my relief she exits and slows down as the road narrows and ascends.

"Get ready for the view," she remarks. "We're driving toward one of the most exclusive developments in Jerusalem. The wedding is being held in a mansion owned by the parents of Gill's friend, a high tech wizard with a heart."

The car groans up a steep incline that finally plateaus. Parking on the side of the road, we take a moment to admire the unimpeded view of the Jerusalem valley, and the soft, rounded hills beyond. Wedging ourselves back in the car we drive a short distance until the road ends abruptly at a rod iron gate. Three men dressed in khaki uniforms spring to attention as we approach.

"They are the valet service," Tamar explains. "And like all the hired help, they are trained security guards as well."

Tamar waves to the men, who recognize her and open the gate. She edges the car smoothly to the far end of a circular crushed white stone driveway that looks like a crescent moon. Several attendants hurry over to help unload the car, but I insist on carrying the oud, which lends me some sense of purpose in this strange and intimidating world. Fluted columns and a robust fountain overflowing into a marble basin, flowers and fruit trees, and rose petals strewn upon the walkway, offer an invitation into a world I can only glimpse. Stepping into the spacious foyer, we are greeted by another uniformed man, well practiced in disguised vigilance.

"Stay alert," he whispers to me through his smile.

Ben Yehuda has disappeared, but Tamar still accompanies me. "This place is a cross between a museum and a palace," she remarks. "I still think I like my Zen lifestyle, but maybe I'm just envious. You all right if I go and take care of things?"

I nod, but as Tamar walks away, I'm seized by panic, as if I've been left in an alien world. I hear someone call my name. Baraka is hurrying toward me, her arms outstretched in greeting. She is dressed in a long, intricately embroidered gown tied with a red sash. She moves with easeful grace, but as she approaches, I note the strain in her face.

"You cannot imagine how happy I am to see you, Ibrahim." She laughs softly. "Your presence here should hardly bring me any sense of comfort, but it does."

"Has anything happened?"

Her smile is strained. "Both extended families are here. Gill's father has brought half his congregation to stage a protest. My family is acting with its usual hysteria. None of them are being allowed entrance, and don't think it doesn't hurt that none of them can step beyond their self-centeredness to celebrate this day with us."

"I'm so sorry, Baraka. You both deserve better."

Baraka smiles. "For some inexplicable reason, I feel there will be magic here tonight."

"I hope you're right, Baraka."

Her expression changes suddenly. "I might be sentimental, Ibrahim, but I'm also a realist. If you feel any sense of threat, if your instincts tell you not to perform, please listen to yourself. I mean that with complete sincerity, and I told my cousin the same thing."

"I will take care of myself, I promise."

"Rebecca, and Tziporah, and your wife are waiting for you to join them. I'll take your oud and lock it up for maximum security."

Reluctantly, I hand over my instrument. "When will we be performing?"

"We'll have the marriage ceremony right away, just to make sure it happens, and then dinner will be served. After that, the night is yours."

I've come to the moment I've been dreading. How will Rebecca and Tziporah react to me? Will I be received with anger, disgust, indignation? How will I respond? I hardly have time to think about it before I'm face to face with Becky, who has come seeking me. We embrace with no thought of etiquette or enmity. She is trembling and her vulnerability calls forth my own sorrow. I'm weeping, and she is weeping, and our tears intermingle.

"We've needed to mourn our sons together," she whispers. "We've needed each other in order to heal."

"Yes," I whisper, "yes."

"Come," she says, taking my hand. "We have a place at the table for you. Let's join this celebration of love."

Transfigured by the holiness of the occasion, Ben Yehuda raises his arms, imploring the divine to bless this worthy couple as they recite their vows of matrimony. Gill and Baraka are now married according to the legalities of state, and the sacraments of both religions. Voices sing praise, wine glasses are filled and emptied and filled again, rose petals are joyously strewn, and love scents the air with intoxicating fragrances. Amala reaches tenderly for my hand, Tziporah weeps softly, and Rebecca and Tamar swirl around the dance floor.

Even the food is intoxicating: minty cucumber soup, lavender sorbet, rosemary couscous, pomegranate pudding, marzipan pastries, cardamom bread, slow cooked and tender lamb stew, pungent feta cheese, and green olives and fig spread.

The crowd is now ripe for music, and Dubaal is already on stage tapping lightly on his drum, offering a subtle invitation to pay attention: something important is about to happen. My fingers ache to play, and my voice is ready to sing out the passion pulsating through me. I take my place on stage next to Dubaal. My oud is awaiting me, and I hold her close, strumming her softly until Dubaal and I exchange the signal, and we both cease playing. The silence is charged with anticipation. Allowing the energy to build until just the right moment, we burst forth with music. The guests shout in delight and jump to their feet to join the line dance led by the newlyweds. The long line slithers like a snake between tables and chairs.

Nobody has the slightest hint of foreboding. But I feel their presence. Hidden among the guests are the vipers, and they are about to strike.

Gunshots, shrieking, people running frantically, chaotically, knocking over tables, chairs, each other, desserts, champagne glasses, flowers. Dubaal shakes me and shouts for me to run, but I don't run. I don't move off my cushion. The thought occurs to me that perhaps I've died. Perhaps this is why I'm so calm. If I'm dead, then my oud has accompanied me into death, and all I can do is play music. And if I'm still alive, and this is the last moment of my life, I will die playing music, my heart on fire with passion, and so I play. I play because a lover must express love, a musician must play music, and life cries out to be lived.

CHAPTER TWENTY-THREE

Raphael

The manuscript still remains unopened on my desk, my plan to work with it having gone awry. With renewed resolve, I move my fingers slowly over the surface of the leather binder, each blemish and scratch a memory of those who came before me. One simple motion is all it would take, and yet I find myself unable to open the binder. My inability is inexplicable, and disturbing, like my inability to respond to Ibrahim, or attend the wedding. I'm a stranger to myself. What has become of the impassioned young boy bedazzled by the shimmering radiance of Her countenance? Just open the binder, I command myself aloud, but my hand will not move.

Exasperated, I push the chair away from my desk, my eyes alighting on the viola, remembering my morning with Yitzhak, and the unobtrusive way he offered me a healing. Inevitably my thoughts turn toward the wedding, and to Ibrahim, his strong, passionate voice traveling the distance to reach me. The voice that I've known to tumble the walls even of those with hardened hearts and closed minds. Is he playing now? Is Becky, in her emerald dress and earrings, swirling about the dance floor?

Have the families of the bride and groom surrendered to the joy of the moment?

The viola comes to rest easily under my chin. Closing my eyes, imagining myself at the wedding with all the people I love, the music arises so spontaneously that I wonder if I'm the player, or the instrument, or the music, or if there is any difference at all. Aviel's presence is suddenly and unmistakably here, at the edge of my perception, but here. He has a message for me, and I listen to his words.

The Cup of Fortune, abba. Ask the Cup your question.

I follow the ritual with meticulous attention, posing my question three times. *Show me how to complete the mission. Show me how best to serve You.* The leaves are settled now, and I peer inside, hoping for revelation, but I see nothing beyond the chaos of leaves hugging the sides, leaves afloat in the shallow pool of remaining tea. My breath catches. I stave off the hurt of disappointment, the sting of failure. There is nothing to offer hope that I might move through this ever-deepening quagmire of doubt. I can do nothing. I am nothing. The truth of this reverberates through me, like a tuning fork, and in this moment all my self-importance, even the self- importance of my suffering, dissolves. This sense of nothing shifts from despair to a deep, spacious emptiness, a quietude undisturbed by the usual constant stream of questions, conflicts and doubts. The truth is that I am nothing. Suddenly, I simply am.

The light is faint at first, like the afterglow of sunset on the mirrored surface of a lake. Has Becky arrived home so early? Is there a fire? Have I forgotten to turn off the stove? The light intensifies, and undulates and swirls in chaotic patterns that finally coalesce into the form of a woman. Her skin radiates light and Her feet are not quite touching the floor. And when She speaks, Her voice is like wind chimes in a gentle breeze.

"Greetings to you, my beloved Raphael, my devoted mission keeper. You have called Me, and I have answered your call."

Overwhelmed by the power and beauty of Her countenance, I stumble with words. "Beloved Goddess, I know not how to proceed, how I may best serve You."

"My dearest Raphael, I am not asking that you serve Me, but that you allow Me to serve you, for in that way I am served. I wish only that peace and happiness be restored to this splendid world that I created in the time before time. I wish only that you who inhabit this world awaken from the spell that was cast upon you by those of selfish intent who long ago took advantage of you by weakening the harmonic bonds of love that ensured abundance, peace, and well-being. When I was forced into exile, I left a spark of My divinity in each of you, hoping that it would serve to guide you toward your own liberation."

"What is the nature of the world that You created?"

"In your archetypal memory, it is what you call heaven. You think heaven is the world after death, but it is the true world that is remembered in the collective memory." Her light flickers momentarily, and then She returns. "My world is a plethora of love's expressions and forms, where the divine infuses materiality, and materiality is an expression of the divine. This is how I dreamed you. Every creature large and small is a unique expression of -life's effulgence, in harmony with its own nature and with the All. This is how I dreamed you, for when each creature is in harmony with the All, then there is no suffering or disease, no strife or war or hunger. This is not heaven, my dear Raphael. This is how I dreamed you. This is the true condition. This is why I must return, to restore My original vision, and to make it so again."

As She speaks Her light begins to fade until She disappears into the dark.

"Goddess," I cry out. "What can I do to help?"

She speaks from far away. "Do your part, my dear one. Do what you know you must do."

CHAPTER TWENTY-FOUR

Raphael

How beautiful the world appears in this moment, even as it struggles to awaken. I've also struggled to awaken, for myself, and for the world that I'm here to serve. I've struggled, doubted, fallen into despair, and ultimately prevailed. I'm ready now to turn toward the manuscript with the level of consciousness needed to complete the decoding. Rushing into my study, I'm prepared to open the binder, but the binder is not where I left it. Panicking, I shuffle through my desk, until I spot the envelope. Calming myself, I open it to discover one thin sheet of paper and two sentences.

You have served me well, Raphael. The manuscript has returned to its source.

I'm ready to leave now, with viola in hand. It is time to dance with Becky in her emerald earrings, time to play music, time to bow to my friend, Ibrahim, and ask for his forgiveness, time to thank Yitzhak for his loving wisdom. It is time to stand before each of my ancestors, because of whose courage and wisdom I stand here now, and honor them all.

I'm all set to leave, having just splashed on Becky's favorite aftershave, when I hear a shattering sound coming from the kitchen. I'm confused more than disturbed. There are no earth tremors today. Has someone entered unbidden? Turning on the light, I spot shards of porcelain scattered all over the floor. Only the handle remains intact. The sight of that ugly, misshapen, mysterious magical Cup strewn all over the floor, having chosen its own demise, evokes a bout of hysterical laughter and joy. I sweep all the shards into a corner. Tomorrow I'll put the pieces back together, not as a Cup but as an exquisite wall hanging, each shard representing a piece of our past, lifted up into holiness.

EPILOGUE

Israel
Rebecca

More than fifty of us have crowded into the courtroom. Dressed in a tight navy blue pantsuit, my sister moves around the floor, her stiletto heels sounding like a flamenco dancer as she cross- examines Mr. Ezra Bloom, who looks bored with the whole endeavor.

"Please answer my question, sir. On what grounds are you refusing to allow yarn to be shipped from New Zealand to Israel? When has yarn been placed on the list of dangerous weapons?"

The courtroom ripples with laughter.

"Yes, there are many shipments, sir. That we are not disputing. I'm sure that you are cognizant of our global knitting project, and this project requires extensive shipments of yarn."

"No, sir, the defendants are not using the yarn for commercial purposes. In fact, there is no money exchanged at all. The defendants are using the yarn to knit the world back together. Have you noticed that it's a bit frayed?"

Even the judge has a good chuckle.

An internet campaign was initiated on our behalf, and close to a million signatures collected protesting the withholding of the gift of yarn sent from our generous New Zealand sisters. We won the appeal, and now we have a steady influx of yarn from all over the world.

We hadn't expected our knitting project to go global, but to our surprise, women began flying in from all corners of the world, begging to join our knitting circles. Our organization, Women for Women, has now taken the name, People for People, as men join our knitting circles, working right alongside us.

Let me be clear. We're not rebelling, or staging a protest. We're not rattling sabers, or raising our fists, or shouting obscenities, or trying to bring anything or anybody down. We're not trying to make trouble, or confront the establishment. We are simply, joyously knitting the world back together.

We are, however, weary of the politics, the bluster, the fear mongers and power mongers, the hypocrisy, the self-serving extremists, the righteous talk of this God and that God, and all the killing that has been justified in the name of whatever God, the endless cycles of violence and retaliation, the name calling and blaming, the broken promises. We are not interested in erecting more walls, or engaging in politics, or economics, or the so-called justice system. They all have a way of making sure their own interests are served, and that nothing fundamentally changes.

We respect the rights and rules of the establishment. We never obstruct traffic, or take over religious sites, or places of commerce. We knit in public parks, donated lawn spaces, median strips on highways, rooftops, subway stations, train stations, airports, mountaintops, and even elevators. Thousands of businesses now sponsor knitting circles, and proudly provide us with sustenance and childcare.

The point is that we are everywhere. In fact, women (and men) in other countries have been inspired to organize their own knitting circles. In some countries women are using grasses or bark, seaweed, hemp, shaved bamboo, and vines instead of yarn. Women in many countries cannot gather without risking their lives, or the lives of their families. We have all pledged to knit in their stead, each woman carrying a sign on her back with the name of the country whose women she represents. We carry them with us, quite literally. The next phase of our knitting project is joining all our scarves together. Can you imagine a scarf that encircles the world? We can and we intend to make it happen.

The media insists on calling us a powerful, unstoppable global movement, and giving us the somewhat demeaning but endearing label of Women's International Knit-In. Nobody can quite believe how a handful of women sitting together and knitting has become a global phenomenon. When interviewed, we shrug our shoulders. Who would possibly believe that we simply are the handmaidens of the Goddess!

We feel Her with us, enjoying and enjoining, sometimes blessing us with a vision of Her radiant countenance, often appearing as globes of light hovering around us. Most often we feel the world come alive with love, and joy, and passion, and hope. And the distance between all of us simply does not exist. We experience this world as one unified body with endlessly diverse and lovely faces. We are all Her mission keepers. We have restored Her to Her rightful place in this beautiful world that She dreamed up in the time before time, and soul by soul it is transforming into a living expression of Her light, radiance, and splendor.

Conference Hall
Amala

"Hello my dear friends,

My name is Amala. Like many women in this world, I was raised to believe that I did not have a right to my own voice. If anybody had told me when I was a young woman that I would be speaking in front of twenty million people, that my words would be streamed all over the world, I would have been horrified. I am here because of a tragedy, and a vision. I am here because my voice is needed. I implore you to keep knitting. Find your own way of knitting the world back together. It might be in our knitting circles. It might be by knitting your families back together, or your tribes or your countries, or your own heart. Keep knitting is my only message to you today, but I can tell you this. If anybody does not believe that our knitting project can heal this world, then wait and see what happens. I assure you that we are no longer alone. She is exiled no more. There is magic waiting to happen."

Raphael

Ibrahim, Dubaal, and I finally completed our first album, dedicated to our two sons, and featuring a photo of our two families on the cover. We named the album, *Tikkun Olam*, healing of the world. We've been surprised at how well it is being received. The profits from the sale of the album are going to purchase yarn to complete the scarf that, belief it or not, precluding oceans, has just about encircled the world.

Shekinah

> I am called by many names and yet I am nameless
> I am She
> Bestower of grace and destroyer of illusion
> Nurturer and protector
> Remover of obstacles
> I am the divine Presence
> The immanent light
> I am the world and beyond the world
> I am timeless and the Creator of time
> I am holy and profane

I am the womb of your creation.
You were created in my image.
I gave birth to you
And then appeared to relinquish you
For that is what you dreamed
And so I complied
Although you forgot your origin,
You worshipped false idols
You created a world of pain
Where there had been bliss
Scarcity where there had been abundance
Cruelty in the stead of compassion.
I am here in your time of exile,
Knowing that the spark of divinity
Within each of you
Will guide you out of darkness
Will guide you home.
I am
You are
Light, Radiance, and Splendor

ACKNOWLEDGMENTS

I wish to acknowledge the Diamond Approach, a contemporary spiritual path offering great wisdom about human potential. I also acknowledge the Zen Peacemaker Order for their practice of bearing witness. Appreciation also goes to Camille Hykes, a superb editor whose wise guidance has been invaluable.

ABOUT THE AUTHOR

Leah Chyten has been a philosopher since youth. Her essay "Life as a Creative Unfoldment" won state recognition as the most original graduation speech in the state of MA. Before attending college she homesteaded in Maine, where she raised animals, children, and vegetables and compiled a collection of songs, poetry, short stories, and a novel. After reluctantly leaving the woods to study psychology and spiritual traditions she became a psychotherapist, workshop leader, and teacher of spirituality. She currently lectures and facilitates groups that explore all facets and dimensions of human potential.

author photo © Jen Dean Studios

SELECTED TITLES FROM
SHE WRITES PRESS

She Writes Press is an independent publishing company founded to serve women writers everywhere. Visit us at www.shewritespress.com.

Elmina's Fire by Linda Carleton. $16.95, 978-1-63152-190-4. A story of conflict over such issues as reincarnation and the nature of good and evil that are as relevant today as they were eight centuries ago, *Elmina's Fire* offers a riveting window into a soul struggling for survival amid the conflict between the Cathars and the Catholic Church.

Dark Lady by Charlene Ball. $16.95, 978-1-63152-228-4. Emilia Bassano Lanyer—poor, beautiful, and intelligent, born to a family of Court musicians and secret Jews, lover to Shakespeare and mistress to an older nobleman—survives to become a published poet in an era when most women's lives are rigidly circumscribed.

A Cup of Redemption by Carole Bumpus. $16.95, 978-1-938314-90-2. Three women, each with their own secrets and shames, seek to make peace with their pasts and carve out new identities for themselves.

The Belief in Angels by J. Dylan Yates. $16.95, 978-1-938314-64-3. From the Majdonek death camp to a volatile hippie household on the East Coast, this narrative of tragedy, survival, and hope spans more than fifty years, from the 1920s to the 1970s.

What is Found, What is Lost by Anne Leigh Parrish. $16.95, 978-1-938314-95-7. After her husband passes away, a series of family crises forces Freddie, a woman raised on religion, to confront long-held questions about her faith.

Murder Under The Bridge: A Palestine Mystery by Kate Raphael. $16.95, 978-1-63152-960-3. Rania, a Palestinian police detective with a young son, meets cheeky Jewish-American feminist Chloe at an Israeli checkpoint—and soon becomes embroiled in a murder case that implicates the highest echelons of the Israeli military.